AN ALPHA'S CLAIM

THE RAYNE PACK SERIES BOOK I

E. BOWSER

CONTENTS

Acknowledgments	vii
Glossary	ix
Prologue	1
1. Dax	11
2. Devana	26
3. Dax	41
4. Devana	54
5. Dax	65
6. Devana	75
7. Aeron	85
8. Devana	92
9. Dax	101
10. Dax	112
11. Dax	126
12. Maeze	136
13. Devana	146
14. Dax	157
15. Dax	167
16. Dax	179
17. Maeze	191
18. Dax	198
19. Devana	208
20. Devana	220
21. Devana	232
Epilogue	240
Glossary	255
Author's Note	259
About the Author	261
Books by This Author	263

I dedicate this book to my family.

Thank you for your love and for supporting me in what I love to do.

Acknowledgments

I want to thank God for letting me be able to write the stories that I love. I also want to thank my mother and the love of my life for putting up with me. I want to thank my friends that keep pushing me and believing in me. Big thank you to Sinful Secrets with a Deadly Bite Group, who always has my back whenever I release. All of you have supported me through this series. Thank you to everyone who read the series that contacted me on Facebook, Twitter and IG. I always love to hear from you, and please leave a review if you can. That is what keeps me writing.

GLOSSARY

Hunter- A Hunter is a human that has been given unique gifts and a mission to keep the peace of all species on earth. A Hunter's primary mission is to hunt demons and send them back to Hell. Five Family Houses lead and train Hunters: Cross, Ryder, Okar, Diya and Wellsley.

True Alpha- A True Alpha is a wolf from the bloodline of the firstborn wolf shifter. They have abilities far past any wolf shifter. The True Alpha is over all wolves and is the leader of all Packs across the world. The True Alpha must protect and guide the wolf shifters according to the laws set by their Deity at the beginning. The True Alpha has Alpha beneath him/her to help accomplish the task and help him/her lead the wolf shifter nation so they may prosper.

Alpha/Luna- The Alpha of the Pack is the leader. He/She is the main one in control and sets the laws of his Pack. They are not required to hunt with the Pack, but most typically do. They demand respect and are in the position to exile, banish, or even kill those who do not show it. Though it is rare, this position can be challenged, and if the challenger wins the fight, the challenger, being the new Alpha, can do what he/she pleases with the previous leaders. This does not usually happen because it would result in a considerable change within the Pack.

Beta- The Beta is the second in command and enforces the law when the current Alpha is not present. If both Alpha dies, the beta(s) take the Alpha position and lead the Pack unless the Alpha has said otherwise. This position cannot be challenged without the alpha approval.

Sentinel- There are four sentinels, two mated pairs, in the Pack. The alphas and betas specially choose each pair. The Alphas and betas train the sentinels to take their places if anything should happen to them. Since becoming one can start as early as one year, the sentinels don't usually have authority over the Pack unless the Alpha or beta have publicly given it to them. They are respected, though. Messing with a sentinel is messing with the Alphas and betas themselves. This rank cannot be challenged whatsoever.

Assassin- Assassin is the most fitting name for this rank because it is self-explanatory. They are also spies for the Pack. There can be a total of only three assassins in each Pack.

Lead Warrior/Enforcer- The lead warrior takes his/her orders directly from the Alpha and sometimes the beta. They are the main leader, general or captain of the warriors in the

Pack. They are appointed by the Alpha and are the best of the best of warriors.

Pups/Cubs- I'm pretty sure that this is self-explanatory. They are the children of the Packs.

Gamma- Those holding this position are usually, if not always, the oldest and wisest of the Pack. They pass on their stories and phrases to the others within the Pack their pearls of wisdom. They delight in telling stories to pups though sometimes what they tell is just legend. Still, each story usually has some moral to it. They may have been the Alpha at one time, and usually, that is true. However, the current Alphas may put others here if it seems right. Those who hold this position are much respected and loved by the rest of the Pack.

Delta- They are the messengers of the Pack, the go-between among the allies, and sometimes even the axis. They risk their own lives by doing so, but it is their duty to make sure that those who need to know are told. Those seeking this position must be agile, patient, and even-tempered while speaking with other packs.

Zeta- They are the war general of the Pack that takes direct orders from the Alpha in case of a war. The Alpha may be the one to declare war, but the Zeta leads the army and come up with the war plans. They also train recruits for a position as an Enforcer and train younger wolves for this position to take their place in the future. Typically, there is only a single Zeta, but there can be as many as three if the populace is high or the Alpha declares it.

Gammazeta- A Gammazeta is a cross between a Zeta and Gamma. They must be born of the two wolves who carry those titles and the True Alpha bloodline. These wolves are very rare, and if you have one in your Pack, you have a wolf full of knowledge of Pack lore and the strength of an Alpha.

Kannuck- Kannuck is the Deity and creator of wolf shifters. He is also the moon god and chooses if you will be an Alpha/Luna and grants each Alpha/Luna some of his powers.

Rogue- Rogues are werewolves that have either been kicked out of their Pack or left on their own free will. Rogues are usually the wolves who have gone against Pack laws and the True Alpha.

Lone Wolf- A lone wolf acts independently or generally lives or spends time alone instead of a Pack. Usually, wolves that have left their Pack are described as lone wolves who is an individual who acts independently and prefers to do things on their own. They primarily prefer solitude or works alone. They are still part of the Pack and will come back when called by their Alpha.

Cadejo/Black dog- A Cadejo/Black Dog will cause disease, destruction, confusion, chaos, and death. It may appear as a dog but do not mistake it for what it truly is a possessed shifter. Once it has possessed a shifter, it can now walk like a human. It will no longer need to hide in the shadows of night to whisper poison from afar. It will now have a voice and a willing soul that will feed it the power of life.

My brothers and I knew things were about to change for the lives of our Pack when Quinn, the True Alpha of all wolves, came to visit us at our home. I didn't know how he would react to my Pack being a mix of shifter species, but I hoped he takes it well. I have always taken in shifters that were in need, no matter what breed they were. I may have been bigger and older, but my wolf knew when to submit to the apex predator in our midst. The only wolf that my wolf has ever submitted to was Quinn.

"Dax, you have done an outstanding job with this Pack. This is what I like to see, and I can feel that this Pack has thrived with you as Alpha. You have cleaned house, right?" Quinn asked as he shook my hand. Before answering, I dropped to a knee and bared my neck to him to show proper respect, and so did my brothers, who stood behind me.

"It is an honor to have you visit my Pack," I said. I stayed kneeling until he allowed us to stand back onto our feet. If his wolf did not find us worthy, he held the right to kill us outright and put in place another Alpha of his choosing.

"Ah, shit! Man, get the hell up. Come on, Dax. It's still me you're talking to," he said, punching me on the shoulder. I smiled and stood, and my brothers followed with smirks as well.

"I mean, power goes to a man's head at times. I didn't want to start no bullshit with you," I laughed. We joked around for a bit, and my brothers took the time to meet Quinn on a more personal level. They also asked him what they should do regarding the plan he was coming up with for the wolf kind. I knew for a fact two of my brothers wanted their own Pack and land but now needed the approval to start one from Quinn. I was unsure if they were ready for all that responsibility yet, but I could feel Max and Alex were close.

"Quinn can get with you all another time for your bull-shit," I said, catching each of my brothers' eyes. Even though we were all Alphas, this was still my Pack, and they each respected that fact. Until they had their own and claimed that right, they were still under me and my protection. Acknowledging that fact made me realize why my brothers needed their own soon enough. Their individual gifts are getting stronger each day, making their Alpha attitudes stronger and more willing to challenge for authority. It was just in our nature to do so, and I had to let them lead their lives one of these days. I was the oldest of them all, and I knew I had to let go, but hell, I have been more of a father than anything.

"I have a plan for each of you, so chill on that note. I hear what all of you are saying, and I got you, but honestly, I am here to speak with Dax on some serious shit," Quinn said, looking at each of us. His entire demeanor changed, and we all could tell this would be interesting.

"Let's talk inside, Alpha," I said, feeling my wolf come to attention. My wolf has been on edge and ready for something. I had a feeling I was about to find out why. He was also clawing inside, trying to tell me something, but I ignored it to focus on healing my Pack members. I looked back to my brothers, knowing they would try to listen to what we needed to discuss. "Two of you take out the pups for training, and the rest go do something fucking productive." They all gave me the finger but did not hesitate to do what I asked.

"If all of you are as good as Hayley, then we should be able to help our wolf nation prosper," he said as we made our way into my office. I closed the massive doors, and we both took seats in the armchairs in front of the large floor-to-ceiling windows.

"Agreed. We all have been too separate for far too long," I said, leveling my violet eyes onto his near-black ones. I could see the slight red ring that told of his True Alpha status and feel the power of his wolf calming my own.

"Before we make that happen, I will need to meet all the Alphas across this land," Quinn stated, looking out of the window.

"I will help with that in any way," He turned back to face me with fierce eyes.

"I need you for something else. You are the Alpha of this state and have been for quite a long time. I want you here, and I know you will continue to make the vision I have for us all come true. It just may come to you having more than just Maryland, but we will get to that soon enough."

"Damn right, I will. I got you, Quinn, just like I know you have my back as well," I nodded.

"There is a problem, Dax, and I need someone I can trust

to handle it. I need someone strong who can work with others who differ from us. We need to figure out what's happening and fix that shit."

"Okay, I am listening," I said, feeling uneasy yet excited.

"There are many who do not believe I am what I am. Therefore, I am going to make it my business to meet all the Packs, to meet all the legit Packs, I should say." I sat back at his words because I had a feeling I would not like what he was going to say.

"Go on," I sighed.

"You know there are rogue wolves out there. Some are just looking for a Pack to belong to, and others are just loners who wouldn't bother anyone."

"Yes, I know a few wolves of that nature. Is that a problem for you or something?" I asked. I hoped it wasn't because one of my brothers was just that type of wolf.

"No. That isn't the problem, Dax. Another wolf is claiming to be the True Alpha, and he is raising an army of his own. He has some wolves believing his bullshit, and he is running on this purity nonsense!" Quinn growled, jumping to his feet. I leaned away, watching him begin to pace. His eyes were a flat black, and his canines lengthened. I could feel his anger, and I felt my own rising at this abomination.

"Purity? What the fuck does that mean?" I asked, standing as well. I looked out of the window to see a vehicle had stopped at my gates, and I saw my brothers moving over to check it out.

"Only born wolves are true wolves. A wolf that is mixed or not wholly a wolf should be killed. Not only is he spitting that bullshit, but something is helping him do it. Something is giving him the power to take out other powerful Alphas and claim their Packs as his own." I was fucking pissed. When had this all started, and how the fuck did we not know about this shit until now?

"How did you find out? I take it he was killing all who wouldn't submit to him?" I asked, turning from the window.

"This has happened before in New York, but this is on another scale of fucking crazy. The person who told me will help with this situation, so I invited her here. They saw it happen, but it was too late to stop it. They can't track this wolf or his growing Pack, but they did sense that there was something of a demonic nature. That is their specialty. I need the two of you to work together on this because I know you can track this motherfucker down, and they can handle the demon aspect of the situation."

"You want me to work with a fucking Hunter?" I asked. The only Hunter I liked was Taria Cross, my sister's best friend. Her pops is cool, but the rest of those bastards are assholes. So why do they give two fucks now? What is happening to us?"

"What I want is for you to work with our allies! I expect you to handle this situation while pulling our brothers and sisters together before they kill them. If this fake ass Alpha isn't shut down and the human world gets a hold of the knowledge that rogue wolves are running wild and killing shit up, they are coming at all of us full force. I will not let that shit go down. Do you understand where I am coming from?" He growled. I knew his anger was not directed my way, but I looked down anyway. I didn't want his wolf thinking I was challenging him.

"Yeah. I get it, Quinn, but when does a Hunter give a shit about what happens to us, or is it just the demon they want, and we are a means to an end?" I saw him pull himself together as he moved to sit back down.

"All Hunters are not the same," he stated simply. I had my doubts about that. However, I was older than he was and had more experience. I would need to see it to believe it.

"That remains to be seen," I growled. I felt the wards being lifted to let the car pass through.

"This is what I need, Dax, but it remains your choice. I will not force my Alphas to do anything." His words soothed the beast inside. Knowing I had a choice in the matter of taking on this mess helped calm me. I did not have an excellent track record with Hunters, not after Cassandra. When I needed help the most, I went to her, and as a Hunter, she should have helped. She should have moved mountains as a friend, but instead, she never answered my call. I never saw or heard from Cassandra, and to me, it showed how much Hunters didn't give a shit about us. I called on other Hunter houses, and no one came, so when the zombies attacked, no one was there to help fight, and so many wolves' lives were lost.

"Thank you for the choice, Quinn," I said as a car came to a stop.

"Well, let's go outside. I will need to know your answer before I leave." We both stood and made our way to the doors.

DEVANA

I pulled to a stop in front of a large home with five tall, sexy as hell men following me. I knew they were all wolf shifters, but I could also sense there were other shifters on this property as well. ***They must take in others***. I hit the button to cut the engine. The brothers weren't hostile towards me, but they weren't friendly either. I could tell they had no trust in others and probably not Hunters. This mission was also a part of fixing the trust issues with the other species in this world. When I had the vision, I knew I had to help in any way necessary to at least make up for my parent's ignorance. I opened the door and stepped out just as the doors to the house opened, and Quinn walked out.

"Devana, thank you for coming and for the call," he said while closing the distance. I could feel his eminent power, and it just seemed to keep growing. I was a seer, but only in the way of demon-related attacks and things that have to do with Hunters. So, when that massacre happened to all those shifters, and I saw the madness in the wolf's eyes, I knew I had to act. The vision was saturated with the stench of a demon, and I could feel the evil surrounding the smoky gray wolf.

"Thank you for taking the call. I hoped you would take that I will help seriously," I said. I felt my body freeze up as my senses became aware of another. It was as if my entire body was on fire. I vaguely saw the other five men walking toward the house when I felt the power that rolled over me. It made every single part of my body tingle with anticipation. I took in a sharp breath and my nose filled with a savory scent of spices mixed with the scent of earth. Finally, a tall, lightly tanned man stepped out the doors with such an intense look I caught my breath. His violet eyes held mine as he approached, just as a predator would his prey. I knew this man to be Dax Rayne, the white wolf and the oldest Alpha brother to a family whose children were all born to lead.

"Devana, this..." Quinn started, but I found my voice. I reached out a hand as I let my eyes travel up, jean-covered muscled thighs and up to a chest that was so damn wide I don't think I could wrap my arms around him. The muscles on his darkly tanned and tattooed arms were bigger than my damn head, but it didn't stop the need I had to feel them wrapping around me. I blinked as he made his way closer when I finally had my eyes on his face. Those violet eyes captured and then trapped me as a slow sexy-ass grin spread across his thick lips. I took a step back because the smell and damn smile had me damn near wet as hell. Even though I could not stop my feelings, I had to get my shit together. I stood taller and kept my hand out as I raised a brow while he licked his lower lip.

"Daxton Rayne." I saw Quinn step away quickly as Dax approached me. He looked at him curiously again, but then smirked. I wouldn't say I liked that smirk or what I thought it meant.

"That's my name, but you can call me MATE." His low growl had my eyes widening in shock. Then he turned to Quinn before I could answer or deny his claim on me. "I made my choice, and it's a go."

DAX
CHAPTER
one

I always knew that being an Alpha would be a challenge but being an older brother to six younger siblings was even worse. They all had distinct personalities, weaknesses and strengths, and I was the one who had to help hone each one of them. Having a sister was the hardest of them all, but I enjoyed raising Hayley. It was one of my greatest joys. I became a mother, father, brother and Alpha when my parents died. It was never easy, but it all worked out in the end. Now, something is coming. This life was changing, and I was tasked with handling Pack justice by our leader, the True Alpha Quinn Savir. I was just happy that I wouldn't have to worry about my little sister getting hurt in the fight to come. I never thought that I would see my sister Hayley so happy and able to accept the Alpha inside of her soul. I didn't expect her to be Mated to a Vampire, let alone an upper class or Blue Blood. However, I could not deny that she and Camron Sloane made a suitable match. I couldn't wait to see them once again, but my Pack has to deal with the issue of traitors to our kind living amongst us.

I knew that nothing would ever be the same, and I was correct. Not only have things changed, but all the trouble and bull shit exposed the rot that ingrained itself inside of my Pack. I never believed that something like this could happen to a Pack as old as mine, but if it happened once it could happen again. After hearing what happened with Xavier's Pack in New York from our Alpha, I knew it was happening to Packs across the globe. When more than one kidnapping happened to the children, I swore to protect them better. I had no choice but to call all of my brothers home. Now all five stared at me with frustration, anticipation and rage. We thought fighting in that battle with the demon Amu would end all this madness, but what it did was focus our attention on more problems threatening our world. Not just the shifter population but the entire world itself, and now our True Alpha has called upon me to help fix one situation. I looked at Max, Malic, Alex, Jarod and Thomas, all Alpha wolves.

"Dax, tell us why exactly we should work with a Hunter? I mean, when in the hell have they given a shit about any species except themselves?" Malic growled. I looked at him and Max, who looked identical and raised a brow. Max sat forward to add more of a laid-back response before his hot head twin could say anything that would make me knock his ass out.

"What Malic is saying, brother, is why do we need their help? We are all here, and we are all Alphas. With you leading, we can handle whatever is thrown our way," Max said to grunts of approval. I looked towards the doors knowing Devana was outside, still speaking with Quinn. I was not thrilled at all working with Hunters, but this was different.

"Would you feel the same if it were Taria?" I shot back. I

looked at each of my brothers in the eye and saw the answer to that question. Without a doubt, they would help if it were her asking. However, I also saw tension with just her name being mentioned. Crazy shit was happening at every turn, and Taria was caught up in a bad way, but our Alpha asked us to take care of business to do what is needed on his end.

"That isn't fair, Dax. She is different. That entire situation is unique when it comes to her. That is one of Hayley's best friends, so that makes her family. Plus, she is cool as shit and acts nothing like the other bitch ass Hunters who haven't been doing their fucking job!" I inclined my head at Alex's tone and narrowed my eyes at all of them. I saw Thomas, the youngest of us, shift uncomfortably at the anger filling the room. He was usually quiet when things got heated. Not taking any sides but always ready to pull us apart and calm things down. That has always been a gift of his since he was born. He did not even cry when he came out. He just opened his large brown eyes and looked around before falling back to sleep. So, it surprised me when he cleared his throat and leaned forward with his arms resting on his knees.

"Normally, I let all of you act like idiots and talk a lot of shit before Dax has to beat your ass into submission, but I cannot sit this one out." Thomas, when he spoke, it was always very calming. You could feel the tension leave your body with each low timbre of his voice. When he was ready for a Pack, I knew that he would be one of the best Alpha wolves in this lifetime. "What it seems like you all forgot is that Quinn requested this from Dax. Our True Alpha, someone we all never thought we would see in our lifetime, came to our home and asked our brother, our Alpha, for help. He could have commanded Dax to do it and work with a Hunter, but he did not. Our brother, hell, our family never backs down from any situation. Our Alpha accepted this mission, and yes, we share our concerns, but ultimately, we follow his lead. We all are Alphas to the core, but we all will follow our brother until we form our own Packs. Things are changing. Our world is changing so, should we? No matter what Hunters have done in the past, we show them that we are better because our Pack does not turn our backs to those in need of our help."

I watched as my brothers looked at their little brother in shock. It was rare that Thomas spoke that much in one sitting. I didn't stop the satisfied smile that crossed my face as each of them looked back at me.

"Shit, kid, I didn't even know you could speak!" Jarod laughed. "I guess we also don't have a choice because big brother Dax is out here claiming his Mate. Did I hear that correctly, Dax? Is that Hunter, your Mate, and that's why you decided to do this?" Jarod asked. He was smiling, but I could tell he was earnest for once. Five sets of eyes landed on me in a challenge. I fought the urge to make them submit to me, knowing it wasn't a challenge of dominance but of the truth.

"Before I even give you that answer, tell me will you help me bring down this fake ass True Alpha or not?" I asked instead. If I gave them the answer that, "your damn right, she was my Mate," I knew without a shadow of a doubt they would do it out of honor. I needed to see if they would ride with me into battle because they wanted to. I saw the glances they threw at each other and wasn't surprised when Thomas stood and took a knee in front of me. I clenched my jaw, keeping my mouth shut and my energy down. I wanted them to have their own will, not the pull of my Alpha energy. As one, the rest of my brother stood and kneeled. Malic looked up at me, and his steel-gray eyes held respect and determination.

"You know we always have your back no matter what the fuck is the problem. This family always rides with each other no matter what is going on." I took a deep breath, feeling our bond as Pack members, brothers and Alpha's woven tightly together once again.

"Now, if all this bowing and bull shit is over, tell us if it's true or not. Is that sexy ass Hunter outside really your Mate?" Jarod smiled. I felt jealousy running through my veins and overpowered me as I tackled his ass to the ground.

DEVANA

My body was still buzzing after being so close to that wolf. Hell, Dax wasn't just a mere wolf, but the way my body reacted to just the presence of him told me I needed to keep my distance. Shit, him yelling out this whole Mate thing was another reason for me to deal with this mission, establish a new relationship with the shifters and get out of here. I could not help that my thoughts kept sliding back to his tanned skin, jet black hair, his tall frame with muscled arms roped with veins. His violet eyes pinned me to the spot, and the heat in them burned every part of my body that his gaze roamed.

"Vana?" I blinked and looked up. Quinn was watching me with concern, but when I met his eyes, he grinned. Oh, no! Hell no! I don't care what he thinks. Nothing is happening with that wolf! Not a damn thing.

"Yeah, yes, I hear you. I know how some shifters feel about us Hunters, but I hope this will help get us on the right track. My parents were in the wrong, and we should have stepped up and thought for ourselves. Still, it's no excuse for how things have been handled." I said expertly, shifting the conversation away from what he was thinking. Quinn nodded.

"Yeah, we learned lessons on all sides. Honestly, all of us on this earth has been played. The games evil has been playing have been happening before either of us was even a thought. My shifters will show you respect. We all need to learn to work together if we are to save everyone." He said, opening his arms wide. I knew what he meant, and he wasn't wrong about it. Things were happening in this world, and not for the better. We spoke for a few more moments before he had to leave. I knew this was all new to him, and he had a ton on his plate, but I wish he could have stayed a bit longer. I took in a deep breath, trying to center myself before confronting this Alpha. I could not believe he announced that I was his Mate like that shit was a done deal. I wasn't a shifter, and whatever his belief, it had nothing to do with me. I turned and looked back at the enormous house when I realized someone was standing in front of me. I looked down into the wide tawny eyes of a little girl. Her hair was a mess of curls that went every which way, but she was so cute I had to smile. I looked, but I didn't see anyone who could help me with her. I knew little about kids at all and even less about shifter children.

"Ahh, hi. Can I help you with something?" I smiled. I glanced around once more and back to the little girl. She cocked her head from side to side while staring at me. I ran my fingers through my short locks, removing them from my face.

"Your eyes are so pretty! They look like a cat's eyes. We have big cats here too! Not just wolves. Are you a cat?" She asked. I knew my mouth was open, not sure what exactly to say to this child. But I also knew how shifters reacted to outsiders speaking to their young.

"No, I am not a cat. Are you a cat?" I asked.

"No, silly! I am a black bear cub, and my name is Meesha." She laughed. She reached out quickly and grabbed my hand. I looked up when I heard a woman calling for the little bear cub.

"Meesha! Where are you? I'm going to find you." The woman smiled. I could tell when she caught my scent, and her head snapped up. "Meesha! Come here right now!" The female snapped.

"Go on now, Meesha," I said, pushing the now scared little girl forward.

"Who are you?!" The woman's growl was low and threatening. Her eyes bled to yellow as she worked to control her shift. This was not the first impression I wanted to make, but I knew how an enraged shifter reacted to strangers around their children. The instinct was so natural

I didn't even realize a blade was on my hand until I tightened my grip.

"Shit." I sighed as the woman pulled the young girl behind her and stared me down. I saw other female shifters coming, and they did not look happy that I was here.

I POSITIONED myself between my car and the female shifters that were approaching. I saw Meesha looking around with confusion written across her face while figuring out what had happened.

"I am no threat to any Pack member here," I spoke loudly enough that whoever was inside the house should be able to hear me. "Meesha is fine. She just came to say hello, and that was it," I said, holding up the hand that was not holding a weapon.

"What business does a Hunter have here?" My eyes moved to another female who came to stand beside the one holding Meesha's arm. She had a Beta look to her and the stance of a fighter. She stood with feet spread apart, arms folded across her chest, but her teal eyes were calm. I couldn't tell precisely what type of shifter she was, which is unusual. I was a Hunter, and I studied things like this and should have placed what she was by sight alone. Her shoulder-length black hair was pulled back into a tight ponytail, and the end of it was the same shade as her eyes.

"Your Alpha invited me here. My name is Devana Okar," I stated.

"I don't care what your name is, Hunter. Our Alpha doesn't deal with Hunters, and since when does a Hunter visit shifter kind?" Her rich cocoa skin made her eyes even more unnatural as they glowed.

"Not Dax, but True Alpha Quinn Savir. I am no threat here to anyone, and yes, your Alpha knows that I am here. I just..." I heard when the front doors opened, and heavy footsteps from six large men came down the stairs. I flexed my hand, making my blade disappear back into its sheath. I did not know why I took my eyes away from the women who were staring daggers at me to look for those violet eyes. It was almost like a compulsion that I had to seek him out, and I hated it. I gritted my teeth together to stop myself from licking my lips when my eyes landed on six feet and seven inches of muscle. The intense way he stared at me had my core clenching in anticipation of what he wanted to do to me. I closed my eyes and turned away because I was losing my damned mind. He was not the reason I was here, and whatever this feeling was or whatever he claimed I was to him didn't matter. Possessing this gift as a seer determined my life for me because anyone I touched or became close to would be pulled into what I saw. The visions I received were nothing but nightmares that I wouldn't wish on my enemies.

"I didn't think this is how we treated guests to our Pack land. Is this how we act, Remi?" Dax questioned the teal-eyed woman. My eyes flicked back to her, and I noticed she now had her head down and eyes cast away. It wasn't a weakness, but their Alpha and his brothers' presence seemed to calm the females. I noticed that others were coming from around the large house. I knew most Packs had acres of land, and I assumed the Rayne Pack was no different. The only difference with this Pack was that it wasn't just wolf shifters present. I could tell they all referred to Dax as their Alpha either way.

"No, Alpha." Remi agreed. I looked down and saw Meesha looking back at me with a smile.

"I thought not. Since it seems like most of the Pack is arriving, it should be easy enough for me to call a meeting. This is Devana Okar, and yes, she is a Hunter. I am sure you were all aware of a visit from True Alpha Quinn, and with that came the news that every Pack member needs to hear."

Dax looked around to every Pack member present at the moment before looking back to his brothers that stood like a wall behind him. I noticed another man standing with them, and he clearly wasn't blood-related, but it was no mistake his position in this Pack. His bronze skin stood out with his short-cut raven hair with a shock of snow-white in the front. He had to be Dax's Beta, his right hand other than his brothers. I didn't know his name, but I knew he was a wolf shifter and a strong one at that. His blue-gray eyes looked me up and down before looking away.

"Max, find out a time when every member will be present and set up the Pack meeting at the pit," Dax ordered. He turned around, and his eyes found mine once again, and the heat I pushed down a few minutes ago came roaring back to life. He walked toward me as if he was on a mission, stopping just a few feet away from me. Then, everyone started going about their business doing what they needed to do before their Pack gathering.

"I know that things are a bit strained with Hunters and supernatural kind, but I hope we can change that for the future," I said, stepping forward holding out a hand. His brows raised as he looked at my hand and back to my face. His brows were the same shade of midnight as his hair, except when the sun hit just right, I could see the violet hairs peeking through the black hair. I almost put my hand down, but he moved more quickly than I expected and captured my hand in his. His hand swallowed mine, and I felt a tug, and I stumbled forward until I caught myself. I leaned into the pull and turned slightly, placing my left hand on his massive bicep to steady myself.

"Good reflexes. That's a plus in my book for a Mate to an Alpha. Follow me, we need to talk, and I rather it was behind closed doors." Dax stated. He let my hand go and moved back to the house before his words registered to my brain.

"Yes! I think you may be right because what I need to say should be private." I grunted, following him as his deep chuckle landed on my skin, sending tingles through my body. We needed to find this rogue and this demon so I could get far away from this wolf.

DAX

I didn't intend to leave Devana outside when I heard Quinn leave. My brothers and my enforcers all but demanded to know what was happening and what I would need from them going forward. I gave them the conversation high-lights, but I knew I would need more information on what my Mate saw in her vision. I took the front steps two at a time, all too aware of her fast-beating heart, her scent of jasmine, lily and vanilla that filled my lungs with each breath. I was not looking for a Mate and definitely wasn't expecting it to be a damn Hunter, but I knew the signs all too well. Well enough. It was no mistake to me, but I didn't know how she felt. There would be recognition between animals if she were another wolf or even shifter kind. It wouldn't matter because she would be mine before we completed this mission. I opened the doors, letting Devana pass by me into the house, and I turned my attention back to my Pack, watching as everyone hurried off to get ready for tonight. I saw Thomas watching me, and before he turned away, he nodded as if he knew something I didn't. I watched as he moved to help Remi gather the shifter children for dinner.

"So has Quinn told you what we are facing?" I closed the door and made my way inside, seeing Devana looking around before facing me. Some of my Pack were still going about their routines in the house.

"He told me what he could, but let's speak in my office. I need to know everything you know before I can figure out where to start." She was tall, maybe five feet seven inches, but she still had to look up at me like everyone else. It was amusing to see her taking a step back so she wouldn't have to look up as far. Her eyes fascinated me the way they changed from green to brown and to gray. Quinn told me she was a seer. Even if he didn't, her eyes would tell that story on their own.

"That's fine. Lead the way." She held a slight accent that I couldn't place. She ran a hand through her locs that reached the bottom of her neck.

"Follow me," I said, moving to the stairs. My house was large by any usual standards, but my side of the house was off-limits to all except a select few. I turned right at the top of the stairs, pushing the double doors open to a large office where Quinn told me about this fake Alpha. I knew shit was about to be a wild ride when even he couldn't contain his anger at what was happening to our kind. I stepped to the side, so Devana had to slide past me, letting her curves brush against my body. Her scent filled my nose, and I heard her catch her breath at the contact. She moved deeper into my office, and my wolf felt content with sharing this space with her. I closed the door and watched her pace in front of the windows, clenching and unclenching her hands. The Hunter was giving herself a pep talk. I could feel my wolf staring at her, ready to claim her, but I knew it wouldn't be so easy.

"Take a seat and tell me about the vision you had. I want to know everything from what you smelled, tasted, heard, felt, and saw. If what you claim you saw had something to do with demons, then I welcome your help as a Hunter. I'm sure you can understand that others in my Pack or any other shifter will not have the same attitude as I do about this... this partnership," I said, moving to sit in the single armchair near where she paced. I hoped that she walked by one more time before my words sank into her brain so I could see her ass in those tight-as-hell leather pants. I tried to see exactly where she hid her weapons. The holster under her leather jacket that held her Glock wasn't meant to be hidden, but I knew Hunters kept blades hidden everywhere on their bodies. I wouldn't mind when this was all over if we played find the Hunter's blades so I could caress every curve of her delectable body.

"Wait. What I claimed I saw? First of all, Daxton, I claim nothing. I know full well what I saw and sensed. There is a demon that has something to do with this wolf! If we have a so-called partnership like YOU claim, you first need to believe that what I tell you is true. Do you think me coming here was easy or that any of this was easy for me after..."?

"After... after Hunters turned their backs on their responsibilities!" I growled. I didn't even realize that I was standing, let alone over her. I knew my wolf was at the forefront, peeking through my eyes, and she could sense it and the danger. Devana did not back down. Not even an inch as my violet eyes blazed down at her, and her catlike eyes glittered right back.

"I can't apologize for every Hunter, but I will apologize on behalf of my family for our role in not carrying out our responsibility to all creatures of this earth. What I will not do is stand here and let you or anyone else make me feel less than when I am here doing the right thing and taking care of my responsibility to wolf shifter kind and this world as we Hunters have been charged in doing," she snapped. I knew it would have been a primal growl and challenge from an Alpha if she were a wolf. My wolf backed down, approving of her courage and of her being Mated to this Alpha wolf. I stepped closer and watched as her eyes darted around, and she brought her hands up, but they just pressed to my chest. I leaned down next to her ear, and I knew that she knew I was scenting her. I licked my lip before I spoke against the shell of her ear.

"My wolf approves, and so do I, Mate. I know I called you Mate earlier, and you dismissed it, but sexy, I am here to tell you I have no problem accepting your apology because you, Hunter, are mine." I couldn't help the growl, and I didn't miss the moan that slipped from her lips.

"Oh, God..." She murmured, and I could feel her nails digging into my chest as she shuttered against my body. I knew she could feel the length of me pressing hard into her stomach when I felt her push closer to me.

"You don't have to call me God. Just call me Alpha." I didn't wait for a response as I licked at her lips, slipping my tongue between them. Then, while holding the back of her neck, I pushed my tongue deep into her mouth, taking what belonged to me. I knew she felt exactly what I was feeling when I felt her fingers grip my shirt tighter, pulling me closer so she could deepen the kiss. Finally, I heard her moan, and I knew she wanted to claim me just as much as I wanted to claim her.

DEVANA

CHAPTER *two*

If I didn't stop this now, things would get so much harder for both of us. Daxton Rayne kissing me, a Hunter, was an impossible thought. He hated us and wasn't afraid of making it known. All Hunters knew of his hatred of our kind because of something that happened long before I was born. He claims that I am his Mate, and I wouldn't lie to myself because I felt something... but I wasn't willing to call it a life bond. This was just an attraction we both held, and I knew all of this could come from me. I am a strong empath and a seer, so I knew what my power could do. This was the exact reason I chose to stay away from everyone but my family. The kiss was hard, but those soft, thick lips felt like silk as they moved across my own. I heard the moan escape from my lips as he trailed his long wet hot tongue along the column of my neck. I had to stop this because I felt his hatred for Hunters would intensify when he realized that this wasn't his emotions. I have seen Daxton in pictures and drawings that were in books and scrolls. I knew it was lust because it was mine that he was feeling. I had to find the will to stop and push him away, no matter how my heart pounded at his touch. No matter how my soul sang at our body's connection.

"Da... Daxton. Stop. Please, we need to stop." I panted. He slowed but didn't stop or pull away. I had to do it because if I couldn't get the strength to do it, things were about to go from hot to blazing. I made my fingers loosen in his shirt and slowed my heavy breathing before gently pushing at his chest.

"The only reason that I am stopping is that you're right. Not right for the reasons you think, but right because we have things to do, and I need to know what you saw. But Devana, when this is done, I hope you're ready." He whispered against my neck. I knew when this was done that I would have to get far away from this man. When I did, the lust would clear, and he would hate Hunters once again because he would believe I manipulated him just like the rest. I pulled away, taking deep breaths, trying my hardest to clear my mind so I could do the mission I came to do.

"When we are done, and I leave, you will understand that this... this thing you believe that you are feeling isn't real."

"I think I would know my Mate when I saw her, scented her, and tasted her."

"Dax, let's get this started. Let me tell you about the vision I had so we..." I lost my breath when a vision so strong slammed into my mind. I felt myself reaching out blindly, trying to find the couch so I could sit down. But, instead, I felt muscular arms wrapping around my waist and being lifted as the world around me fell away.

As the vision shifted, the shapes that were shadows became clearer. I stood in a large open wooded area where motor homes made a circle around something. I

took a step forward, and I could see the shifters standing inside this circle, and one man taller than the rest was in the middle. I wrinkled my nose at the scents filling my nostrils and knew precisely what it was. The scent of death, loss, loneliness and demon. The place had a heavy weight of evil surrounding these shifters. As I got closer, the words the shifter was saying became clear to my hearing.

"As we take down Alpha after Alpha, we show who is the True Alpha of this nation. I will give the faithful the gift of power and the ability to transform into the third form. We kill those who stand in the way of this Pack! We kill the ones who aren't pure in blood! We are the chosen, and we will own it all. Now it's time to show how my ultimate strength will have every other Alpha kneel at my feet. Once we take the Rayne Pack's Alpha down and destroy a family of Alphas that are un-pure, they all will bow. This so-called True Alpha Quinn is nothing more than a puppet propped up to control you. He claims a Witch as a Mate, and she has birthed bastard un-pure pups. Follow me to cleanliness and to rid this world of the abominations of half-breed wolves. Follow me, and your children will have a chance to live. Disobey and suffer just as the un-pure wolves in your Packs. Follow me as I become Alpha to all Packs across this nation. Once that is accomplished, we will take this country, and everyone will bow at our feet. I Aeron Alpha of the Breaker Pack True Alpha to all wolves will wash this land in the blood of all who stand in our way! We take the un-clean Rayne Pack, and then we kill the man who calls himself the True Alpha Quinn Savir. Who's ready?" I watched the man grinning at the howls that filled the air while also scowling at some who stayed silent. Aeron was almost as tall as Dax, standing at least six feet five inches, with light brown hair and full bread. His darkly tanned skin was at odds with his eyes. I moved closer to get a better look at Aeron as he looked over his crowd. His dark brown eyes held a crimson ring, just like Quinn's. The difference was that ring wasn't from any natural-born power but one of a demon. When his gaze landed on me, I knew he could see me because I saw the demon looking back through his eyes.

"Hunter, Hunter, Hunter. This isn't the first time you have been spying. Come here!" Aeron leaped down from the platform he was standing on, coming directly at me. I put up both arms and screamed as I readied myself for an attack.

"Devana! Devana! You're safe, you're safe!" Dax repeated until I calmed down enough to relax my body. I have had a vision just suddenly come on me without me sleeping or looking for one. It felt as if the vision was forced into my mind, but how was that even possible?

"I'm good. I'm okay." I said, panting. I blinked rapidly, trying to clear my racing thoughts, when I realized two of Dax's brothers were in the room staring at me with concern. "Shit," I whispered, and Dax looked at me before looking up at his brothers.

"Give us some space. I will explain later. Just give us space."

"Dax, we could feel your alarm. Shit, man, we felt the terror! What the fuck is going on in here?" Malic asked. His pensive eyes looked at me as if I had caused this pain. I looked away, feeling like shit because I knew that I did.

This was the exact reason that I had to leave when this shit was over. Dax was already too close, and I would not let my curse affect him. I looked up at Dax, who was still hovering over me, and met his violet eyes as they burned into mine.

"I said I would explain, and that is exactly what I meant. So, do your Alpha a favor and get the fuck out. It's all good here, brothers." His tone was sharp, but I could hear the affection in the word brother. No one spoke, and I didn't hear any footsteps leaving when the door shut.

"Daxton, I'm okay, really I'm good," I said as I tried pushing him away. He moved, but it wasn't from my advances. Instead, he moved to sit down next to me and pulled my body into his lap. Dax was a large man but an even larger wolf. I imagined myself in this position many times in my life, but I knew that shit was just fantasy. Now it was as if my fantasy were coming to life, just like my visions.

DAX

I saw and experienced everything in her vision as if I had it myself. Of course, I held Devana even as she tried to wiggle her way out of my lap, but that made it all the better.

"You can keep moving that sexy ass around, and we can end up in another position, or you can stay still while I hold you. Then you can explain what just happened and how it's possible." I knew my voice held a little of my Alpha command laced through it, but that I couldn't help. I also knew that even though I was strong and enormous compared to her, she was still a Hunter. Their kind was known for taking out things I wouldn't want to face. So, if she truly wanted, she could move. I leaned back as she let out a sigh and stopped struggling, which were good signs for me because she felt something as well. "Talk to me, beautiful. Whatever it is you feel like you need to say, I can handle it," I stated.

"What exactly did you see?" She asked. I watched as her hands clenched and unclenched as if they itched for a blade.

"I saw the fake ass Alpha who believes that he is the True Alpha. I also saw former Pack members of Packs from across different states. What pisses me off most is that a few of those wolves aren't there by choice but out of fear. That's what has me ready to tear out the throats of not only Aeron but the ones who follow him willingly."

"So, you saw it all, and you heard what he said about you?" Devana finally relaxed. I rubbed small circles along her honey brown skin as I let the calming energy of my wolf radiate out of me.

"Yes, but I don't give a fuck about that. He doesn't scare me nor worry me because I can handle my shit. What worries me is that the demon knew you were there and knew you saw the first vision. It knew your name, and from what I know about demons, that isn't good." Before I could react, Devana jumped up, spinning around to stare at me. Her cat-like eyes glittered in aggravation and pride.

"I am a Hunter, and the only thing that should worry you is if you don't get the chance to take down this wolf before I do. Well, after I finish with this demon." She panted, and I couldn't look away from her lips, her curves, but what held my attention most was her iron-clad will. I love it, but she needs to learn anything that has to do with wolves, or a Pack is our business.

"Hunter, you are here about the demon, not the wolf. He is my problem. Aeron is my Pack business, and we handle Pack business. Not the Vampires and for sure not no fucking Hunters." I heard the disdain in my voice, but it was too late. I saw her jerk back a little, and I was on my feet, reaching out to her. This shit was all new to me, and I damn sure was not expecting my Mate to be a part of the one group I hated the most. "Devana..."

"No. No, you're right, and it was my fault for saying that. Let's get to business, Daxton. You saw this vision, but not the first one, so let me clue you in on what we are dealing with," she said. I could see the steel door slamming shut, and when it did, it left just a Hunter. It was all good because we had time, and she would forgive me. She would stay whether she thought so or not.

I closed my mouth and moved over to the windows, watching as the sun started to set. I made it a point to shut my mind about what we should be discussing. Just seeing what I did told me my Pack was in serious danger and that Aeron and his crew were getting closer.

"I'm listening, Hunter." It was silent for a moment as she stared at me. I could feel her fiery gaze roaming my body, but I couldn't look at her.

"My first vision of this wolf was in the middle of him killing a Pack in Alabama a few months back. I was confused at first because I could tell this hadn't been the first Pack to die. He started with smaller Packs at first, which wouldn't be considered missing. I should have known this first vision was different when I saw everything through his eyes."

"You saw him kill the entire Pack or just a few?" I turned to face her to see the answer to that question. By the looks of it, that had never happened before. She grimaced at the memory of the vision, and it told me it had to be gruesome.

"I don't know what I came in on or where exactly it happened, but my vision started when he tore the throat out of a Beta. The Alpha was already dead, and he stood over this Beta waiting for him to die. I could smell the death and hear the screams of frightened children and adult shifters. I already knew I would have to report this, but I wasn't getting involved. I knew our help wouldn't be appreciated or wanted, but all that went up in smoke when I heard the voice.

"What voice? From someone around him?" I pushed away from the window to sit down at my desk. Devana came over as I started going through names and numbers of other Alpha Wolf shifters in North America. We had to stop this crazy fucking wolf before he or his message spreads overseas. We all knew of wolves who thought the same way, looking down on wolves who were transformed or half-breed. Those kinds whispered about it behind closed doors and never acted on it, but if they caught wind of it, things could change. Their words may become action, and none of us needed that shit.

"No, not from around him, but inside him. The voice was in Aeron's head. It was a demon that is when I knew whether a wolf kind accepted my help or not. I had to get involved. So, I did what I could and reached out to my contacts, which put me in touch with Quinn."

"Okay. This is what has to happen now. Aeron is close to my state, and he already made it clear he was coming for me. We need to stop him and his followers before they even think of stepping foot onto the soil of my state. Rogue wolves that deal in the type of violence his ass is doing doesn't get the grace period of two days to make themselves known." I finished emailing my contacts to ensure them that it stops here. Even though I knew I would beat his ass down and make him submit, everyone else still should be on guard.

"Has anything like this ever happened before?" Devana asked as she picked up a picture of Lily and Garrett from Halloween. I saw her small smile before placing the picture back on the desk. I waited for her eyes to look into mine. Instead, her eyes changed again to a deep green that held flicks of gold around the irises.

"I thought Hunters kept records of everything?" She rolled her eyes and waved me off. "Naw, I'm serious. I thought you all kept a running record of everything in supernatural history. That's what I was told, but it could have changed by now. It's been long enough." I shut my computer down, pushing thoughts of Cassandra away.

"Who told you that? I mean, we do, but I figured you could give me a first-hand account since you... since you are a shifter." She hurried to finish.

"Why would I have a first-hand account? Maybe the

question should be, how would you know that I would have a first-hand account?" I asked.

"Never mind. Do you have a room where I can put my things and make some calls? How long do we have before your Pack meeting?" She inquired. I pressed for more information, but time wasn't on our side at the moment.

"Yeah, sure. My room is across the hall. Use it in any way you need. There are fresh towels in the master bath." I smiled. I saw the instant heat in her eyes and the blush that colored her cheeks. I couldn't wait to strip her out of those clothes and show her this wasn't something she could walk away from permanently.

"I'm not using your damn room. Do you have a spot for me or not? I could always just use my car. Unfortunately, I have been in worst conditions." She cocked her head to the side, raising a perfectly arched eyebrow.

"There is a spare room next to mine and a bathroom in the hall next to it. Feel free to use that room while you're here. As for the meeting, it's Pack only." I stated. I moved around my desk, heading for the doors to get up with my brothers and Beta. They needed this information, and we needed to double down on our defenses. Shit was getting hot, and I refused to let my Pack suffer any more of the bullshit. I moved fast, probably faster, than her thoughts could comprehend what I had said. I wasn't about to argue with her about my Pack. I was out the door and down the stairs when I heard her yell my name.

"Daxton!"

Few people knew that Daxton was my given name. The only person who used it was my mother, and she died nineteen years ago. Since her death, no one has used it, not even my brothers. So if I were real with myself, it felt good to hear it again, especially from my Mate. Still, no one outside of my mother and Cassandra ever called me that. So how would she even know it?

DEVANA

Dax was down the stairs and out of the door before I even made it to the top. I looked over and saw three doors and started for them. I had a bag inside my car that I would need to bring up, but I just need a breather for now. I opened one door leading to the bathroom, so I tried the other and saw a modest room with a king-sized bed, two dressers, a large window and a tv on the wall. I went in and closed the door, seeing a massive closet on the far side of the room and another door next to the one I had just came through. I opened that door and verified that it was a connecting door to the bathroom in the hall. I stepped inside, locked the door leading into the hall, and left the one open in my room. Dax may think I wouldn't be at that meeting, but he had another thing coming. I moved over to the plush bed and sat down. I pulled my cell out and hit the speed dial to call my sister. I had little time to fill her in on what I had to do because I knew she would run to our parents. They supported getting back into what we were meant to be doing and realized how their beliefs had been wrong. They spoke of days in the past where this was exactly what we should do, and they knew they weren't living up to their responsibilities. Still, it wouldn't stop them from forbidding me to go to Pack lands and getting involved this way.

"Vana, where are you? Please don't tell me you went alone to deal with this demon," Dali asked. I could hear the panic and irritation in her voice.

"Chill out Dali, I'm good. I have a backup if I need it. I just wanted to check in and let you know everything is cool."

"Everything is cool, you say? Is that the story you're sticking with, Devana?" I rolled my eyes. I slipped off my leather jacket and hung it on a nearby desk chair. I saw the computer and wondered if I needed a code. I hit the power button and waited for the screen to light up.

"Yes. What else is there to say? When I find the demon, I will deal with it. I shouldn't be any longer than a week or so. Any longer, then maybe you should start looking for me."

"Devana! You got to be kidding me with this shit! Mother and Father know exactly where you are and want a video call at nine tonight."

"What the hell do you mean, know where I am? I know they didn't have me tailed or tracked! I am a grown-ass woman who has been dealing with demons for over eighty years, sister. This has to stop." I said, shaking my head. "They had their time and fucked it up. I will not sit by while innocent shifters die. Not this time," I snapped.

"Quinn called Vana. He spoke to Father about the situation. He said, and I quote, 'Thank you, sir, for sending your daughter Devana to help the wolf shifter nation with this problem. I believe this may be a start of mending the broken relationship between our people.' Father told him that it was no problem, and he knows you will do what needs to be done!" Dali was pissed, and I knew it. I made my way back to the door to get my bag out of the car. I was going to need a hot ass shower after this conversation.

"Just tell me how bad it is for real, sis." I sighed. I reached for the door when it opened, and I looked up into teal eyes.

"Naw. You left me in the hot seat of bullshit and worried as hell about you."

"Dali, come on," I said, taking a step back. Remi slipped inside and held the door open while watching me silently.

"Fine, fine, let me see if I can figure out exactly how mad they are, and I will call you back," Dali murmured.

"Thanks." I ended the call and thanked Remi for holding the door as I stepped out. I jogged down the stone steps and unlocked my car.

"Hi!" I stopped with my hand on the back door and peeked around the back of the car. I saw a mess of curls and the cutest smile.

"Hi, Meesha. Aren't you supposed to be getting ready for dinner?" I asked, looking around.

"I finished early so that I can tell Alpha Dax good night. He checks my room to make sure no red eyes are in there," she whispered. I frowned because usually, shifter children aren't scared of such things.

"Red eyes?"

"Yeah, the bad ones that came before. They took me once," Meesha whispered. She looked to the ground and clutched her stuffed white wolf tightly.

"Well, we won't let that happen," I smiled.

"Meesha! Meesha, it's time for bed!" I heard the voice of the woman from earlier. I looked back down, but Meesha was already running off.

"Bye, cat lady!" She laughed. I grabbed my bag, curious about what she could be talking about, when I felt someone behind me. I turned on my heel and slid to the left, pulling out a blade simultaneously. I held the blade at my side as I faced Remi, who raised her brows at me.

"Nice moves. You are good with the child. She seems to like you without knowing you. Sometimes a child has good instincts, but other times they do not. Which time is this?" Remi's voice held a slight French accent, but I knew it wasn't. I couldn't place where she was from or what type of shifter. I also did not hear her until she was just a few feet away from me, which wasn't like me.

"I said it before, and I will repeat it. I am not here to hurt anyone, especially not a child. I am here for a purpose you will learn about soon." I stood up straighter, lifting my bag onto my shoulder. I made a show of sliding my blade away, and those glowing teal eyes followed the movement.

"So you said before. It's just so much mistrust about you, Hunters. Now I need to be sure these shifters will be safe with you here." Her gaze held mine, and I inclined my head.

"The harm is not from me."

"Maybe not the physical harm, but it doesn't mean that you, Hunter are safe." My brows pulled together, but Remi turned and walked away. I couldn't even hear her footsteps on the dirt. I didn't know what she was, but it was ancient. My phone beeped as I started for the house. The sun was setting, and I could hear the surrounding homes getting their young to bed.

"Dali, what's up?" I answered.

"You are at Dax Rayne's house right now. Are you crazy?" Dali screamed into the phone.

"Yes, it's fine. I'm fine."

"You're fine. Right, and I believe that because you say so. Devana, you do realize that he dies in your vision. You died in that fucking vision! I'm on my way."

"No! No, you will stay home where you can carry out our family name if... if it plays out the way, my vision went."

"Hell no! Fuck this, Vana! Are you crazy! We can handle this a different way," she cried.

"Dali, you know every time I decided on what should be done, it all ended the same. The only way things changed is when I went alone and spoke with Quinn. When I awoke from that last vision, my time was out, and this, this right here, is the only way we have a chance. I need all of them to trust me, at least a little, for us to win. If this is the only way to bring shifter and Hunter kind on one accord once again, then so be it. I love you, sister. I will not be on the video chat. When this is over and we win, I will deal with the consequences."

I ended the call and debated to hit the button to cut off the power, but I decided to leave it on. I never knew what might happen or if someone needed to get in contact with me. I stepped inside of my temporary room and closed the door. I leaned against it, praying this is what had to be done to save this entire Pack.

DAX CHAPTER *three*

As I left the house, I saw Thomas and Jarod doing a perimeter check-in in their wolf forms. I knew that we would face this threat together and take them down with my brothers all here. Right now, I needed to find my Beta Dimitri to discuss powering up our wards around the property. I seldom called on the Witches that we are contracted with, but I had to take every precaution if this bastard is coming for my Pack. I saw the fire blazing at the pit where the Pack meeting would occur and made my way over to it.

"Alpha?" I turned to see a lion shifter looking up at me. Her medallion gold eyes held a steely expression.

"Yes, Leodora."

"Do you think it's safe that you have a Hunter on these lands? I mean for the children, and we know what happens when they are trusted," she said. She wrapped her toned, tanned arms around her waist, but her eyes were hard.

"All of that will be answered during the meeting, but I understand why you feel the need to speak up. I am doing everything I can to protect you all, and when it comes to demons, a Hunter is the best thing to deal with them."

"Yes, Alpha, I know it's... Dax, you know what happened to me, and I don't want what happened to me to happen to anyone else here. If Malic, in all his asshole ways, hadn't stepped in when those monsters were transferring me somewhere else, I would be dead. Hunters sold us out, and...."

"I understand. I promised that we would find a way for you to get back to your pride when it's safe. I have relayed all the info I had to the correct shifters and friends that I trust. I know for a fact the Delioness is in this state and tracking down any missing along with who is responsible." I promised. I reached out, placing a hand on her shoulder when both her hands flew to her mouth.

"Delioness knows what's happening? *Apademak* heard my prayer. There are many more of us still missing. I trust you, Dax, but I do not know if I can trust a Hunter. Not after what they have done." Leodora sighed. Her long brown braids almost touched the ground when she looked down with the shake of her head.

"I understand exactly how you feel, but I was reminded recently that not all Hunters are the same and that things are shifting in this supernatural world. If you trust me, then know, I believe it's for the best when I say that things are changing. Your Queen has been told about you and will make this one of her stops as she finds the remaining lion shifters. You can tell her your story if and when you want to. Another thing Leodora...."

"Yes, Alpha."

"This will always be your home as long as you want it to be." I could see the stress leak from her body as her shoulders dropped. I smiled at the young lioness and turned back to head for the pit. I walked in to see Dimitri speaking to another Pack member who stood nose to nose with him.

"Lennox, Dimitri, what is the problem?" Dimitri narrowed his eyes at the wolf and took a step back.

"Nothing, Alpha. I just had to make the rules clear once more for this one." Dimitri said without taking his eyes away from Lennox.

"Yeah, yeah, Alpha, we all good here." Lennox sneered.

"Look. At. Me." I know they both heard the low growl in my voice. Dimitri wasn't too bothered by it, but he still obeyed. On the other hand, Lennox listened to the command in my tone and faced me immediately. His eyes were cast down and away, but I could see the sneer on his face.

"If my Beta tells you again what the rules are to my Pack, you and your brother will be gone. I don't set many rules, but I expect every last one to be followed. You get me, Lennox?" I watched as he reflexively swallowed and nodded his head. "Out loud!"

"Yes, Alpha."

"I will speak to you later about this. Get out of here until it's time for the meeting." I grunted as he dashed for the exit. "Tell that brother of yours not to be late to this meeting like the last one, or he will deal with me!" I called out at his retreating back. I looked back at Dimitri as he ran a hand through his hair in frustration.

"These young ones get bigger balls by the day but don't know shit," Dimitri grunted with a laugh.

"What the fuck was that about, and is it something I need to be concerned about at the moment?"

"Naw, nothing too serious, but I will keep my eye on

them. His brother was messing around with the wards. When I came close to them, I overheard Lennox telling him it wasn't just a rock and to leave it alone. So, I pulled their dumb asses up on it and sent them on their way. I came here to get this place ready, and here comes big brother. Saying some shit like I don't have authority over them because they aren't real Pack members and that I shouldn't be speaking to his little brother that way. It was some bullshit, and you walk in as I was setting his ass straight about how this shit works."

"Lennox is a hot-head, but he never goes against Pack law. His brother questions a lot of shit, but Lennox saying all that to you smells like bullshit to me. It sounds like the words of his brother Lindell. They have been here for six months, but I consistently hear about Lindell complaining about working beside Magnus. He thinks of him as prey and not a part of the Pack. So, I had to snatch his ass up about that as well."

"I remember, but he hasn't done anything too crazy lately. He's lucky you stepped in with Magnus. Just because he is a Stag doesn't mean he is prey. Now that would have been some shit to see, but Magnus is too patient to rise to Lindell's comments. This situation with Lennox does seem out of left field." Dimitri muttered.

"Monitor it."

"I got you. You know that. Now, what brought you down here? Isn't it time for you to "check" for monsters?" Dimitri grinned as he lit another torch.

"Shut the fuck up. If that eases my young Pack's minds, then I will do it every fucking night and have "Beta Tree" right along with me if he doesn't wipe that smile off his face." I crossed my arms and stood to my full height, feet apart, waiting, so he knew I was dead serious.

"Oh shit, you're for real! Naw, you got that. I still can't believe the kids call me Tree. How hard is Dimitri? Fine, the smile is gone. Now tell me what you need." He said seriously.

"I need you to hit up the Witches to come set up some additional wards around here. I want them placed a few feet from the ones we have, and while we are in this meeting, I want them placed around my house and keyed to myself, you, and my brothers. That will be the last defense if anything gets through. You and Thomas will defend the Pack and its young."

"What! I am going to fight! That's how I am going to defend this Pack, Dax." Dimitri shook his head in irritation. I knew what he wanted, but this is how I needed it.

"No. You will do what I told you to do because you know how much the safety of those pups and cubs means to me and because your Alpha commands it," I said with force. "Do you trust me?" I asked. I knew my violet eyes were burning bright because my wolf was close to the surface. Dimitri felt it as well and what this request meant to me, and why he was chosen to handle it.

"I trust you, Alpha. You know I got you and will do whatever it is that you need me to do."

"Thank you."

"I will hit up Peter and his sister. I will double the rate, so it gets done tonight."

"Triple it if need be, Dimitri. I don't give two shits what the cost will be. So, get it done and fast."

"I got you," he said and pulled out his cell. I nodded and

turned away. I started for the homes of each young shifter, doing what I promised them recently. I would keep the monsters away from them. If that bastard Aeron thought he and whatever demon could come for my Pack, they both had it wrong. I would protect my Mate, my Pack, and my brothers by sending them both to Hell.

DEVANA

I moved over to the bed, throwing my bag down and hating that I had my family worried. Watching Dax and his Pack die gutted me when I continued having that vision. For so long, I studied the Rayne Pack shifters and Dax especially. I opened the book of scrolls entrusted to my sister and me by our father to learn the Rayne Pack's history. The two Alpha parents produced seven Alphas children and the prophecy that came with them. It had drawn me to him from the start. The vivid way the drawing captured his violet eyes haunted me at night before I fell into sleep. It was just something about him standing bloody in one of the most significant wars that destroyed the trust shifters had with Hunters. I never understood why we stayed out of that war, and when I asked about it, I was told it had nothing to do with demons, therefore, nothing to do with Hunters. I turned to the page with the drawing of his face and remembered how those eyes caressed my skin. How his mouth felt on mine as I rubbed up against him placing my feelings into him.

"Shit," I muttered and slammed the book closed. I threw it on the bed and dug through the bag for my Hunter clothing. I looked toward the bathroom and at the clock ticking on the wall and figured I still had some time before the meeting took place. I read in the book that at 12:12 am, wolf shifter kind comes together for their Pack meetings: unless it was for punishment, it could be immediate. It was close to 9:30 pm now, so I had a few hours to spare. I put the book back inside my bag, grabbed my lavender vanilla sugar scrub and soap. I undressed while walking into the bathroom. It was larger than I thought, with a walk-in shower that seemed to have a button for anything you may need while washing. The double sinks with clean towels and clothes sat in a neat pile. Next to the sinks sat a claw-foot tub opposite the shower, and I forgot about the large shower. I had to relax and reign in my gift to make others feel what I wanted them to feel. "Hell, maybe Dali is right. Being here can't be a good idea." I mumbled as I ran the water, letting it get hot. I placed my clothes in a folded pile next to the sink and stepped into the water.

As I slid down, I found the tub was deeper than I thought and moaned at the scalding water massaging my body. I could tell that I was drifting in and out of consciousness. I didn't want to sit in the tub for too long and pass out, missing the meeting. I had to have been in the water for twenty minutes or so, but I knew I had to get out. I wanted to walk around the Pack lands and find the pit where the meeting will be held that he thinks I am not attending. Quinn did not ask me to be here and not be a part of whatever defense or plans the Pack will decide on doing. I knew the other shifters here did not trust me, so I wanted to be upfront about what I was doing here, not hidden away while Dax spoke for me. This is a turning point for our *kind* to reconnect, and that is how I had to look at it. Just thinking his name brought up his violet eyes, massive frames, and powerful hands. My core ached, and I couldn't stop myself from letting a hand that rested on the side of the tub slip beneath the waters to run over my throbbing clit. I was tall, but Dax was a tree, and I wanted to climb him and feel his heated skin against mine.

"Fuck, Dax..." I moaned as my fingers moved faster.

"Shouldn't you moan my name when I'm inside you, Mate?" I gasped and leaned forward as my eyes flew open. I used an arm to hide my breast that had been on display beforehand, but I would not give his ass the satisfaction.

"What the fuck, Dax? Does a locked door mean nothing to you?" I gritted. I knew my eyes were flashing with irritation, so the usual green was probably hazel now. His heated gaze ran over me, and I could tell by the bulge in his jeans if I gave in an inch, he would take a mile. I watched as his wolf pulled back inside, barely able to contain the attraction I was throwing off. This was a bad idea, and I should have thought about coming here. He reigned in his hunger and then narrowed his eyes at me as if I had done something.

"Locked doors don't mean shit when it's in my home, but fuck all that, Devana. If you think I will not enter after I knocked for ten minutes to check on my Mate, you are seriously mistaken. We will get to that MATE fact later. How about we talk about this," he growled. That was when I noticed he held up the book of scrolls, and it was opened to the picture I stared at not too long ago.

"Shit!" He raised a single midnight black eyebrow, waiting for an answer I didn't have. How do you tell a person you have a book about the complete history of his family?

DAX

I left my Mate in the bathroom to finish up and moved over to the window. I pulled the curtains closed even though she faced away from any other houses on the property. There was still a possibility that someone could be roaming the woods or grounds, and I wasn't having that. No matter how irritated I was at the moment, no one saw my Mate's body but me. I didn't plan on walking inside at first, but I felt a fear I hadn't before when I didn't get an answer. I knew once I was inside that I was irrational, but the thoughts of something happening to my Mate on my land had my wolf seeing red. Once inside, I knew exactly what happened and where she was, and the wolf backed away from the edge. I always held tight control over my wolf, but I would have to work on it when it came to my Mate. If I hadn't gone inside, I would have never spotted that book, and if not for Cassandra, I wouldn't have known what was inside. I knew the cover and what was written inside of it. What I couldn't understand was how would Devana had gotten it. This was one of Cassandra's personal Journals that I teased her about writing. I never tried to see what was written inside, but she told me it was about her and me.

I reached inside her bag, grabbed the journal, which I realized was now a complete book. I opened it, seeing the pages or scrolls inside. I could smell Devana's scent all over it as if she carried it with her daily. I brought it closer to my nose and found the scroll that most held her scent. I stared at a picture of myself on the night I called for Cassandra to come, but she never did. I knew this was her book, but she was not there. If she wasn't, then who was to capture this drawing correctly?

"Dax, it's not okay for you to just go through my things." Her melodic, slightly accented voice had me turning away from my thoughts. I watched as she carried her clothes to her bag in one hand while holding her towel tightly.

"This isn't your thing, Devana. This book doesn't belong to you nor your family." I tried to keep the anger out of my voice, but I failed. I watched as the green eyes flared and her honey brown skin flushed red.

"That book has been in my family since before I was born! Give the book to me, please."

"This book is about me! Without me even reading it, I know because I fucking know who wrote it!" I saw Devana's eyes widen at my words.

"I need to get dressed, and you need to leave. You want the book, take it." She snapped. She turned her back to me and grabbed her clothes that were on the bed.

"Are you sure that is what you want? You don't want to tell me why your scent is so heavily on my drawing? Or where did your family get this journal of my fucking life? Why would a Hunter family even keep something like this?"

"A journal? What are you talking about, what journal? That book was written to tell the counts of your family. It is not a journal. It is meant to help learn your wolves' strengths and weaknesses so that younger Hunters can be taught how to survive against your kind. We have stories about all wolf shifter kinds that first walked this earth. This one is just about your family and what happened."

"So you mean to tell me there isn't anything inside about Cassandra and me? Nothing at all about the Hunter that wrote this book?" I asked, getting closer to her.

"What? How the hell do you know Cassandra Cross? She wrote the beginning, but I don't know who else finished it to this point. It has become harder to keep the records." Finally, I was close enough that she took a step back, craning her neck to look up. Her green eyes danced between grey, green, and brown as she glared up at me.

"What exactly do you mean up until this point? The picture of me drawn in here shouldn't even exist because not one of you, Hunter, showed up to help with that battle." I heard the growl, but I couldn't help it. Devana stepped back again, but my arm grabbed her free hand and stopped her from moving away from me.

"Hunters were there, but they did not feel as if they should interfere with your troubles. So they recorded it but stayed out of the fight," she whispered. I could feel through the bond-forming that told me that she was reciting something that was said to her. She had no firsthand knowledge of how much damage the Hunters had caused by not stepping in to help.

"You come here and tell me that I am supposed to trust that you, a Hunter, are here to help? You bring the very proof that Hunter's do not deserve our trust." Devana held my eyes, not saying a word. I doubted my mating bond at this point. How would I know if she didn't just come here to do what was done years ago? Devana is a Hunter, and that is someone I could never trust.

"I am here to help, Dax," she said firmly.

"No. This doesn't seem right, no matter what my wolf is telling me. You can't be my Mate because I can't trust you, Devana. You need to leave. Thank you for at least giving us a heads up about the situation. We can handle it from here. I... I just don't trust Hunters, and I don't think that will change." I let her arm go, taking a step back even though it physically hurt me to do it. I couldn't get around the fact that Hunters stood and watched as pups died alongside their parents and did nothing. I couldn't trust my Pack in her hands to find out she would stand by and let it happen again.

"Daxton! Wait! You can't walk away like this! I am here to help!" Devana moved quickly to get in front of me.

"How am I to believe a Hunter? How?" I shouted. She stared at me with her mouth open and glared at me like I was the one with no loyalty. "Get your things and go," I growled.

"You don't need to believe a Hunter! All you need to believe in is me, your Mate!" Her furious cry made me stop in my tracks, but the word Mate had me looking back at her.

"That's right! Believe me, because I chose on my own to be here. I made this choice to come, even knowing it could mean my death. I am not asking you to trust in any other Hunter; I am asking you to put your trust in me. You claimed me, so I am not going anywhere."

DEVANA
CHAPTER
four

Dax turned around to stare at me, and his eyes grew an intense violet as he stalked back over to me. I swallowed because I could not help the words that spilled from my lips, but he had to trust me. My feelings were a mess, and I didn't think Dax would have this intense attraction for me. Even with my gifts, something had to be there for him to look at me the way he does right now.

"What did you say?" His low growl vibrated my clit as if he was speaking to it.

"I said I am not going anywhere," I whispered. I was losing my mind, and the fact I couldn't even control my breathing told me maybe he was right, and I should leave. Every time the thought crossed my mind, the pain in my heart damn near stopped my breath.

"No. No, not that. Say it again," Dax commanded. He was in front of me before I knew it. I heard the book hit the floor. Dax's hands reached up, grabbing my hair, making sure I couldn't move an inch. His grip was tight, but it didn't hurt as he held my face making us eye to eye. "Say it."

The command in his voice had a horse moan leaving my lips.

"Mate. I said, Mate," I whimpered. I didn't know what was wrong with me. I was a Hunter. I'm not weak. Damn, he had me weak in the knees. But when it came to those violet eyes and his domineering presence, something just switched off. I didn't feel like a Hunter, but like a woman who needed his mouth on mine.

"This is my problem, Devana. My wolf knows you are mine, but my mind tells me you are not telling me everything. You call me your Mate, but I don't know if you truly believe this is a fact or not." His words ripped at my soul, but logically, I knew this could be my out. I could pull away and go after this demon alone so no one would get hurt. My heart told me that was so damn wrong, but could I trust myself that these feelings were genuine?

"I make this promise to you that I am not here to hurt anyone and that I am here to help." He searched my eyes for the truth of my words. I was losing the grip I held on my towel. I wanted to run my hands up his body and take his shirt off. "Fuck it."

I reached up to pull his face to mine, and his lips devoured me. I felt his fingers leave my hair. They worked their way to my ass, squeezing my cheeks and pulling me closer. The towel was long gone as we demanded more from each other. Dax pulled back only to place his lips on my neck, licking and sucking. He had me going into a frenzy trying to climb his ass like a damn tree. Finally, Dax stepped back and pulled his shirt off, and my mouth went dry. His chest was covered in tattoos of so many animals, but the massive red wolf over his heart stood out the most. I didn't have time to ask about any of them because he dropped his sweats and my core throbbed. I never knew I could crave a person until Daxton Rayne. I was soaked before he even touched me again.

"Get on the bed." His voice was almost incomprehensible. I moved and climbed onto the bed when I felt his hand on my ankle, pulling me back and flipping me around. I groaned as Dax stalked over my body. I fantasized about this, but my feeling was more than lust. I wanted him. I wanted to protect him and give everything I am to this man, this wolf. The realization of my feelings slammed into my chest as Dax grabbed both breasts together and sucked.

"Ohh...oh shiii..." I moaned as he rubbed his thickness against my core. He didn't stop teasing my nipples until my body shuddered beneath him.

"I hope you know what you are in for, Hunter."

Dax grunted as he leaned down to kiss me quickly. He moved back down my body, giving each breast attention one last time before his tongue slowly drifted down my body to my navel. I couldn't help the shudder as his hands glided over each breast and pinched my nipples hard.

"Oh fuck!" I cried. I felt the tingle in my clit. I moaned in pleasure as he kissed every inch while moving between nipples, pinching them, making my thighs clench tight around him.

"I wanted to taste this earlier. I have been thinking about it ever since I smelled your scent. I need it on my tongue." His low groan had my eyes rolling as he made his way to my core. I shuddered again as he teasingly began licking my clit, working me as he watched me. My eyes were heavy, but I couldn't mistake the wolf peeking through, ready to claim what was his. His tongue slid between the edges of my lips as his hands traveled down to rest on my legs. He began teasing and playing, avoiding what I wanted. I reached down, trying to move his head up so he could suck my clit the way I needed him to. He caught my arm, and I saw the cocky ass smile as he slammed it to the bed. I rocked my hips, trying to get him where I wanted, when he slid his tongue deep in my opening, making me arch up with a desire for more. I whimpered in time with his tongue thrusts into my opening, making a mess on his face. I swear his tongue got longer as it hit spots inside of me that it shouldn't have, making me call out his name.

"Dax, Dax! Please!" I moaned. I felt my climax building, and I was going to explode. My entire body needed him in ways I couldn't fully understand. The first time I ever saw his face in the drawings, I was drawn to him. I didn't know how long he would keep me on the edge of coming, but I need the release and for Dax to give it to me. His tongue teased my clit, while occasionally traveling back down to swipe at my opening, teasing me as if he were going to shove his tongue back deep inside of me. I felt his thick finger slide in deep as he crooked his finger to hit my G-spot. I couldn't help the cry of pleasure, and I moved my hips without control. I wanted more, and I wanted him inside of me.

"You called me your Mate, but I don't think you believe it. But you will." His words were rough and laced with a hint of a growl, making my entire body vibrate.

I felt tears gather in the corner of my eyes as the agony of just being so close to release was driving me insane. I knew he was tormenting me for the use of the word Mate. I knew Dax as an Alpha ached to hear those words leave my lips in submission. Not being able to take anymore, I tried to wiggle away from his grip, but his growl stopped all movement. His violet eyes snapped up to meet mine, and I felt as if I would growl right back.

"I need to come, Dax, please?"

His chuckle sent more vibrations through me and was almost enough to cause me to climax. Dax leaned back down without answering me, and his tongue circled and twirled at my clit while his fingers thrust deeper into me. I couldn't stop the moan from escaping my lips as I let my head fall onto the mattress. I gripped the sheets with one hand as the other found its way into his thick hair. I pulled at it as I rocked my hips, "*Dax.*"

I knew I was close, but I wanted more. I opened my mouth but slammed it shut when I realized I almost asked for his mark, for him to bite me in the way that would make me his. Dax pushed another finger into my tight core, stretching me out as he hit that spot repeatedly. I clenched onto his fingers and gripped his hair tightly as I rose to make him give me more. His large hand pushed me back down on the bed as he looked up to meet my heated gaze. I couldn't tear my eyes away from his as I gasped out loudly as his finger made a move that had me crashing into bliss.

"Oh...fuck!" I screamed as I came feeling everything drain out of me. All the worries, stress and fear were gone in the minutes my climax lasted. I felt his lips on mine as his fingers kept up the motion giving me aftershocks of plea-sure. I felt as though I was drugged or buzzed in a good way. I didn't know that my eyes lids had slid closed until I tried to open them.

"Shh..you have time, Mate. Just rest for now." I felt him move away from me and then his heat around me as he adjusted my body to lay on his chest. I couldn't stay awake for anything else.

DAX

I knew this was my Mate, but it was still something she wasn't telling me, and I did not like it. I watched her sleeping on my chest for a few more minutes before moving her carefully onto the mattress and slipping out of bed to get to my Pack meeting. As a Pack Alpha, I had to make sure my lands would be safe while I dealt with this imposter running around as if he is the True Alpha or even an Alpha at all. I put my clothes back on and headed to my room to get cleaned up before it was time. I knew Devana wanted to be a part of the meeting, and maybe she should since she was my Mate, but she wasn't truthful. I could sense it and feel that even though she used the word Mate, she did not mean it. "I don't have time for this. What the hell was Quinn thinking?" I grumbled as I showered quickly. I stepped out with a towel around my hips to see Thomas standing by the window overlooking the entire property. "What are you doing here? Should you be at the pit?" I said, looking at the clock. Thomas said nothing and didn't make a move to face me, so I moved over to the old oak dresser that belonged to my parents and pulled out a pair of black sweatpants and a long-sleeve black t-shirt.

"Someone here is up to something, and I don't like it. I don't like it because I can't figure it out just yet. Who would want to work with a fake wolf who calls themselves The True Alpha in their right mind? It makes no sense when Quinn has shown not only to be the real True Alpha but also has the eyes to prove it," Thomas said. He finally turned around to look at me. I could tell this shit was getting to him, because his empathic gifts could typically find the deceit in a shifter as well as keeping a Pack calm. The fact he wasn't getting anything was telling the wrongness of this entire situation. Something or someone was hiding this person from his gift, which was never a good sign.

"Little brother, as long as I have lived, there has always been a reason that humans or supernaturals follow the wrong side. Everyone chooses what they believe in, and sometimes they make the wrong choices or choose to follow the wrong person. The problem with this is that some have their choice taken from them. For example, we have a demon possessing a wolf shifter because this shifter wants power. That rogue wants a title that does not belong to him and believes that only born wolves are the true shifters, which touches on shit that other shifters believe in. He speaks the words that others want to say but are too afraid to say, so they follow him no matter how wrong it feels. It's fucking with me, brother. What is the endgame to all of this? What is the endgame for this demon?" I asked. What does this demon get from this chaos because we know it isn't to help this wolf?

"That is what is honestly bothering me the most. The others are looking for a fight. They want to bring this Alpha and his Pack down before…" I looked up from lacing my boots to catch Thomas's eyes before he looked away. I stood and made my way over to him and grabbed his shoulder so he could look at me.

"This will not end up like the last battle. I know what you lost…" Thomas pulled away, and I could feel the control over his emotions slam into place.

"I know it won't. We will not let it happen again. If this Hunter can give us an edge this time, I have no problem working with her or any other Hunter. Just know that it will be few who have my point of view." He said, turning to face me once more. He could almost be my twin except for the eyes and the height. I looked at him more like a son than my other brothers because he was the youngest and smallest when he was born. The only one who actually saw me as more of a Father was Hayley.

"Yeah, I know. I appreciate that, but my word is the law whatever they have to say. This is not a democracy in this Pack, and I will ensure every wolf understands that tonight. I will always do what is best for my Pack and my family." I held his eyes until his shifted away and down.

"I got you, Alpha," he said. We both turned as a howl filled the night and knew it was time to get things started.

DEVANA

I could barely see through the smoke as I ran into the field, searching for Dax. The screaming and howls of pain coming all around me had me spinning in circles. "Dax!" I screamed but immediately started to cough. I tripped over a body and looked down to see a partially shifted wolf lying face down in the dirt, rapidly decaying in front of my eyes. I scooted back on my hands and feet only to bump into another body, but this time, it was an entirely shifted wolf staring at me with blank eyes. I looked closer and saw the twisted remains of the wolf that looked to be transforming into something else. "What the hell is going on here!" I stood up and moved through the smoke, searching for the violet eyes that had to be here. I heard the howling and growling coming behind me, and I spun around in place with my blade up and ready. A large wolf with crimson eyes that burned as if they were the gateway to hell growled deep. I narrowed my eyes, preparing myself to take this thing out when it began to shift into a tall figure of a man, but the crimson eyes never left mine.

"You again, Hunter. You should not be involved in

this matter of wolves. You have no truce and no loyalty to each other." The bass-filled voice echoed around me and inside of my mind. The demon seemed confused about why I was still around or trying to help. It had me thinking if this separation of Hunter's from the supernatural species was all in a grand design.

"You are the one who doesn't belong here, demon!" I gritted. I tightened my grip on my blade and readied myself for the attack. A hiss of laughter crawled along my skin like a thousand spiders.

"You will fall, along with the wolves, if that is what you wish. I have created my *Cadejo*. My Red Eyed Wolf will destroy them all." The demon laughed, and I attacked. I went for his neck with my blade. I wasn't Taria Cross, and I couldn't kill a demon without a demon blade. Lucky, I had plenty of them. I was close, and I spun on a heel to go right when the demon shifted into the large smokey black wolf and faded into the smoke. My demon blade came down in the spot it was in and slammed into the ground.

"Shit!" I screamed, pulling the blade out. I spun around just as the wolf leaped from the shadows. I knew I wouldn't have time to get my arm up before the demon caught me in its jaws. "No!"

BUZZ... BUZZ...BUZZ

"Holy! Oh....oh my...shit!" I jumped up from the bed and slid to the floor as I tried and failed to catch my breath.

BUZZ...BUZZ...BUZZ

I looked around for what the noise could be when I figured out what it was making it. "Damn," I said, shaking my head. I blinked a few times before pulling myself to my feet and looking for my phone. I was still naked but sated and feeling good. "Hello?" I said, wiping my eyes.

"Vana! Are you sleep? Well, if you are, you need to get up. I don't care what you say, Devana. I am coming to help you. I don't know if I trust these shifters to have your back."

"Dali! Wait, what time is it?" I said, looking at the clock. "Shit...listen, I have to go. Don't come here. I am good. Everything will be fine, just trust me. Everything is good, plus we don't need mom and dad mad at you as well. One of us has to stay in their good graces." I said as I moved around the room. I disconnected the call as I began to pull my clothes on. I shook my head in agitation with Dax. He could have woken me up, but I knew it was because he didn't think I should be there. He wanted me as a Mate. He claimed me as his Mate, but he didn't trust me, and I didn't blame him.

The fact that I was a Hunter would make everything about this partnership harder. The fact that I possessed a book that told of his past and how my people did nothing to help his people. I would try to right that wrong starting here. The vision came crashing back into my mind, and I saw pieces that I overlooked while I was inside the vision. Whatever attack that was in my vision is going to happen soon. It wasn't here on this land but not too far away from it. I knew most of his Pack lived on this property, but I was sure some didn't. I promised to help protect his Pack, and I promised myself to protect Dax. I would keep both promises, even if that meant I had to save him from myself in the process. I made sure to have all my weapons secured before I moved to the windows. Dax probably had someone downstairs waiting for me, but they wouldn't get the chance to stop me. I opened the window and jumped out.

DAX
CHAPTER
five

I looked around at my Pack and could sense each shifter's anticipation, fear and anxiousness. I stood in the center of the pit along with my Beta and brothers so everyone would know that we would protect them.

"I am sure all of you know that we have a Hunter on our lands," I said. I was connecting eyes with each member to gauge who would show to be a problem.

"A Hunter! We don't need a Hunter to help. We can deal with whatever issue on our own!" The murmurs and mumbles of "hell yeah," and "damn straight" followed Braxton's statement. I knew it was him that spoke. I turned to pin my gaze on the black bear shifter who stood with his massive, fisted hands. His Mate Diana looked at me with pleading eyes to not throw them out of the Pack. I wouldn't do anything like that, but Braxton wasn't about to start some shit in my meeting.

"Sit down, Braxton. That decision is not up to you. You found a home here with your Mate and cubs. I don't ask for much except that you follow Pack law and my commands. So when I say we have a Hunter here, that means they were invited, and they are here to help with the problem." I stared at Braxton for a minute before he sat down with a nod.

"Yes, Alpha," he grunted. I didn't miss the touch on the shoulder that Lindell gave Braxton. I didn't need to say a thing because I knew Dimitri saw it as well. Something was up with those two, but I didn't know what it was yet. I understood Braxton to a certain extent because his Sleuth of Bear family was all but decimated, and the Hunter in charge of that state did nothing.

"Good. I knew everyone's feelings about the Hunters very well. All of you shifters know me and how I feel about them, but times are changing. There has been a shift in this world, and we all feel it. Some of us saw it up close and personal. Evil has come, and it is coming for every being on this earth. Now, something is coming for our Pack and others around this country, and our True Alpha has asked me, and by asking me, he is asking this Pack to be the ones to stop it. Quinn, our True Alpha, has connected us with a Hunter because not only will we need to handle rogue wolves but a demon as well." I looked around at the shocked faces, and some faces with panic etched into them. I looked over to Thomas, and he took a step forward, holding out a hand to calm the Pack so we could get this done. I could feel the energy of Thomas, like a soothing breeze that soothed the soul. The Pack began to ease, and I saw when it was safe to continue.

"Alpha, why would this Hunter help us at all? I mean, they normally just stand by and do nothing. Are they only here because of the demon? Did they bring the demon to us?" I saw Nessa standing with her arms folded. She looked afraid but eager to fight if called to do so.

"No, Nessa, this demon was not brought here by the

Hunter. Our task is to find out what this demon is trying to do and stop the shit. But, first, we have to put this shifter to bed before he does any more damage."

"But...some are saying he is the True Alpha. I have heard from other shifters in different states that there is another True Alpha. Is this the one we are calling the rogue?" Nessa asked. I looked at my brothers and Dimitri before answering Nessa.

"When and where have you heard this information?" I asked. Nessa looked around before meeting my eyes, and she looked away.

"I have spoken to other friends from different Packs around the nation. I didn't think it was a big deal because when would we really see the True Alpha, anyway? Plus, I didn't take them seriously. I just thought it was Pack politics or something. I mean, how long has it been since an actual True Alpha has lived among us." She said, dropping her arms to her side.

"I have heard rumblings as well, Alpha. I mean, just questions about who this Alpha is and whether we are sure he is the real deal. Not to mention the whole purity of his children is a question because they are half Witch. How could he actually be a True Wolf Alpha when his Mate is not even a shifter?" William said.

"Purity? Is that what you're thinking, William? Is any other wolf shifter here carrying these same thoughts as this fake Alpha?" I asked. I felt Malic move out of line and slip into the shadows of the pit. My eyes had never left the wolf William, who I knew cared little for others in this Pack if they weren't wolves.

"I...I never said I did, Alpha. I...I am just stating what we have heard, and these are valid questions. I do not doubt that Quinn Savir is the True Alpha." William said quickly. His eyes darted around frantically, looking for Malic.

"A demon possesses this rogue, and none of his words are ever to be trusted. Now, who else has heard this talk and never thought to bring it to your Alpha!" The growl and command that were laced in my words had each head bowing. I knew some of the wolves here only cared for their species, and nothing would change that fact, but I never thought they had a problem with a turned were-shifter. I knew there were very few who kept to themselves off-Pack lands. I saw Malic appeared behind two male shifters that sat behind William. He placed both hands on their shoulders and pulled them from the seats. I felt Jarod step forward as I waited for any more to be removed to the side about their beliefs. This Pack served one Alpha and one True Alpha. I understood that maybe this rogue had infiltrated packs before they even got there. The Packs that were taken down and Alpha killed were because they had inside knowledge. This demon started its infestation before it even came to town. Jarod stalked back and forth as he eyed each Pack member before he spoke.

"This Pack has always been a mixture of shifters. We never and will never turn our backs on any shifter in need. We accept all with no question of heritage, and we only ask that you believe in your Alpha and wolf shifter law. I know that many of you do not trust Hunters, but they are best at hunting demons. Suppose this demon has already gotten into the minds of a few of you. What will happen when it comes, because it is coming. We need every advantage, and at the moment, we have one of the best advantages, thanks to our True Alpha. That is a Hunter who can find, fight, and destroy a demon. Who here can tell me that they have done the same?" I listened to each of my member's murmurs and thoughts as what Jarod said hit home. He was already thinking along the same lines as I was, and that was that shit had already started. This rogue and demon would try to destroy my Pack from the inside out.

I could feel that my Pack began to see the need for a Hunter. I could also sense their fear about trusting a Hunter who may leave us to die because they don't consider it their problem. I completely understood it, and I could not fault them for it. This is the main reason why I did not want Devana at this meeting. No one trusted her, and I still felt something was off even knowing she is my Mate. It was lucky for William that Malic took him as well from my sight because I almost tore his spine through his mouth. Devana is my Mate, and she is not a shifter, so William's feelings about that matter hits close to home. Not only that, but we have others here who have been bitten or scratched, and they should not have to hear his hatred.

"Alpha, I know that we may need this, Hunter, but...how are we supposed to fight beside someone that we do not trust?" Nessa asked. I looked at the others in the Pack who would be fighting and saw the same frustration in their eyes.

"What about our pups and cubs? How will we protect them from this rogue?" Another member asked.

"I will protect my Pack. Nothing will touch our children." I stated. I felt my brothers lock eyes on me as I made that statement as a law. "Who of this Pack will put aside their misgivings of Hunters and trust their Alpha in this decision? Who will make sure that rogue will never touch another Pack?" I knew my eyes grew a burning violet as I spoke, and I knew my words instilled courage and a sense of purpose for my shifters. I took in a breath and caught a scent that should have been in bed and not in my pit. I turned my head to the opening, but I saw nothing. It didn't matter because my wolf saw all on this land. Devana was here, but she chose well to stay out of sight for now. I let my Alpha energy flow through the Pack to feel the safety they craved and expected to feel from me.

"Tonight, we will prepare our land and protect our children. OUR True Alpha has chosen this Pack to handle this, and we will. If you hold the same beliefs as these fake ass wolves and that fake Alpha, this is no longer the place for you to live. This family has always taken in others of different species and protected them as well as bitten wolves. Tonight is the only night you are free to leave this land and Pack. If I find that any member of this Pack is working in the same belief system as this possessed wolf, you will become my enemy." I looked around to each pack member so they could see the deadly seriousness of my words. "All of you know how I deal with my enemies, and you will not receive any mercy from me but a quick death. Am I clear?" I heard some whimpers from Pack members who weren't as strong as others from the pressure my power put on their bodies. I knew everyone needed to understand that I meant what I said and that this wolf and all of his followers would suffer Pack law. Their actions meant death, and every Pack member in this meeting knew it to be law.

DEVANA

I knew Dax could feel me just as his Mate pull called out to me as well. I couldn't shake the vision of what happened or forget the words that the demon spoke. As I listened to the meeting, I heard all the concerns, knowing these shifters would not trust me. I couldn't blame them because we have ignored our mission and purpose for far too long. I slid along the wall of the pit and overheard shifters being dragged out of the meeting. It didn't matter what race, breed, or species you were. There would always be others who think they are superior to the rest. I pressed my back to the wall and slowed my breathing as I listened to the shifters.

"Malic! Malic, this is crazy! I said nothing about disobeying my Alpha. I should not be prosecuted because I have stronger beliefs!" An older wolf shifter spat. I watched as Malic and three men stood facing each other. They were all huge men, but Malic was larger, and his Alpha influence pressed down on the senses. My gaze flicked to the opening, and I saw the Beta Dimitri coming out to stand next to Malic.

"Cut the shit, William. You just keep running off at the

mouth and digging a deeper hole for yourself," Malic growled. Malic took a step forward, and the other shifters took one step back.

"Fuck this, Will! It was all funny at first, but they are serious. I have a family I need to think about, and this Pack provides that safety for us." The shifter moved away from William and the other shifter, putting him outside of Malic's metallic gaze.

"Smart move, Cecil, but don't move any further," Dimitri grunted.

"Listen, Malic, Dimitri, it's like he said all fun and games. Yes, I believe that a born wolf is true, but I don't harbor ill intentions toward anyone! Hell, I have a family and just want what is best for them! So just listen to what..."

"Malic! I don't know what Will has going on, but I was just in it for the free alcohol and boredom. I don't care if you are born, bitten, scratched, or hell, even if you are a damn alien! I have no problems!" The other wolf said, holding up his hands.

"Joel, get your ass over there with Cecil's, simple ass!" Dimitri growled. Joel moved quickly to the side without hesitation.

"Now, hold the fuck up!" William said as he pulled himself taller. My eyes narrowed on the wolf. His movements were jerkier than they should have been. All supernatural creatures have a grace about them that looked effortlessly beautiful, except for a demon. I knew that William wasn't possessed as the wolf running around claiming to be the True Alpha, but he was being groomed for a possession. The darkness that surrounded him gave me an eerie feeling. The mostly invisible scratches on his neck that should have been healed were made in a pattern. No one but another Hunter would notice or understand its meaning. William was marked, and his soul is in danger of being taken.

I knew I had to act fast if I wanted to help this man and everyone in this Pack alive. God only knows how many others here have been marked like him.

"William, you need to calm down, or I will have to put you down. All of you will wait for the Alpha to finish, and he will deal with you himself!" Malic growled. The other men looked down and away, but William didn't. I saw the mark extend further down his neck, the more his anger grew.

"You, Malic, are not the Alpha of this Pack and are a pup compared to me. I am an elder, and you should learn some respect!" Spital flew from his lips as Malic's eyes blazed in the night. I saw Dimitri reach out and grab Malic's arm, and I noticed his hand was formed into the claws of his wolf. William looked down and backed up with a sneer.

"You best keep your mouth closed, William, because I cannot hold Malic back." Dimitri glared at the man.

"Fuck you, Beta!" William snarled as he dropped to all fours. His clothes began to shred as he began shifting into his wolf form. I couldn't wait any longer because they would kill this wolf. I moved out of the shadows in one step and flashed forward. I saw Malic and Dimitri's eyes flick toward me as I moved in their direction with quick steps. I crashed into the shifting wolf, knocking the giant creature to the ground. I rolled to my feet, making sure my blades were away. I didn't want to kill him, only help this wolf.

"A Hunter! She's attacking William!" One of the other men that were with William shouted. I looked into the brown eyes of the wolf as he shook himself. William's wolf is dark brown, but his ears were tipped black with a gray muzzle. He growled, showing me his sharp fangs. I could see the faint red glow in his eyes.

"He's gone feral! Get away from him. This is Pack business!" Malic growled. I knew he was moving over to me, but I wasn't about to give him the time. This type of mark is like an infection, and if another gets bit or scratched, it will move onto the next. So this one wolf could infect the entire Pack.

"Stay back!" I shouted. William howled and leaped for my throat.

DEVANA
CHAPTER
Six

I didn't have time to look toward Malic when William came at me with teeth bared. I dropped low, letting the wolf sail over my head. I came up as the wolf hit the ground and spun around in place to face me. It felt as if everything was happening in slow motion, but I knew it had only been seconds. I moved while I took out one blade to remove the infected skin before it was too late. I took in a breath and could taste Dax's scent in the air and feel his power as if it caressed my skin.

"She's attacking him!" A woman shifter screamed, but it was too late for anyone to stop me. I let the wolf land on top of me as he leaped to meet me. Its jaws were clamped on my arm, and I could feel the pressure, but it wouldn't break through my Hunter gear.

"Devana!" Dax roared. I knew he and everyone else would be on us in a hot second, but that was all I needed to get the job done. I jammed my blade into the wolf's neck and twisted. The wolf's head was angled the exact way I needed to reach the spot where the marking was hiding under the fur. William pulled back and roared in pain, but I held on to my blade and grabbed his head, and I began digging out the rot that was trying to settle into his flesh and soul. Blood began to pour, and I smelled the wrongness of it, but I kept up the pressure until I hit bone. Then I spoke a few words that made my blade flash with pure white light, making everyone blind for just a second. William howled, but I felt him weaken, and his blood began to smell of shifter once again. Finally, the light blinked out, and I pulled my blade out as William fell to the ground.

"She killed him! She..."

"Devana!" Dax was in front of me and pulling me out from underneath a now sleeping William. I could hear the growls and snarls coming from the Pack. What I didn't expect was Dax pulling me into him as he checked me over for what he probably thought was a severed arm.

"What the hell? Where are you hurt? You could have been killed." His voice was rough, but his touch was gentle as he maneuvered my arm.

"I'm good. I need..."

"Alpha! We can't trust the Hunter! She killed William!" I tried pulling away from Dax, but his grip on me was like iron. I wiggled to turn and face everyone when I heard two shots ring out in the night.

"Every round I have is silver, and every weapon I possess is coated in it. Now get your damn hands off of my sister. If it weren't for her, that wolf...well, he probably would have killed his family later tonight." I knew the voice as if it were my own. I didn't know how or why Dali was here, but this was about to be a shit storm in two seconds. I felt Dax tense and knew that he gave an order to someone on some level, but I wasn't able to hear him mentally. At least not yet.

"How the fuck did you get on my land?" Dax growled.

"Dax, hold up. Dali, what in the hell are you doing here? I told you to stay away!" I said as Dax finally let me go after he realized my arm was fine. Dali strolled down a hill toward the growing crowd and agitated shifters with two guns held high. Her silver-lined, dragon-skinned Hunter gear would make it hard for any of these shifters to get close to her, but it wouldn't stop all shifters.

"Saving your ass just in time! I told you they wouldn't..." Dali stopped talking, and I saw a large form seeming to peel out of the darkened tree line. He moved so fast I only glimpsed amber eyes with gold flecks. He was in front of Dali in a second. Her gun shifted to point at his chest, but his clawed hand was around her silver-covered neck. Except she didn't seem to notice it or move when her trigger finger spasmed slightly. I knew the silver had to hurt, but Max was also an Alpha. A powerful one at that.

"I don't have time for this," I muttered. I turned and moved for the down wolf, but a female shifter growled at me when I was two steps away from him. It didn't frighten me, but it made me pause. She was small in human form, but the yellow eyes that looked at me were predatory. "I need to finish the ritual if you want me to save his life. The demon has already gotten to him, and I don't know how long he has been marked. If you want me to save him, then let me do what needs to be done." I stated. I was always taught never to take my eyes from a predator, but I needed Dax to see what I was saying is the truth. I turned away from the woman who had to be William's Mate and stared at my own.

DAX

I knew Hunters were fast, but I never saw a Hunter other than Taria move the way Devana did. Before I could move, William had his teeth in her as he shook her like a rag doll. This was why I did not want her at this meeting because, Pack or not, Devana is my Mate, and I would kill William if he harmed her. I moved, but a sudden flash of light filled the night, blinding me. It didn't matter because I could still scent my Mate. The light was gone just as suddenly as it came, and Devana pushed the large wolf to the side, and William laid still. "Fuck," I growled. I couldn't help but pull her into me to see how bad the damage would be. I didn't know what to expect, but I should have known that a Mate of mine would know how to handle herself. As the words she spoke filtered through, I filtered out all sounds too narrow in on William. I knew my brother had the other Hunter, so I wasn't worried about an attack from her. His heart was still beating, but it was at a slow pace. William's temperature was low, too low for a pure-blooded shifter. It only took a moment for me to see the truth in Devana's eyes, and I knew if she weren't here, my Pack might have been decimated overnight.

"Jayla! Stand back."

"Alpha! She...you can't let this Hunter...."

"I said stand back! All of you stand back!" I growled. I knew my eyes burned, and I could see the effect my power started to have on everyone present. Devana had a slight limp, but she kneeled beside William and placed her hands on his blood-soaked fur. She whispered in a language I only heard two other people use, and they both were Hunters. I wasn't sure if it was Enochian or something similar.

"That's enough, Devana!" The woman screamed in our direction.

"You give no orders here, Hunter." I heard Max growl. It wasn't his usual growl to an enemy, but something...else. I took a step forward, not caring what would happen because if I was correct, the intruder is my Mate's sister, and she wouldn't tell her to stop if it wasn't doing Devana any harm. I could feel the heat coming from her hands, but I paid little attention as I reached down and snatched her away from the wolf.

"Wait! Dax! Wait a minute."

"He's fine! He is waking, and you look..." I looked her over, and the dark bruises under those cat-like eyes held all of my attention. "You're exhausted." I gritted.

"Jesus! Can you tell your mutt to stand down! I need to see my sister."

"I am nothing but Purebred Alpha over this way, sexy. There isn't a need for orders because you aren't moving an inch."

"I...I'm fine, Dali I..." Devana's eyes rolled back in her head, and that was that.

"Dimitri! Take William to the clinic and stay there with him until one of the enforcers gets there. Max, stop the bull shit and get that Hunter to the house. Everyone else, you know what needs to be done, so fucking do it!"

"A...Alpha I would..." The shuddering came from Jayla, but I knew what she wanted.

"You may go with him, but you will stay there until I speak to the both of you. Now Move!" I shouted as I took quick strides to the main house.

Remi had the doors open before I made it to the house's front steps. But I didn't stop as other Pack members darted questioning looks at the other Hunter that made it onto our land and at me holding my Hunter in my arms. The fact that Dali made it onto our land in itself should have been impossible. I was up the stairs and inside my room before I knew it. I laid Devana on the bed, not knowing exactly what I should do for her when I heard Dali raising hell. I needed answers from her about what to do with Devana. I also needed to know how she managed to step foot on this property. My wolf refused to let me move from this spot, so I had no choice but to have Max bring the Hunter to me.

I moved toward the door, but I didn't make it a few feet before my wolf went crazy at leaving Devana's side when she was vulnerable. "Bring her here, Max." I knew everyone heard the low growl. I was trying to hold back my anger, hatred, and fear all at once. Just because Devana is my Mate doesn't mean I put aside my disdain for Hunters. Now I have two of them on my land and inside of my home. One of which was not invited and will not be staying.

"Da...Dax." My body moved to the bed before I realized it. Her eyes opened, and I knew my wolf was peeking out, and it was the first time I couldn't control it.

"Devana, what were you thinking? I told you not to come to the meeting." I knew damn well my first words shouldn't be a command, but what else would she expect. I was Alpha, and my word was law, no ifs ands or buts about it. Her face scrunched up with a frown as she tried to sit up.

"If... if I didn't, this entire Pack..."

"Vana! This is what I was trying to tell you! They would have killed you even though you were saving their Pack member's life," Dali interrupted. I looked back as the Hunter snatched her arm away from Max and gritted her teeth as she rushed forward. I growled, and she stopped just two feet away from us. I couldn't stop the growl, but I didn't even try it. We were not like her people that stood by while others died. "Vana?" Dali said as she looked between her sister and me.

"Dali, I told you not to come here. I'm fine." I felt Devana's tiny hand on my forearm, making me take my glare away from her sister.

"If I hadn't shown up, they would have killed you for helping their Pack member! They wouldn't even have heard you out! You put yourself in danger to help people who wouldn't do shit for you."

"Dali!" Devana snapped. She sat up, but I placed a hand on her to keep her from getting up. "Dax, let me..."

"No."

"But Dax she..."

"No," I said again and turned to face the Hunter. I looked over at Max as he rubbed at the burns on his hands. "Listen, Hunter. I do not appreciate you assuming shit about my Pack. We do not leave people to die or kill them for no reason. You do not get to come here and be self-righteous about shit the way YOUR people have let all species down over the years. You do not know me, and I sure as hell don't care to know you, but your sister is my MATE, and I would never let anyone, not even my Pack, get close to killing her. So, what's going to happen here is you will go with Max to my office while I make sure my MATE isn't hurt. This is not a request. It is a fucking order." I bit out each word as slow as I could. I held on tight to my wolf. I could feel that my wolf wanted to lash out at anyone that came close to Devana at this moment. Max understood what was up, but I saw the defiance on Dali's face. Before she could open her mouth, and Devana managed to get up, Max moved. He had the Hunter by her waist and hauled her out of the door. I caught the flash of heat in her eyes before the irritated mask slipped back into place.

"Daxton, we don't have time for all of this." I turned back to look down at my frowning Mate. Her eyes glittered with irritation, but I knew my own burned with it.

"I told you not to come to my Pack meeting. Not only did you not listen, but you could have been fucking hurt in the process." I couldn't help but to check her over once more. I knew about the Mating bond and how it can cloud the mind initially, but that was after the mark.

"Yeah, well, you can't claim a Mate and then tell her she isn't welcomed! It doesn't matter anyway because we have a problem, a huge problem." I was about to give her the many reasons why her ass should not have been there when I felt the fear coming off her body.

"The demon has already begun to infest my Pack," I growled. I stared into those eyes that flashed from green to hazel and brown before she looked away.

"Yes. Yes, it has, but that isn't what concerns me the most. The demon we face is a *Cadejo*."

"The Black Dog?" I asked, confused as to why she believes that it's so bad.

"That is just a simple term. I know that you are older and may hold more knowledge of supernatural things, but you do not know demons. Not like a Hunter. This...this *Cadejo* is here to cause disease, destruction, confusion, chaos and death. Which one will it go with at the end? No one knows. It may appear as a dog but do not mistake it for what it truly is, evil walking. If a *Cadejo* possessed a wolf shifter, that means it can now walk like a man. It will no longer need to hide in the shadows of night to whisper its poison. It now has a voice and a willing soul that will feed it the power of life."

As Devana spoke, her words slowly clicked into place about what was happening and what would happen to my Pack. I remember learning about this Black Dog that I took for a joke long ago, just something said in passing. Cassandra once told me it was lucky that my family was blessed with all Alphas. ***Seven Alpha children born to one family will contain the gift that will push the darkness of the Black Dog back into the pit.*** A prophecy that was spoken about and confirmed by the Hunter. A prediction that didn't seem as if it genuinely meant anything other than calming the fears of one family being too powerful. No one has ever seen this *Cadejo*, but I can't deny that Devana's words rang true. Unfortunately, none of us ever took stock in those words because what canine could stand up to the apex predator? What type of Dog could compare itself to a Werewolf?

"Tell me what I need to know to protect my Pack. Tell me everything I need to know to protect all of my people. I need the truth, all of it, and whatever it is you aren't telling me. I can't have you at my back if I can't even trust you. I should be able to trust my Mate." I growled. This moment right here and now would tell me if she would stand at my side or be just like the Hunters of old. Devana held my gaze, but I wasn't about to back down from what I asked. I needed to know what she knows and what exactly she is trying to keep hidden from me.

"Let me tell you of the vision," She said softly.

"You had another?" That was possible, but that isn't the thing she was keeping from me. My wolf could taste it. We could feel it.

"Yes, but before I tell you of that one, let me tell you of the very first one." I leaned away as she maneuvered herself up. I could sense her fear, apprehension, and resolve. Her cat-like eyes hardened, and she sucked in a breath as she began telling me of a vision of a wolf with violet eyes that turned crimson as he slaughtered his entire Pack.

AERON
CHAPTER *seven*

I felt it when the connection broke with one of the shifters in the Rayne pack. It wasn't one I spent most of my time working on, but another. It was one of the older shifters that could have been an addition to my army. I stood up from the kneeling position and kicked over the bowl of blood I used to see through the eyes of the shifter. The dark, now black blood pooled on the ground, and I watched it spread until it hit the arm of the shifter I used to fill it. I didn't know what it was about this wolf that her blood gave this spell such a boost of power, but I would find out.

"A...Alpha...can...can I..." My lips pulled back in disgust at the female shifter. Her long black hair was matted and knotted in places. Her once rich brown skin seemed to have dulled, and the defiance in her eyes was now gone. I liked her defiant, but I wanted her broken. I didn't understand the feelings I had when I am around this wolf, which always angered me every time I used her for this purpose. I narrowed my eyes at her, and she glanced away quickly, but I saw the spark in those lavender eyes.

"Clean this mess up and then tell the Pack females it's time to move. We need to go and free more wolves from the service of this False Alpha, but first, we need to deal with the Pack in that state. Make sure those females in this new Pack know the rules this time, Maeze. You know what the price for you will be when they fuck up," I growled.

"Y.. yes, Alpha. I understand," She whispered. I cracked a smile because I heard the distaste in her voice and the slight growl she tried to cover. That just means she isn't as broken as I thought. That was good. Her blood connected to **Abadozui** stronger than any other, but I didn't know why. I was close to getting my answer to that question. She just needed a little more alone time with her Alpha. I bared my teeth at her before I turned on my heel and stepped out of the windowless room. I felt the crawling, stinging sensation along my skin and smelled the foulness of the demon before I heard its voice in my mind.

"Aeron, we have a problem."

The deep voice still scraped against my senses, and I felt as though blades stabbed me repeatedly in my brain. But it didn't matter because it was well worth it.

"The Hunter. Yes, I saw her, but she is just one. We are many," I answered. As I walked, I caught the eye of Keys, my Beta that was once an Alpha. It didn't take much for him to see who to follow, and I didn't have to do a damn thing. He spoke to another wolf, preparing the Pack to move, but he joined me as I walked out of this rundown house and into the woods. He knew not to speak until I spoke first. That was the first lesson he learned, and it didn't need any repeating. His left eye still hadn't grown back, and I knew that it would not.

"Yessss wolf. I give you the gift of my power so that

you could right the wrongs of your species. Show the purest wolves that you are the True Alpha. All I ask for is one thing from you once you gut the white wolf. One of the great Alphas that stands in the way of your greatness."

The words the demon spoke sparked a fire deep inside of me. But, of course, there was always a give and take when dealing with demon kind. I would fulfill my destiny by sacrificing the cursed bloodline of a family of Alphas.

"That is exactly what I am doing. You want the white wolf's violet eyes and his cursed bloodline dead, and that is exactly what you will have."

"This Hunter is formidable, but we are more powerful. Her demon blades mean nothing to us, but her eyes mean everything. You have my power, Aeron and the Hunter knows that I am with you. She will think it easy to hurt us, but she is wrong. This Hunter isn't like the rest but is a seer. Get me her eyes, wolf, and you will gain another gift indeed. Bring me those jeweled eyes and make sure that Hunter diessss."

The hissing echoed in my thoughts as the face of that Hunter flashed in my mind.

"I will take care of her, Abadozui. After that, the Hunter eyes will be mine, and the eyes of Dax Rayne shall be yours." I could feel the surge of power burning through my veins as my wolf paced and growled for the blood of my enemies. This power needed to be fed, and it always required the blood of an Alpha.

"Gooddd...goood. It's time to feed now. You will need the strength when fighting this wolf, Aeron. Now feed well tonight." I felt the demon fade, but I knew it wouldn't be far away.

"Keys. We may encounter a Hunter when taking this Pack."

"Hunters, do not get involved in Pack business, Alpha."

"Yeah, they normally do not, but somehow this Hunter is involved, and she knows we are coming." I stopped because I knew we were far enough away from the others. I looked down at Keys, who stood five foot seven inches with a stocky frame and mahogany skin. His yellow wolf's eyes burned in the darkness of this night.

"What do we need to do? How do we need to fight this Hunter? I have never encountered a Hunter before. As a rule, they don't fuck with us, and we don't fuck with them."

"You are right about that. Hunters used to Hunt things like us Keys. Hunters are strong and know details about every sup's weakness."

"Well, too bad for the Hunter that she doesn't know you don't have a weakness." His white teeth flashed in the night as my crimson eyes began to glow.

"Yeah, you're right, Keys. Too bad for the Hunter I will not have a weakness." Keys frowned at the low growl but never had the chance to scream as I devoured him in bite after bite.

MAEZE

Aeron didn't know that I could see what he could see each time he used my blood. If he didn't realize that, it meant he did not know what type of wolf I am. I pulled myself up and swayed at the blood loss. It didn't last long as my shifter blood restored itself just as fast as an Alpha wolf could. It took everything inside of me to hide my power from the demon riding inside of his body, and I wasn't sure if I could much longer. I stood up and felt for the wall as I made my way to the only door in the room. Even though I shouldn't have a problem seeing anything in the dark, this room was unnatural. The darkness seemed to seep through the walls as if it was alive. I felt the knob of the door and pushed through, shielding my eyes from the sudden light. I had to get to the other female shifters and the children because this might be the only moment we had to escape. I would have left this Pack long before now if it weren't for the others. I couldn't leave those who want nothing to do with this madness with a rogue wolf claiming that he is the True Alpha.

I knew he was not the True Alpha, and when he conned his way into the Pack, that was giving me a safe haven until I grew stronger and caught up on the current events. I only needed a few more days of rest before traveling to find the True Alpha, but I knew I couldn't leave them once he came. Once he started talking all that bullshit about purity and hate, I knew he was trouble. My wolf and I knew this creature was no Alpha, and we felt it deep in our bones. It definitely was not a True Alpha because the True Alpha blood runs deep in my veins. This beast was not a Savir. That bloodline alone carries the gene to be the one True Alpha, and my Father and Mother were bitten by the very first. They weren't Alphas nor Betas, but something else altogether, making me unique and something that shouldn't exist. The daughter of a Zeta and Gamma wolf, making me the only of my kind. I should have never left the human world to roam as my wolf until another True Alpha rose. I was just so damn tired, and it seemed as if we were in a time of peace, but I was wrong. Many things have happened, and maybe I could've prevented it, but it was too late for that now.

Once I felt the disturbance of a full demon walking on earth, I knew I had roamed far too long. I was weak, lost in my animal form, and did not know things had changed so much. As I pushed through the sweaty bodies of wolves, amping themselves up for the fight to come, I forced those thoughts out of my head. I had to get the others ready because this will be their only chance to escape this hell. My strength returned, and I knew I could fight my way out of here, but I could not take all of these wolves who wanted to go with me. Too many would die, and I wasn't about to have that shit happen. I looked at these wolves covered in blood, smelling of hate and rage, and just shook my head as I moved through the fools. They did not know that this Pack would not go down without a fucking fight. The Rayne Pack had a Hunter on their side. I felt the hesitance in both Aeron and the demon. This Rayne Pack may just be the ones that could help me end this nightmare for these wolves Aeron has kidnapped.

After telling Dax about the first vision, I had of his Pack. He stared at me in anger. His violet eyes glowed brightly at the horrors that his Pack would face if we didn't stop this shit right here, and right damn now. I watched as he visibly reigned back his wolf as his face began to ripple. He was on the verge of a transformation and unable to control his shift. That for an Alpha shouldn't happen, but with the knowledge thrown in your face that you would be the one to cause the pain and death, I could understand it. I didn't think before I reached out and placed both hands on his face, making him focus on me.

"We will not let that happen. We will stop the bastard, and I will send that demon straight back to Hell," I promised. Dax didn't pull away from my touch as I expected, but he seemed to get a handle on his emotions.

"I would never harm anyone who doesn't deserve it. I... that is impossible."

"Yes, normally, yes, it would be impossible, but this demon is nothing nice. It wants your species erased from existence. I don't know why, and I don't know the endgame, but I do know we will not let it happen," I said as I dropped my hands from his face. I watched him as he ran his large hands through his jet-black hair and growled.

"Okay...okay, we will stop this from happening. We need to move quickly and get things set in place," he said as he stood. I pushed myself up and swung my legs to the side of the bed. I stood up, feeling slightly shaky, but I managed it. I looked up, and Dax was standing in front of me, looking down so intensely that I caught my breath. I hated that my body instantly responded to his scent and closeness. I blinked a few times and made my way to step around him when he caught my arm.

"Dax...",

"Oh no, no, no Devana. I want everything. I want to hear it all because I know you still hold things back from me, and I will not have anything like that between us." I didn't even realize that he was pushing backward until my calves hit the mattress.

"Daxton, we don't..."

"You like to use my given name because you think it puts distance between this Mate bond, but it doesn't. I know you feel it, just like I feel that you are still hiding things from me, and I will not let that shit ride. Not with everything happening. You feel it's fast, maybe too soon or that this wolf Mating thing doesn't apply to you, but baby, you got that shit wrong."

"No, no, it isn't that, Dax! We don't have time for this shit right now. We have other things that need..." My words were cut off when I felt his hands grab me around the waist, and he pulled me to him. He leaned down, and his smooth skin rubbed against my cheek as his scent made my eyes slide shut.

"I am the Alpha, and if I say we have time, Mate. We have time. Now let me know what keeps those shadows of doubt in your eyes and the smell of deceit anytime I get close to you." I shook at his low rumble with a slight growl. I could feel my heart pounding and hear it in my ears as his words sank deeply into my heart and soul.

"What...you're feeling...it isn't real, Dax. It's a gift of mine that I try to..." I could feel his breath on my neck as he breathed in my scent.

"What other gifts do you possess?" He asked. His voice was so rough, deep, and sensual. It crawled along my skin and over my body, making me wet without a touch.

"We should get...we need..." I shuddered and couldn't help the intense feeling of pleasure that ran through me. His long tongue licked the side of my neck, and I knew he felt my pulse jump. Hell, with his hearing, I knew he heard my heart pounding. I reached out, gripping his muscled arms, and I felt a sudden need to just grind myself all over him.

"This is where I think you're not grasping the fact that you, Hunter, belong to me. You are my Mate, and I belong to you. Secrets or just withholding information will not go down between us. It will become increasingly harder for you to hold back from telling me everything. Either way, I will not permit it. It will not matter what you tell me, Devana, because you being my Mate will remain the same." I wanted to believe his words, but I knew all too well how shit went down. Too many past lovers left me when they found out, thinking I intentionally messed with their emotions. They weren't sure if what they felt was true or me fucking with them. It was best to get this shit out and over with now than later. At least this will put some distance between us, and I could focus on what I came here to do.

"I have the ability to manipulate emotions or affect someone close to me with my own emotions." I pulled away from him as I said this so I could stare into his eyes. I wanted him to understand what I was saying and know it was the truth. I waited for his stare to reveal the disgust, anger and hatred. Dax stared down at me for what felt like hours when it was only minutes. His violet gaze seemed to intensify as his dark brows furrowed. He leaned away, looking me over, but it felt as if he was staring into my soul.

"So, you feel as if I don't know or have no control over my feelings? Devana, I am an Alpha. No one other than my True Alpha can have dominion over me. No gift or power can take control over an Alpha. Why don't you know this?" His usually serious face softened slightly as he watched me. His hands slid down my sides and gripped my waist, pulling my body closer to him again.

I shook my head, "Dax, you don't understand." I closed my eyes because I knew what I would say sounded crazy even to myself, but I knew he wouldn't get it unless I told him everything. "You feel this way because I have these feelings and have ever since the first time I saw the drawing of you. Then again, when I saw you in my visions. This shit is not real and is just the lust I have for you."

"Oh, I can most definitely smell the lust, Hunter, but you aren't listening to what I am saying. Alpha wolves are not affected by gifts of this nature unless it is demonic. You are thinking along the lines of a human Devana. Yes, I feel the same emotions, but my wolf can smell, taste, and sense you are mine. The emotions of it are just another bond. So don't even try telling me what I feel because it's bullshit. I know what I want and what belongs to me. Did you ever stop to realize why you felt that way without even meeting me?"

"Dax, this...this doesn't make..."

"Oh, it makes perfect sense. Your soul already knew what you keep on denying." I had to shake my head because how? How would I know something that I didn't know? That thought made no sense to me at all.

"Dax, you are tripping! You just don't get it. Once I am away from you, then you will see. The need or claim for me will dampen and fade away. It's not real, Dax." I looked up at him, and he glared at me with the shake of his head. Before I could step away, he crushed me to him and lifted my body, triggering me to wrap my legs around his waist. His lips were on mine before I could say anything else. I barely felt my back hit the bed because his hard body was all over me. I moaned as he licked at my lips, and I dragged in a breath before he kissed me again. My arms found their way around his neck, and I pulled him closer. I felt every hard angle of his body and felt his length pressed against my core.

He pulled his mouth away and watched me. The hunger in his eyes told me all I needed to know at the moment. "No, no, no! This isn't helping the situation, and we need to."

"Let me show you Devana how I know you are my Mate," he grinned. Dax reached up to grab my hands from around his neck and slammed them to the bed. "You probably already feel it eating away at you. You want my mark on you when I am deep inside you. You want to feel my fangs claiming you as my Mate. I know you can feel it, Devana. I can scent the need in you that wants it. It calls to me. It calls to my wolf." How did he know what I was thinking or that I just about craved for him to do it? Maybe I was the one who was trippin because I was starting to believe it again that it could be true. I could tell he saw my thought process in my eyes because he began to smirk as if he had won. I opened my mouth, but he was already moving before any words came out. I felt his massive weight lift off of me. I didn't think a person this big should be able to move that fast. Dax stood in front of me, naked, and I could not help my eyes from scanning him from head to toe. The long thick length of him had heat rushing through my body. I sucked my bottom lip into my mouth, wanting to taste him as he tasted me earlier.

"Take your clothes off, Devana." I sat up, holding his intense stare as I removed my fighting clothes piece by piece, and his eyes never left my body. I stood up to take off my pants after kicking off my boots when he moved. I was pushed flat on my back as he stalked over me. I was wet as hell as he licked a path up my neck and lightly bit down exactly where I wanted him to mark me. My eyes snapped open at the thought, and it was like he knew what I was thinking. He moved his hips, and I felt the head rub against my clit, making me moan. I used my hand to press him closer and to give me what I wanted, what I needed.

"Beg." His growl of that one word snapped me back to attention. I couldn't understand how and why I was lost in every movement he made. My finger rubbed along his light brown skin over the colorful tattoos and muscles. "Mate." His growl of warning had my eyes looking back to stare into the burning violet of his eyes.

"No," I muttered. Every rule or restriction I placed on myself was being knocked down as if I never had it in place. Now he wanted me to give in and let myself be claimed. None of this shit made sense because we were still the enemies to everyone in the supernatural world.

"No. Really? Oh, you will beg for me to mark you, Mate,

but I won't until you scream it while I am buried deep, and you accept my claim as fact," He promised.

"Wa..." I moaned when his right finger slipped down and entered me. He kissed me deeply, sucking my soul from me before pulling away to run his tongue along my neck and down to my breasts. His tongue snaked out, licking each nipple as he added another finger inside me, making me groan deeply in pleasure. My hips bounced wildly on the bed as I squirmed and quivered beneath his hard body. Those violet eyes never left mine no matter what he did, and his grin grew wider. I dug my fingers into his hair as I cried out.

"Dax, please."

"Please, what?"

"Ohh my... please, I need...."

"Tell me. You know what you need to do if you want to come." He whispered into my ear. I wanted to scream, cry, and beg all at the same time. He was hard as fuck, and each time he moved, I could feel him rubbing my clit.

"I'm waiting."

"Fuck me. Please just fuck me," He laughed at me. His chuckle had my eyes blazing at him, but I couldn't move. He had me pinned and panting in every way.

"I couldn't hear you." He added another finger, and I shook with need.

"Dax, I want you. I need you to fuck me, please!" I was panting so hard I couldn't catch my breath. I knew if he didn't do something, I was going to lose my fucking mind.

"That's a good Mate. Get nice and wet for me," he groaned into my mouth. He pulled his fingers out, and I missed them only for a second. He guided himself into my opening and gently eased his head into me. We both gasped at the tightness and the pleasure.

"Devana, fuck baby...." As he pushed deeper, his grunt of pleasure had my entire body on fire.

I groaned loudly as he slammed into me again. He leaned back, using his hand to press down on my chest, holding me in place. Dax pulled my leg over his arm with the other. I lifted my hips to slam my ass back on him, making him throw his head back in pleasure. "Shit!" He growled, dropping my leg to pound in deeper.

"Yes! Right there... Dax. Oh..." He leaned away again, lifting both of my legs up in the air, spreading them wide apart, and started pumping relentlessly into my heat. I never knew what I would get next, as he would give long, hard, fast, and deep thrusts. Then he slowed to almost a crawl, going all the way into me with long and deep, powerful strokes. My muscles grabbed him, holding him tightly inside of me as I screamed his name repeatedly.

Finally, Dax brought me to climax after climax, making me beg him not to stop. My nails raked down his back and his arms as I clutched him. His face was in the side of my neck, kissing and licking my skin at the spot I wanted him to bite. It was driving me insane with the need to be claimed. I felt the tips of his canines scratching along my throat, and I wanted his mark. I needed his bite so badly I began to come again. Confusion clouded my mind but hope-filled it, and his words of me wanting to be marked circled around and around. Could he be right, or is it my lust for him so blinding that I'm losing my mind. Dax sucked at my neck as his rough finger rubbed over my sensitive nipples. I gasped at the sensation as it felt as though it had a direct line to my clit.

"Do it! Do it!" I moaned. The pleasure had me in a haze; I didn't know what was happening.

"Not yet, baby. Not yet. You are not ready, but you're close," he growled as he licked at my lips. I opened, needing to feel him everywhere. He kissed me through my orgasms as my core squeezed tight around him. I came so hard I pulled away from the kiss, gasping as he pushed deep and grunted. He jerked as he climaxed behind me, grinding his hips into me as he filled me. As he pulled out of me, I was a quivering mess of nerve endings and emotions. He didn't claim me even when I begged for it, and I didn't know why. It hurt that he didn't, but I should have expected that. I promised myself that I would figure this shit out when we killed this possessed wolf. Dax seemed so sure that he knew the truth and that I was his Mate. I looked into his eyes, seeing a spot of light blue in the irises. I blinked, and it was gone as if it were never there. I wanted his mark, so could it be possible that he was right and that I already knew he was my Mate as I was his? He smiled at me and licked my lips as he leaned down. I cupped his face in my hands and kissed him passionately, showing him what I was feeling rather than words. This just got more complicated because I feared he was right and if so, this would change everything in my world and in his. I vowed to myself as he kissed me that I would not let this demon get anywhere close to my wolf, even if I had to die to save him.

DAX

CHAPTER *nine*

I knew that time was short, but I had to settle some things with my Mate before moving forward. Everything wasn't solved, but it was enough that I wasn't worried about her fighting beside me. I get why she didn't want to say anything about her gifts initially because I sure as shit might have accused her of doing some bull shit. It would have been nothing but the hate I had for Hunters as a whole because my wolf knew instantly what she was to me. The man inside of me just didn't want to admit it or didn't want to believe it. I lived this long without a True Mate, and when she came, she had to be a Hunter. We both showered quickly, knowing we took too much time for ourselves, but it was needed. My wolf was settled as much as he could be, but I knew I wouldn't be able to hold him back the next time I needed to claim her rose up. When this was done, and I had that fake Alpha's head, she would take my mark and beg for it. I brought my thoughts back to the present. I turned my head and caught her cat-like gaze on me as if she knew where my thoughts had strayed. I looked away and looked over my brothers and enforcers. I noticed Dali glaring, but it wasn't at me. I followed her gaze over to Max, who watched her while licking his lower lip. I couldn't tell if he was fucking with her or if something was going on between the two.

"Listen up. We need to head out to each home that isn't on Pack land. They all need to be brought back here, but I do not want them traveling here alone. We need to bring them in and fast. Dimitri, have you made the calls?" I looked at my Beta. His quick nod was all I needed to move on. Some of these shifters have children, and from what I know about this bastard, he likes to take prisoners. He will have none of my shifters." I folded my arms across my chest as I took in each of my brothers. I looked at my eight enforcers, who I wanted to be paired up with each of my brothers. "Remi, I want you here with Thomas, getting everything in place. Thomas knows what I need and want."

"Alpha, I don't think Thomas needs me with him. He has the other shifters here that can help with this. I want to..."

"Remi, it shouldn't be too hard for you to take direction. What needs to be done here is just as important as what needs to be done out there. Right?" Thomas said. I saw a muscle in Remi's jaw tick, and her teal eyes flash with anger, or was its attraction?

"Remi, I want you here because, as Thomas said, it is important also, if necessary, you can get the children out of here if the land is breached," I said, holding her eyes. I watched as she caught my meaning and nodded. She shifted slightly, trying to put distance between her and Thomas, but Thomas just moved with her with a micro flash of a smile.

"Yes, Alpha, I understand," she sighed.

"Good, because the cubs and pups trust you. Also, you know that Meesha wouldn't listen to anyone but you two and could easily get lost or left behind." I saw both Remi and Thomas sober at that thought. Remi caught my eyes for just a second and nodded once more. The teal of her eyes blazed, and I could feel her age press against my senses. I didn't know precisely where Remi came from or why she came here, but I would never turn away a shifter in need. Now I was glad at that decision because her age and experience will help protect my Pack through all this.

"Nothing will get to our Pack Dax," Thomas stated this as fact. I turned my head toward him and saw he meant every word.

"Good. Now I want the enforces with an Alpha while we bring in the rest of the Pack who is living off the property."

"And the Hunters?" Max asked, and Dali blew out a breath but didn't say anything. I could feel that she and Devana were communicating somehow, which was intriguing.

"Dali will go with you and one enforcer," I said.

"Wait one minute! I am not a part of this Pack, so you do not give me orders!"

"Just like a Hunter to turn their backs on their responsibilities," Max grunted. There were mummers of agreements, but I held up a hand. Dali stood now with a blade in her hand as she stared Max down. Regardless of who she was or the fact she wasn't a shifter staring at any Alpha in the eyes is considered a challenge.

"You don't know me! You don't know shit about me! I did not say I wouldn't give my help. I said I do not take orders as if I am a part of this Pack! I am here to make sure you all don't fucking kill my sister for trying to help you animals."

"Dali! That is enough! We need to talk right fucking

now," Devana shouted. I had too many other things to worry about than the ego or ignorance of a Hunter.

"Either you can help, or you can get the fuck off my land." Everyone, including the Hunters, felt the command in my voice. Devana's lips thinned into a flat line as she looked at me. I saw the flash of anger, but she also understood that we didn't have time for the bullshit. She made a quick nod in acknowledgment. I watched the sway of her hips as she walked over to her sister, grabbing her by the arm. She pulled her toward the back of the house with a look of irritation. The wolves parted to let them through, and my eyes went back to my brother. Max stood rooted to the spot with both fists clenched tightly. His pale gray eyes with a hint of amber tracked Dali's movements until both Hunters left the room.

"Now everyone split up, and let's get this shit done. I want everyone here on this property in less than two hours." I made my decree, and I wasn't about to hear any complaints or comments. "Let's move," I growled.

DEVANA

I was pissed and happy that Dali showed up, but I couldn't have her challenging any and everything someone said.

"What the hell, Vana?" Dali shouted as she snatched her arm away. I rounded on her, ready to tell her to leave and go back home, when I caught her eyes. I saw the fear and uncertainty in them that had me pulling back.

"Dali, why are you here? You already know what is going to happen and why I am here. Fighting and arguing with the people I am trying to help ain't doing shit," I said calmly. She shook her head and closed her eyes. I knew she was counting backward from ten to calm herself down.

"I know! I know. It's just...that I can't let you do this on your own. I know what you are trying to do here, and I get it. It's just they think that we are supposed to just bow to them as if we were the ones who did whatever to them back in the day. And that damn Max thinks he can just put his hands on me or tell me what to do! None of them trust us, so why the hell should we trust them?"

"I get it, Dali, but I chose to come here to make a better relationship with them. At least start a better relation..." Dali threw up her hand, cutting me off.

"No! Naw, Vana, you came here because of HIM. Yes, you may want to bridge the gap between Hunters and Shifters, but this is about Dax. He called you his Mate. Don't try to make this out to be about anything else. You do know whatever you two have going on isn't going to work. They will never accept you as one of theirs, and I doubt our parents are ready for anything..."

"That is none of your business or theirs. I am a grown woman, and if I choose to be..."

"It can't be real, Vana! Or have you forgotten about your gift and what it does?" Dali stared into my eyes, and I know she saw the flinch. Her anger died out as she reached out for me. "I'm sorry, I didn't mean..."

"No, you're right. I haven't forgotten anything but..." I stopped because I felt him before I saw him. I looked past Dali and directly into violet eyes.

"Devana is my Mate. Neither you, her parents, Hunters or my Pack will impede that. What I am to her and what she is to me is nobody's business but ours." I swallowed, trying to moisten my dry throat.

"Dax." I cleared my throat again. Dali spun on her heels to face him with her arms crossed.

"Let me just say this, Dax. I will not get in the way of my sister's happiness if this is true, but I will not let anyone or anything hurt her again." I drew in a breath at Dali's sharp words and then understood why she was so upset. I have had others in the past, mainly Hunters or humans, who couldn't handle my gifts. Once I told them about my gifts, they didn't believe if in what we had because they didn't know if it was real or not. I got why she was so extra about all this but...but this is entirely different. I blinked a few times and looked up as Dax's eyes narrowed. Then he took one step forward, completely erasing any distance we had between us.

"Who the fuck hurt her before?" His voice was a growl, and the question was deadly. Dali sucked in a breath, and I knew she saw something in his aura. I stepped around her and held up a hand.

"That was many years ago, and I'm fine. We need to get moving. We have wasted enough time already," I said. Dax stared at me, and I swear he was trying his hardest to see into my thoughts.

"Yeah. Yeah, you're right. We do need to get moving, but first, I need to know how you made it onto my land?" Dax asked. I turned to Dali, wondering the same thing. I watched her eyes begin to focus again, and she looked at me strangely before answering.

"I see now. Well, anyway, there is an un-warded part of your land in the dense part of the woods. I figured you all knew about it because it was dug up from the inside," Dali frowned. I looked at her because that "I see" meant she saw more than she was letting on. Then her words registered about the grounds not being as protected as we believed.

"No. We didn't," Dax said as a scream ripped through the quiet of the night.

I WOULD BE dead wrong if I ever entertained the idea that I could run from Dax. As Hunters, we are fast, we are way faster than an average human, but we didn't match shifter speed. Dax was an Alpha making him extremely fast because he was there and gone in seconds. I didn't even see the change between wolf and man. He was in motion as he took one step, then shifted into a giant white wolf without breaking his stride.

"Beautiful," Dali said as the howls filled the air. I completely agreed as my feet started moving while I took out a blade. Dali was next to me as we made our way to the screams.

"Dali, do you sense anything?" I said as we leaped over a car and landed in a crouch.

"No! There is no demon anywhere near here!" She said as we started moving once again. I couldn't deny that I was happy my sister decided to show up, anyway. Having her unique gift of remote viewing always came in handy at times like this because something was wrong. I saw at least fifteen wolves squaring off with the wolves of the Rayne Pack. It looked like Dax had his other enforcers spread across the property, and the ones in the house were going to go with us.

"Dali!" I said as we slowed down. Dax was larger than any wolf I had ever seen in my life. His fur was pure white, but the violet of his now enormous eyes lit the night with an eerie glow.

"Devana, something...no this...we need to go. This is a distraction!" Dali yelled. I hadn't noticed that Max and Thomas were beside us until I looked at my sister. Her eyes were unfocused as the brown swirled with a mix of gray. I knew she saw what we could not and that it would be happening soon, whatever it was.

"What the hell is she talking about?" Max asked as he kept an eye on our surroundings.

"There is no demon here. Something is up, and the fact that those wolves are cowering in Dax's presence means they are weak. They are a distraction and were sent to be slaughtered. The rogue didn't count on Dax's significant Alpha power. We need to get to those other Pack members who aren't protected. Now!" I saw Max and Thomas share a glance before Thomas shifted into a large white wolf with a sable tint. His wolf was just as beautiful as his brother's. It wouldn't matter because whatever it was about that white wolf with the violet eyes, I could never truly see another wolf.

"Thomas will be able to handle these Betas along with the enforcers," Max said as he stared at his brothers. I knew they were all communicating mentally, and it stung that I couldn't do the same with Dax.

"I will help as well. I do not trust these wolves whether they submit or not. They will not stay on these lands," Remi said. I looked to my right, where the sultry voice came from, and found Remi watching the wolves with glowing teal eyes. It was almost as if her eyes were pools of ocean water. I started to ask what she meant exactly, but then Dax howled, and the rogue wolves all dropped to their belly, whining.

"Dax agrees, Remi. He wants you and Thomas to care for the land in his absence now. Hunters, let's move," Max said as Dax turned and pinned me with his eyes.

Dax looked at me and then at the truck that was pulling up with Dimitri inside. "Dax has said plans have changed and wants you with Dimitri," Max said before taking off. I looked back at Dax when he took off in a blur of motion as the SUV screeched to a stop. I looked back, seeing Dali blinking, and noticed Max holding her hip lightly.

"I'm good, Vana. Go! There is no time. I will go with Max," she said. I wasted no more time as I dove inside the truck, and Dimitri took off in the same direction Dax ran.

"Did I get this right that this was a distraction and the others are the target?" Dimitri asked. The truck hit a bump, and I grabbed the handle so I could hold on. He spun the wheel hard and damned near just about tipped us over as he hit a hard turn. It brought us out onto a paved road in the back area of the property.

"Yes."

"How do we know which house the demon will show up to?" He asked. Dimitri kept darting quick glances my way, but I didn't have an answer. How would we know which home of the Pack member he would show up for personally? "Well? Think Hunter! You know demons better than any of us, so where would he show up?"

"It's not as easy as your..." My words cut off at the memory of the vision I had earlier. The one I had before all the drama got in the way. I closed my eyes, slowing everything down in that last vision, ignoring the Black Dog's red eyes, and focused on the surrounding land. The smoke and smell of death clogged my senses, but as I looked around, I saw it. A black truck turned on its side and small faces peeked through the windows of a one-story house. One face I focused on damn near stopped my heart from beating.

"Turn around! Turn around!" I looked all around us, but there was nothing but trees on both sides of this paved road. Dimitri hit the brakes hard, good thing I put my hand out in time to catch myself before my head slammed into the dash. "The vision changed at the last minute! I didn't notice it at first because I was pulled out of it, but it started to change when he knew I could see...he...we need to get back to the house!" I said firmly. A deep growl filled the vehicle's space, making the hairs on the back of my neck stand on end. Dimitri spun the wheel and started back to the house.

"Fuck! Fuck!" Dimitri growled while hitting the stirring wheel. I pulled out my phone to call Dali as the truck sped up. "Who are you calling?"

"My sister! They..."

"They still need to check on the Pack members. The bastard still could have sent others there to hunt them or kidnap them. I sent out a call for the Alpha. It will be up to us and whoever is still on the property until he gets back."

"You're right, but they will need to check the house we were going to as well."

"Vana!" My sister finally answered.

"Dali! Listen, the demon is at the house! I know it."

"We're on the..."

"No, no, you need to check on the other Pack members to make sure they are safe and let Max know he needs to get to the house we were going to check out."

"Devana, are you sure? You know demons, and they are fucking tricky as shit. It could be fucking with you."

"It already did, but I saw it. I caught the change just like the one that made me come here in the first place."

"Shit! Fine, fine, we will, but I will be there as soon as we get these wolves safe. Don't do anything that will get you killed or..."

"It will be fine. Just...just watch your back. I'll see you soon," I said, ending the call. I knew what she wanted to say, but I wasn't trying to hear it. Since I started hunting demons, they have always wanted my eyes. Too many legends say eyes are the doorway to one's soul. They should say that eyes are the doorway to a Hunter's soul, and without their eyes, they will never see the gates of their final home.

DAX CHAPTER *ten*

I held a mental connection with everyone that is a part of my Pack, but it was stronger when it came to my brothers and my Beta. Many shifters sometimes can lose themselves to their animal, if only for a moment, but being an Alpha, that has never happened. When I stood looking at these weaker wolves who thought to attack my Pack on my land, I felt the need my wolf had and struggled not just to kill them all. I could see that they were all just sacrifices to this fake Alpha's cause. Before I heard Devana's words, I knew that they were not the enemy, but I would be damned if they harmed anyone.

"Alpha! Turn back!"

"Dimitri, what the hell is happening? I am near to Matthew's home, and he has four pups..."

"No! Shit has changed. Your Mate said the vision changed, and he is going to attack the Pack land."

"Fuck!"

I could see the house up ahead, but I knew Devana would not have me turn back if she was not absolutely sure her vision had changed. What did she see that made her come to this decision? If I had given her my mark, I would have known what she was thinking and seeing. I felt the rumble in my chest as my wolf agreed with my thoughts. It didn't matter because some damage would be done to my people before I made it back. How could I continue to call myself their Alpha when I failed to keep them safe once again.

"You are not the one who chooses to be an Alpha. That choice and privilege belong to me."

As an Alpha, there have always been talks of the creator of shifters, more specifically wolf shifter kind. It is instinct to know when that being is speaking to you as an Alpha.

"Kannuck."

I stopped in my tracks, even though my paws and heart wanted me to keep moving when he spoke. When *Kannuck* speaks to you, you stop whatever you are doing, no matter what is happening.

"If you want the children of Alphas who are all Alphas to succeed in saving your species, a sacrifice must be made. If you, Dax Rayne as Alpha of the Rayne Pack, want to fulfill the prophecy, you must first claim the gift that has been given to you. The power that will be needed to save all my children will lie in your willing-ness to claim."

The thoughts rushing around in my head from his words had me confused. The problem is that the God of wolves was gone instantly, leaving his cryptic message behind. I didn't have time to understand what it meant, but I knew a part of it had to do with this rogue. I was the Alpha, and I knew all my strengths and weakness. I knew the gifts I possessed and what I did not. Whatever gift belonging to me, I would find, and I would claim it if that meant saving my Pack. I refused to let them down again. I would give my life before letting this rogue tear through my Pack like he did others before mine. As I ran through the trees at a speed I knew my brothers would have trouble keeping up with, I thought about the words that weren't all meant for this moment. They weren't even meant just for me, but for all of us. The Rayne Alphas all had a part to play, and we all had to play our role in saving not just our Pack but the entire species of wolf shifters.

I KNEW Devana and Dimitri would make it back to the Pack before I would. Once I reached my home, I thought of what I might find almost had my wolf in a blind panic. I was Alpha, and I wanted my family and my Pack safe. That had my wolf moving at a speed that made the trees and the stars in the sky seem as if they were nothing but smudges. The violet of my eyes burned as they lit the night. I had no problem seeing every branch, animal, hole, or fallen tree in my path. I moved through this land as if it were nothing because I could feel every inch of what belonged to me as Alpha. I could feel the battle taking place and feel the pain of my

Pack members as they fought. I knew that many wolves were attacking, and that concerned me. I knew there was a breach in my wards, but I also knew that it was closed as soon as I went to bring the rest of my wolves home. My anger spiked to new heights. Now that I know that someone is removing the wards placed, I stretched out my energy to all the wards surrounding my property. That is how I knew when the fucking demon stepped foot on my land and how I could feel that not only one ward had fallen, but another and another after that. I sensed the magic in the air just as I felt all the wards to the property began to crumble.

Suddenly, like a punch to my senses, I could feel the hidden presence of over seventy wolves, and they had my entire property surrounded as they moved in on my Pack for the kill. No one, not even Devana, had sensed this demon or Alpha was using a Witch. Only a Witch stronger than the one I had could have destroyed the wards from the outside. Or the Witch that made them in the first place was the one who broke them. "Peter!" I let out a howl of rage just as another scent filled my nose. The rumbling growl deep in my chest grew violent, as my rage at the scent I already knew like it was my own, almost broke the spirit of my wolf. Damn near my heart as a man.

I knew I was still miles away, but I could smell the blood in the air. A lot of the blood is from wolves on both sides, but the sudden sharp scent that crashed into my senses had me shifting into the third form. The shift was done in an instant. I went from standing on all fours to standing on two legs with long claws as hands. I already stood at six feet and seven inches, but I knew now I was over seven feet tall. I drew in a long breath, and that scent I knew so well and so quickly was coming from my Mate, and it was a deadly amount! After over two hundred years, I just found my Mate, and I would not lose her. I was an Alpha, the Alpha of this Pack and state. This rogue will not take another wolf, Pack, life, breath, and for damn sure not my MATE!

DEVANA

The truck hadn't even reached the start of the homes on Dax's property when we noticed the wolves hidden in the trees. They were waiting for something, but it didn't matter because I could feel the demon and the heaviness of evil that hung in the night's air.

"How did we not see them when we left? This is impossible!" Dimitri grunted. He spun the wheel as we hit a curve at top speed. The tires slid on the dirt road, but he course-corrected so we wouldn't tip over, and then he pressed harder on the gas. I could see the wolves hidden in the tree line. Their eyes glowed bright amber or yellow as we flew by, but I didn't feel the demon was with these wolves. He was here, though, but maybe on the other side of the property.

"They had to have been here, though. We would have seen them when leaving," I said. I reached down to the holster strapped to my thigh and pulled out my P17 .22 pistol.

"You a thug now or something? I thought all you Hunters used blades or the ninja swords," Dimitri asked.

I doubled check that my ammo was werewolf-friendly. I wasn't sure about the numbers that this Alpha had amassed, but I was glad I brought my moonlit ammo. I knew Dimitri didn't really care what the hell I was doing, more so trying to keep his cool.

"I have those as well. Not the sword but the blades and this..." I held up my pistol and just smiled. "You should never leave home without one," I said.

"Almost there! The wards should have...what the fuck?" I looked at Dimitri and saw the color drain from his face before he squeezed the stirring wheel.

"What?" I screamed. I whipped my head to my passenger side window when I felt magic. There was a Witch here and working a powerful spell. Right at that thought, I knew what Dimitri would say, and my blood ran cold.

"The wards...they're down." I could see the property's lights now and the wolves behind us catching up to attack.

"Stop the truck. We need to slow them down! Send out a message to whoever is on the property and get into the main house! That is where they will be the safest at this point." No other words were needed as Dimitri slammed on the breaks. I wasted no time waiting for the vehicle to stop before I opened my door and dove out. Apparently, neither did Dimitri because he was out of the truck and shifting as I rolled to my feet. At the last minute, he must have spun the wheel because the truck slammed into the trees, hitting a few wolves that didn't get out of the way in time. I took the time to note Dimitri's wolf and saw that you wouldn't mistake him for any other wolf. Like his Alpha, Dimitri's wolf was different in color than most wolves. His fur was unique enough that no one could ever forget him. His coat split down the middle, leaving one side an inky black and the other snow white like the shock of white in his hair. His eyes weren't amber or yellow like the ones coming at us. They were a glowing cobalt blue when he turned to me. He was larger than the wolves coming at us, but I saw no wolf near Dax's size. I wasn't Pack, so I couldn't understand his mental speech, but I knew the game.

I moved just as he leaped in the air, taking down a wolf that came from my left. I was already ducking and bringing up my pistol and letting two shots ring out before slipping it back into my holster. I was already moving as howls filled the night, and my blades found their target. I managed to stab one wolf in the throat as I flipped over its back and kicked another in the head. Dimitri was next to me as we continued to move. I knew if we stopped, they would drag us down. I dropped low to the ground as Dimitri used his paw to swipe at a wolf that was coming up behind me, and I used another blade to stab an amber eye. That wolf almost took a bite out of Dimitri's flank, but I wasn't letting that shit go down. I rolled under Dimitri and got to my feet just as a giant brown wolf leaped from the side and came at me. I threw up an arm as the pressure of its massive jaws clamped down on my arm. I knew there would be a bruise and pain, but I could deal with that as long as I still had my arm at the end of the night. I brought up my pistol and shot the wolf in the face.

"Dimitri, down!" I screamed as the moonlit bullet crashed into its skull and exploded. The jaws didn't loosen, but it wouldn't matter in a moment. I dropped to the ground and closed my eyes as the woods lit up in a blinding flash of light. The first two shots I fired were just silver mixed with wolfsbane. A wolf shifter could survive if those were dug out immediately, but the rest loaded were a mixture of silver nitrate, wolfsbane and the magical essences of the New Moon. I managed to move enough to cover Dimitri's large head as the blast took out whatever wolf was in its path. The explosion only lasted about a minute, but that was all we needed for a head start. This type of ammo is scarce because of our status with the supernatural community and involved Witches. "Move, move, move!" I shouted as I shook the ashes of my freed arm. Dimitri was up in a second, shaking his head. The wolves in the surrounding area were all stunned, and this was our chance. I looked at Dimitri, and he moved his head with impatience. I realized what he wanted and almost said hell no, but I remembered we had no vehicle left. I reached out without another thought, gripping the soft black and white fur. I climbed onto his back as he shot through the darkness, heading for the screams.

I LOWERED myself to lay on Dimitri's back. Branches and trees whipped across my arms, legs, and back as we moved. I knew the wolves that didn't go down would soon shake off the moonlit effects, but I could hear the fighting as if we were already there. Dimitri was fast, but I managed to see an older, chubby, red-headed man pushing himself up from the ground. I saw him grab a pendant that was around his neck before Dimitri slid to a stop. I whipped my head around in time to see what had to be the other set of wards shimmer and fall. That was when I saw the glow of the red eyes, but he wasn't in wolf form. He stood tall as he raised his head to the sky and howled. More wolves came from his end, joining the others that were attacking the Pack.

"Go! I will be fine!" I said, sliding off his back and pulling out my twin pistols. Tonight may be the first time I would use both weapons at once, and I pray that enough wolves get hurt by the aftermath because this was all I had with me. Dimitri hesitated, but I didn't because I saw exactly where the demon-ridden wolf was heading. To make an Alpha such as Dax surrender would be to kill the soul of his Pack. He was going for the children. A wolf landed in front of me, and this was the first time I hesitated. I had no clue who the fuck was, friend or enemy, unless they were trying to kill me.

"FUCK!" This wasn't like when we were outside the property when I used my gun. I could hurt someone in the Pack, someone on our side.

"Shit!" I roared as I put them away and reached behind my back, pulling out a thin sword with a pitch-black blade named *Krisha*. I took a step, but before I moved, I saw the white and black wolf jump out from the side, taking down another tan wolf and ripping out its neck. Dimitri pulled back, and his glowing eyes met mine. "Fine! We need to get to the house!" I said, knowing exactly what he was saying without the benefit of a Pack bond. He would know Pack members in an instant. We moved, and I followed his movements as we made our way through the chaos.

"Devana!" After taking down a wolf coming up on Dimitri, I saw Malic running toward me when I looked to my left. He was still in his human form, but his strength as an Alpha was unmatched by these lower wolves. He used his massive fist to punch one wolf and grabbed another by the throat while kicking a large black and tan wolf in the chest. He threw the one he was holding into a group of wolves that were running toward us.

"Malic, we need to get to the house! The demon!" I said, spinning back around in time to duck. As the wolf leaped over my head, I came back up with *Krisha* and split the wolf's belly open. I felt a wolf at my back, but Malic was just there beside me, ripping out the throat as if it were nothing.

"Let's go then, Hunter," Malic said in a deep growl. I stood to my full height and nodded. I wanted to know if Dali and the others made it to where they were going. I wanted to know where Dax was and if he would make it in time because I knew deep in my bones that I couldn't do this alone.

Dimitri was now able to move ahead since Malic was with me. There were shifted wolves and unshifted everywhere. Everyone was fighting as if their lives depended on it. I noticed a woman with a group of other women and children huddle close to a building, trying to stay in the shadows. I caught her eyes, and hers widened when she saw me. I started to head for the group, but the smell of death, evil and madness filled my nose. All of my Hunter senses went on full alert, and I moved quickly to put myself in front of Malic.

"Devana, what…" He never got to finish, as deep laughter began to fill the night, and everything stopped. The wolves pulled back from whatever fight they were having, and the men who fought on the side of this demon pulled back as well. I flicked my eyes toward the house and saw the same short, pudgy man with his hand pressed against the massive doors. "Peter, what the fuck are you doing?" Malic growled. He started forward, but I held out my arm to stop him in his tracks. This demon was powerful and glutted on the blood sacrifices. "Devana…",

"Listen to the Hunter Malic! You step one foot in that direction, and I will have your head as my next trophy." The Alpha grinned. I could see the blood coating his teeth and smell the death on his tongue at this distance. I knew what he was doing, and I was subtly undoing the demonic spell he planted. One step, and things would get bloody and fast.

"Fuck you! I don't know about these so-called wolves who follow you, but I don't need to listen to shit you have to say. You are not my True Alpha Aeron!" I could feel the growl building in Malic's chest. He was pressed right up against me, and I could tell he was trying to push me slowly out of the way. The problem with that is I was the only one holding back the spell this bastard was weaving. All of his wolves knew what was up, so they stopped and moved closer to their Alpha. I didn't understand why the other women and children who had to be with them didn't cross-over to him.

"Malic, No!" It was hard trying to carry a conversation when working this type of spell. I wasn't a Witch. I was far from being that magically inclined, but all Hunters knew the words and spells that have to do with anything demon-related. It had something to do with our blood-lines. The purest of Hunter's bloodlines was the Cross family. It probably would have taken a drop of blood to break this spell if I were one of them, but I wasn't. One of them trained me very well long ago, so I knew I could do this. I just prayed it was in time. The Warlock's chants were growing louder as the demon wolf laughed at Malic, but his eyes shined with a small amount of surprise at his name.

"Bring her to meee," Aeron hissed. My eyes never left the wolf, and his crimson red eyes bored into mine. I didn't see the man or wolf shifter. All I saw was something evil watching me back. The hate that I felt coming from him would crush a lesser soul if they could feel this type of hatred. It knew I was here to stop its plans, and the demon would try its damnest to kill me. I heard the struggling and screaming, but I didn't dare lose concentration.

"No! No! Get the hell off of me!" I saw when he reached out and pulled a female in front of him.

"Leodora! Fuck this!" Malic roared as Aeron smiled coldly at us.

"Malic! No just..."

"If you give your life to me, Alpha Malic Rayne, I will

spare this one. It seems you have a strong attachment to this feline."

"Fuck him, Malic! There isn't anything he can do to me... you know it!" Leodora grimaced. I was almost done with the spell. I had to make sure I found every drop of blood he spilled that kept us on this side.

"She isn't even one of us, Malic. She's a feline and not worth walking in our presence. I should just do you this favor."

"No! You son of a bitch! You came here for Alphas! Here I am, but you hide behind a female!" I could feel Malic's skin rippling as if he couldn't control it, and he could shift at any moment. Dimitri's eyes never left the house, and the Warlock stood with his head to the sky, chanting.

"Malic! No!" Leodora cried. Just a few more seconds, and I could sink my blade deep into his heart.

"I am here for Alphas, yes, but I am also here to rid this earth of the unworthy." Aeron grinned, and it seemed to stretch unnaturally across his face. My eyes widen in horror. The words of my spell became faster. His mouth split up the side, and his teeth turned a rust-brown with sharp points. His mouth opened, and his teeth came down into Leodora's neck.

"Leo! Fuck this!" Malic roared as he smoothly shifted and charged at the demon wolf.

"Malic! Wait, I need..." I screamed, but it was too late. He was moving, and I knew it would snatch his soul and kill him if he reached the barrier. I launched myself at the giant dark red wolf while pulling out a silver-lined blade. I managed to stab him in the flank, but I knew it wouldn't kill him, only slow him down. Malic howled out in pain, but my forward motion had me falling to the ground and sliding along the grass directly into the barrier. I said the last few words as I pulled out my pistol and slammed hard into the blood barrier. It made my vision fade, but I was glad to have been taught to shoot while blindfolded. I pulled the trigger as blood filled my mouth while howls and screams ripped through the night.

CHAPTER
eleven

I reached my property, and everything was in chaos. Homes were burning, and screams in the distance rang in my ears. None of it mattered at this moment because all I could scent was the blood of my Mate. The foul smell of demons saturated this entire place as the voices of my Pack, brothers and Beta filled my mind. I couldn't answer them due to the rage and anger I felt. I was about to lose my Mate before I even had the chance to claim her as mine. If I had, she would have been able to draw on our Mating Bond for healing. I knew Hunters were better at healing than average humans. But that was just it, Hunters were still human, so if she was severely wounded enough, she could still die. I felt my property had a split or some kind of barrier dividing it in two. I couldn't reach Thomas or Remi. I couldn't feel the wards placed around my home, so I knew exactly what was cut off from me. The scent of another familiar presence brought a growl to my lips as I moved through the fires that burned newly built homes down to the ground. I saw dead or wounded Pack members scattered everywhere, but I didn't have time to stop. I turned my head, and my eyes locked on a pair of glowing lavender eyes that did not belong to my Pack. I saw her dip her head in submission as she crouched protectively in front of other female shifters and cubs. This female wasn't an Alpha nor Beta, but she gave off those vibes to me. As an Alpha, I should have known what she was, but I didn't have time to focus on the female.

I shifted into my human form in one fluid movement just as a light flashed and burned bright. I shielded my eyes but kept it moving toward the scent of my Mate.

"Alpha!" Dimitri's voice slammed into my thoughts. I focused on his thoughts as I pushed into his consciousness so I could see what he saw at that moment. It wasn't what I thought or who I thought he would have been looking at right now.

"Where is Devana?" I growled. I was close as I moved through the thick smoke that surrounded everything.

"They will get in the house! The pups! The cubs!" I could feel Dimitri's rage at not getting to those who needed him. He was Beta, and all children trusted in him just as much as their Alpha to protect them.

"She did it!"

"I am here, Dimitri. Save them. I will deal with this fucking demon and all of his followers. The light died just as suddenly as it appeared, and I saw my Mate choking on her blood with more running from her nose, eyes and ears. Malic held a badly wounded Leodora across his lap while an open wound appeared on the side of his stomach. Aeron stood watching my Hunter as if she was a prize or something with distaste. Her eyes never left his as the demon wolf took a step. I was there in a second and backhanding the rogue Alpha away from my Mate. I looked down and saw those eyes flash green to brown to gray. The look of happiness and fear crossed her face as I leaned over and scooped her into my arms. The still alive wolves began to move after her, but they weren't getting the chance. I took her small pistol from bloody fingers and aimed. When I hit the Alpha, some of the further away wolves had already runoff.

"Those magic bullets won't do shit to a True Alpha Daxton Rayne," Aeron said, pushing to his feet. I didn't respond to his bullshit. I fired, aiming directly at his chest. I didn't stop there but moved slightly and shooting at each wolf who dared to fucking stand up. I did not know how many bullets were left, but I fired until it locked back. The bright light from each shot knocked down every wolf who thought they could come for my Pack or me. I knew he was coming. I could smell his foul stench, but I didn't have time to deal with him. I had no clue how to kill a demon without my Hunter. That knowledge came crashing down around me when I heard a shriek from behind me. The brightness of whatever type of bullets she had in her gun had already died out, and Aeron was coming toward me. He shifted into a dark gray and black wolf with crimson red eyes as he moved. I didn't expect the wings that unfurrowed from his sides. I felt something brush my arm as Dali ran past me with two swords held high. The screaming wasn't just screaming but a spell in a language I could never learn. Devana coughed, and I looked down to see her eyes wide as she watched her sister run toward the demon.

"Dali!" Her crocked cry and her hand reaching to her sister had me moving. I don't know the reason, but if I didn't, Dali would surely die. I made it to her side as she finished the chant, as the demon started backing away with a snarl. Dali's two swords glowed white as gold symbols shone brightly, and she slammed both together. I didn't have time to think or figure out how I knew this had to be done; I just did it. I grabbed Dali by the waist as the ripple of gold light shot out. I threw Dali back in the direction she came and leaped into the air, away from the light as it exploded. The sound was like a bomb had been dropped as the golden-white fire burned, began to eat away everything in its path.

"Dax! What in the fuck was that?" Max said as he held a dazed Dali. Her face was snuggled into his neck as she tried to lift her head.

"It...it didn't kill it...it's strong...this won't stop... Devana...where is..." Dali could barely keep her eyes open, but I couldn't focus on anything at the moment while Devana hung limp in my arms. I laid her down and searched her body, but I could find any wounds, but her light brown skin was getting pale.

"Devana! Tell me what I need to do! I just got your ass, so you can't...Devana!" I leaned down, placing my ear to her chest as if I needed to do any of that shit. I could hear shit hundreds of feet away, but I needed to listen to her heartbeat. "Devana!"

"Dax she..."

"NO!" I roared at Max, who took a step back. My growl must have given Dali what she needed to open her eyes and focus.

"Devana. Oh God, no! Devana! She hit that thing, but..." I looked up and started CPR to see Dali's watery gaze on me.

"What! What do I need to do?" I heard the weakness in my voice, and I couldn't give a shit. I could hear and feel the pain of my Pack, and I did not give a shit.

"She is your Mate. Your bond should have..." I knew the violet of my eyes burned, and the grief was written in every line on my face. "Do it! Do that shit right fucking now! Save my sister! She wouldn't be here if it weren't for you, and she wouldn't have gotten hurt!"

"This is my fault. If I wouldn't have..." Malic said, coming up beside me. The dark circles and blood staining his side made him look as if he had just escaped a horror movie. There wasn't time to think or consider that she could hate me forever doing this without her consent. I couldn't do this how it is meant to be done. I knew she was my Mate, and she wanted my bite, but I knew doing this in this state would change everything. I looked down, and everything else faded into the background. Nothing else mattered at this point. Either our Mating bond was strong enough to withstand this, or it wasn't. I would live with her hate, but I will not live without her. I leaned my head back and let my canines lengthen and bite down into Devana's shoulder until I hit bone.

DEVANA

I knew that I was dying, but I couldn't let that demon steal another soul, especially not Dax's brother. That spell the demon cast would have taken any soul, but not one of a Hunter. I could see now how it got so many to follow him as he took Pack after Pack. The demon started with taking souls and letting the others in the Pack see the power. I knew for sure that I would not have that problem, and I would still have my soul. I also knew that there was a possibility that I wouldn't have my life. That didn't matter, but it was what we do, and I would do it again if that meant I saved someone else of that kind of fate. I couldn't tell if I passed out or where I was, but it was entirely black, all except that faint light in the distance. I felt as if every organ in my body was liquifying. I wasn't expecting to have a vision or see slightly further ahead in the future, but I was glad when the vision came. The darkness became suddenly light as different visions moved through my mind at a speed I wasn't accustomed to having. As I watched, the pain faded somewhat, and the screaming and crying of the others drifted away. I saw glimpses of each of the Rayne brothers in different situations, but one thing remained the same in each one. A demon was always present in every one of them.

"Devana Adria Okar...it is now time for you to choose."

"Who...who are you?"

I could feel a power I had never felt in my life. It was almost close to my feeling when I met Michael Vaughn for the first time. He was a Vampire King, but this power feels slightly different. It felt older, wild, and predatory. I knew that I was dying, but I wasn't expecting to hear voices or see soft light. Everything around me was dark except the light in the distance, which felt like the moon. My thoughts were scattered, and I couldn't make sense of how something felt like moonlight.

"What you feel is my power, and what you sense as moonlight is your Mate."

The voice spoke again. It was deep and almost a growl of words. As the words of the voice sank in, I began to look around.

"Dax? No, he can't be here. He has to live!"

"Do you want to live?"

"What I want doesn't matter. If I die, then that is *His* Will. I knew the consequences when I chose to save Malic, and I was right to do so! They all must live, and now they will. My sister can carry on what I started."

I didn't much care who this was speaking to me. Of course, I wanted to live if that meant I got to find someone who finally saw me. I got to experience a man who could look past my gifts and just see me! I didn't have that feeling long but saving Malic wasn't a question. A Hunter protects all beings on this earth from evil no matter the form it takes.

"You have taken the first step in the redemption of

House Okar. You may not have been the Hunter who chose not to help *MY WOLVES*, but you have been chosen to walk in both worlds as Hunter and Shifter. Your fellow Hunters may choose to turn their backs on you, but you will bear that cost. You will bring both together. If you choose this path, there will be much agony. Everyone has a choice, and now is your time to choose your destiny. Will you, Hunter, fix the wrongs that your House has committed by becoming the very being they turned their backs on?"

His wolves? What did that even mean? And who…it was as if every lesson, book or conversation I had about wolf shifters kind slammed into my mind. I knew exactly who this voice was and what he was asking. The voice speaking to me with this much power had to be *Kannuck.*

"I cannot fix wrongs that were done before my time. I could only work to regain the trust now, and hopefully, my death will show everyone we need each other and will bring Hunter and Shifters together."

It wasn't that I wouldn't walk this life. It was more that I felt if I took this lifeline, it would be meaningless. I would be looked at by others as if I took this as another grab at life, but my death will show wolves what Hunters will do to protect and Hunters what they should have been doing, so something like this will never happen again. If we were together, a demon would have been hard-pressed to gain control of a shifter. We would have been called in at the start of this situation.

"This is your cross to bear, Devana Okar. Would you leave a Mate who would risk your hatred just to save your life?"

I opened my mouth to speak as a sharp pain ran from my

neck and down through my entire body. I wanted to scream, but I couldn't make a sound. It felt like my bones were being crushed and like every organ was being remade while I was awake. My blood burned inside my veins, and it felt as if my skin was too tight. I couldn't move, as the pain in my mouth felt like my teeth were being drilled.

"Devana, you will not leave me." That voice I knew for sure. That voice was full of command and... "Devana!"

I screamed at the pain in my body and cried at the pain in the voice of my Mate. Just the thought of that word had my mind focusing. I didn't care what anyone thought, said, or accused me of doing. I may not believe I was the one for this destiny, but I knew I would not leave my Mate. Whatever the price I had to pay to get back to him to be with him and save his Pack, I would pay.

"Then it is done."

The deep growl of words sent another wave of pain through me as my back and neck pressure increased horribly. I felt like my skin was being ripped to shreds. As if someone was taking a blade and digging it into my bones. All of my bones began to move and shift as if I was regrowing my entire body. I couldn't tell if I was screaming aloud or if this was still all in my mind. Sharp stabs of pain raced down my right shoulder, and my back like it was running from something. I felt like my skin had been torn off and was slowly knitting itself back together just for it to happen all over again. I didn't know if I was still crying, but I held on to what I knew was waiting for me. Dax would be on the other end of this pain. Light began flashing around me, and I could hear voices and noises that were too loud. I could hear the crackling of the fire and smell the dead or dying. That couldn't be right because I couldn't figure out where I was or what I should be doing. I tried to move, but I felt the weight of something holding me still. I tried moving my body, but it felt wrong, like I had too many arms and my head felt too heavy.

"Devana, baby. Open your eyes."

"Is she…"

"Quiet!" I knew my sister's voice, and I felt myself calm slightly because she was safe. That meant she could carry out what I started when…shit! My eyes were so heavy, but I had to open them. I needed to see Dax and make sure he knew that everything would be fine, and Dali would make sure his Pack took out that demon before…

"Devana! Open your eyes, Mate." Dax's voice weaved around me like a caress, but I also felt the commanding ring laced in it. I had the immediate urge to bite him for even trying to order me around, but that settled when I felt his touch and smelled his scent. As that thought played over in my head, I wanted to know why I would say scent. I felt when my brain kicked in, and the words of what the wolf deity said came crushing over me. My eyes flew open, and everything looked the same but also different. Things I wouldn't usually see became more precise, and the pain I experienced seemed almost a dull ache. I lifted my arm and expected to see a hand, but all I saw was a white paw.

"Devana?" I knew that voice was Dax, but when I opened my mouth to respond, all that came out was a howl.

MAEZE
CHAPTER
twelve

I stood up when a gigantic man stepped out of the smoke with glowing terracotta eyes. He looked us all over with a deep frown and then back at me. He was an Alpha, but he wasn't the one I saw in Aeron's visions.

"None of you are Pack. Why didn't you leave with your True Alpha?" Disgust was laced through his voice as he crossed his massive arms across his chest. He talked to all of us, but he was staring at me.

"That is not the True Alpha, nor is he my Alpha," I snapped. I was tired, irritated, and wanted to get these women and children somewhere safe. I looked up, realizing I was speaking to an Alpha I wanted help from, and they usually would take my tone as a challenge. The man dropped his tattooed arms, and he laughed. His smooth, bronzed skin seemed to gleam in the light of the fire, and when the glow of his eyes dimmed, they turned a dark brown.

"What are you doing here?"

"Who are you?"

"Who exactly are you? I can tell that you shouldn't even

have been caught up in this mess, but I think I understand why you didn't just escape on your own. So again, why are you here?"

"They need a safe place. I couldn't leave them with...that piece of shit that calls himself an Alpha. My name is Maeze Aiman of the Savir Pack."

"Savir!"

"Yes. I was born into the Savir Pack and have served the Pack of the True Alpha." I heard the gasps and whimpers behind me, and I turned to the females. Before turning back, I looked at the pups, making sure they were all still accounted for.

"You are not an Alpha or a Beta, but you are not just a normal wolf..." His head cocked to the side, but I could tell he was still watching for threats. He was checking us over, and I could also feel him press against my mind. My mental shield held, though, and I saw his eyes on me again. He pulled back and looked around as if he sensed something.

"My name is Alex Rayne, and what I can sense so far, you all aren't a threat. About the safe haven, that is usually what we do here. Yesterday I would have said this was a safe place, but as you can see..."

"Yes, but this is better than with him. At least better until I can track down the True Alpha."

"Track down..." His words were cut off as a scream ripped through the night on the heel of the loudest howl I have heard. "Fuck!" Alex turned back to us, looking us over and making a quick decision. "Follow me! Make sure you keep up. I am not sure this place is completely safe yet," he growled and started to move. I looked back to my charges and saw hope filling their eyes. I prayed this was the right move.

"Let's go!" I said and followed after the Alpha as he disappeared into the smoke. It was almost as if he turned into the smoke surrounding us until a large arm reached out and pulled me along towards the painful howls of what seemed to be a newly turned wolf.

As I was pulled, I made sure the other females were close behind me. Alex let go of my hand and stumbled out into a small clearing facing a massive house, but I could only focus on the giant white wolf standing over another smaller white wolf whose howls pained me. The wolf was confused and in pain because of the transformation. I stepped forward, wanting to help, when the large wolf turned its head and growled low. The violet eyes were shocking, and the large sharp teeth stopped me in my tracks. I knew this was the correct Pack when I saw him, but I wasn't expecting to face this type of wolf. Very few Dire Wolves are left, and not even a True Alpha may carry that gene. A True Alpha was something else altogether. Dire Wolves were the guardians of the True Alphas sent out to do what had to be done before the True Alpha stepped in to handle it. If a Dire Wolf was here and being attacked, then Aeron may have bitten off more than he could chew. I backed up, holding out my arm so the other females wouldn't get any closer. I stared into the violet eyes, but I didn't see the green for the pupil that all Dire Wolves were said to possess to deal with any supernatural threat. I didn't know everything about these wolves, but I could tell this wolf was unique but missing the piece that may be needed to kill this wolf and banish this demon back to Hell.

"Thomas! Is it safe?" Alex asked of another wolf. When the younger shifter lifted his head, I knew instantly he was another Alpha. What I also felt was a sense of peace roll over me, and I could feel the females behind me breathe out a sigh as if they had been holding their breath this entire time.

"Yes. No one will hurt any who is inside this house." His smooth bass voice further intensified the feeling of safety and peace.

"Maeze, please take the females and pups into the house." Alex directly positioned himself between the white wolf who could have killed us with one swipe of its claws and us. As we moved, another female shifter appeared in the doorway, but she wasn't a wolf. I did not know what she could be, but it was old. Older than I was, and I would be considered ancient nowadays, or so I thought. We made it up the stone steps, and the female with the teal eyes stepped aside as we passed through the doorway and into an ample space that looked as if a bomb had gone off. I turned to make sure all were accounted for once more before I felt my inner wolf relax a fraction. I could tell that coming here was the right thing to do. I took a breath and categorized all the scents that surrounded this area, and what caught me was the scent of home. I could smell other pups and shifter children. I could also smell the Warlock that had to be here still and death. There were so many scents, but the scent only the True Alpha carried was faint. He was here, so that meant I am closer than I thought.

DIMITRI

I shifted as I made it into the house. I reached out and grabbed a wolf that made its way inside the house before I did. I grabbed the large wolf by the neck and threw it against the wall. I heard growls and screams from the children coming from the Great Room. I could smell the magic in the air, and I knew Peter was still there. Why the fuck would he help this deranged Pack to attack us? We have been in an alliance with the Warlock's family for decades. I smashed through the double doors to see Remi holding the Warlock above her head. Her skin darkened as the teal of her eyes glowed with power. She threw the Warlock across the room and away from the children as she worked to control her shift. Her face would remind you of a shark because of the rows of sharp teeth, but she wasn't. I don't think anyone truly knew precisely what Remi was, but we knew it was old. I turned to see Peter trying to push himself up from the floor as he grabbed a pendant around his neck, but I didn't give his ass a chance. He betrayed us, and that would not stand. We couldn't trust him, so that meant we couldn't trust the rest of his Circle either. I moved in a partial shift in my third form. I worked hard to achieve this state, but there was still a time limit on how long we could hold it.

"Don't kill him!" Thomas growled. I grabbed the short Warlock by the back of his neck and ripped the necklace off.

"No! No! What have you done? None of you know power!" Peter screeched. He reached out to the pendent that went crashing to the floor.

"Shut the hell up! You have broken the vow the bond with this Pack," I growled. I kicked the pendent over to Remi. I watched her out the corner of my eye pick it up while making sure the children stayed far behind.

"What is the need to serve this disgrace of a Pack! The True Alpha grants powers that far surpass the fraud you call Alpha." Spittal flew from his lips as his eyes began to get a faint glow of red. Before I thought about it, I pulled the little man to my face and snarled. Everything went quiet, and the level of magic died down when the Warlock slumped into sleep. I rarely used my mental abilities. The fact that I could enter your mind and change your perception of what you're seeing is fucked up. Peter had decent mental barriers, but it wasn't good enough. I pushed into his thoughts and used the gift given to me at birth. If I enter your mind, you will only see your never-ending death by what you fear the most.

"You will endure until I pull you out," I growled in his thoughts. Those words would repeat until I released him. I dropped the sweating man to the floor and looked up to see Thomas partially shifted, holding two wolves by the throats. I felt myself shifting back as I looked around to see Remi directing the female shifters and our children to the lower level of the house. I could tell that some made it downstairs to the tunnels, and who was left didn't make it before Peter managed to get inside. I cocked my head side to side to crack my neck while I cataloged everything that went down.

"Thomas."

"I'm good. I am taking our guests to their new accommodations while I speak with them," Thomas grunted. I looked him over, and I could see he vibrated with anger.

"That will have to wait. We need to secure them and speak with our Alpha," I said as I made my way over to a closet. There were always clothes in every part of the house in all sizes. They were primarily sweatpants or shorts and a tee. I reached in, knowing exactly what I was getting while I watched Thomas. He was usually the peaceful and calm out of the brothers, except when it came to the children. His "talks" usually ended up with the other person's head either bitten off or cut off if you didn't answer every question truthfully. His unique talent of knowing when others are lying leaves no room for doubt, and it actually gets the answers we need by the surviving "guest", as he calls the prisoners.

"Have all my brothers, Remi, and..." Thomas stopped speaking as a group of female shifters, and Alex stood watching in the doorway. The woman who stood in front of the rest rang many alarming bells in my head because I couldn't figure out what type of wolf she could be. Whatever she was, her wolf was ancient.

I LOOKED over the group and then to Remi, who stared at the wolf with lavender eyes.

"These shifters need sanctuary. They escaped from that wolf's Pack. Remi, can you get them settled?" Alex asked.

"No, Remi, tell Lena to get them settled and meet us in Dax's office. If what I felt is real, then he will want answers after he finishes caring for his Mate," Thomas said. He was still in his third form, and every word was a deep growl.

"I have it handled, Thomas. Just take care of your little pets quickly so we can get to the planning. I also think she..." Remi pointed at the female shifter, who raised a brow at Remi.

"You may call me Maeze *Great Livyatan*." I looked at Maeze and back to Remi, whose eyes glowed brightly as she bared her teeth.

"Just as I thought. You are more than what you appear on the surface." Remi smiled, but that shit looked as if you just came face to face with something in the deepest depths of the ocean. Remi turned her gaze to me and then back to Thomas, who was squinting back at Remi. "She may know how we can hit back and hit back hard," Remi said. I agreed, but we didn't know this shifter, and this is one call I would not make.

"If she is to join, that will be the Alpha's decision. As of right now, we need to secure these assholes. We also need to figure out exactly how we are going to ward the fuck out of this house." I could feel my wolf pushing against my skin. I took in a breath, and something was off and smelled a bit different from just a few minutes ago. I could tell when the brothers caught on as well. We all turned to the women, and I moved forward.

"You might as well step forward. I know you don't belong here, and if you are coming to save this piece of shit right here, you are mistaken," I growled. The female shifters moved out of the way, and I stopped short as a female with rich brown skin with eyes so dark they looked as if they could pass as black. Her braids came past her shoulders, and my eyes kept moving down, taking her all in. The oversized white tee shirt and distressed jeans couldn't hide all her curves. I got to her waistline and noticed her holding a hand that was way too small, and when I looked over, I stared into the dark gaze of a young boy who narrowed his midnight black eyes at me.

"Well, I wasn't trying to hide, just getting a sense of this house and land before getting it warded properly."

"Who sent you here?"

"Quinn asked me to come and give my assistance, and it appears...y'all need it." She said, looking around. "Oh, and that Warlock over there has been warding this place in a pattern to form a Hellhole." She said, looking uneasy.

"Our True Alpha sent you but hasn't called to let us know about it?"

"He is the Alpha. I don't think he needs a reason to do

anything. Since he and his family saved me, my son, and our Circle, I will do whatever I can to help you," she sighed. She reached up to run her finger over a necklace. The charm seemed to be a triangle with a circle inside it, and inside the circle were three ovals. Each oval ended at the tip of each point of the triangle. If I remembered the teachings from my Mother correctly, that symbol meant fire and protection. I just didn't know why they were fused in such a way.

"We will see," I said as I tore my eyes away from her necklace. "What Circle do you claim that you are from, and what do we call you?" I asked, but something was telling me I was missing something. They should be obvious. She smirked as she dropped her hand, placing it on her hip.

"I am part of the Grey Circle, and you may call me Journee, and this little man is Zaccai," She said. Journee looked down at the little boy who glared at me. I did not know why he glared at me when any other kid wouldn't leave me the hell alone, but...wait. My eyes shot back to her, realizing she said the name, Grey. Journee is a part of the Circle that belongs to the wife of our True Alpha. I guess she caught the realization in my eyes because she smiled as if saying, "now we shall see."

DEVANA

CHAPTER thirteen

I wasn't actually sure when the pain faded, but I knew things had changed on a cellular level. I had heightened senses as a Hunter, but this had them turned up to one hundred percent. I could hear, taste, smell, and feel everything around me. I knew we were no longer close to the house, and no other wolves were near me except...except one. This wolf I knew and one I needed to see and to have closer to me, but my eyes just felt so heavy. I wanted to open them, so I knew that Dax was safe. That one word had my eyes opening because I had to know if everyone was safe. The rogue wolf had us, found us slipping, and could have killed...

"Devana?" The voice in my head sounded so deep and melodic. The very sound calmed me enough that I looked around. I knew it was morning already. I could see every damn thing clear as fucking day. I turned my head, and that felt so wrong because it was too big and heavy. When I stared into the violet eyes of the largest wolf I had ever known, those thoughts fled my mind. I reached out, wanting to feel his fur and make sure he was really there and that I wasn't dreaming. When I did, I knew something was way the hell off. I saw another wolf reaching toward Dax each time I tried moving my arms. "Mate!" I went to open my mouth to tell him not to shout in my mind and ask him how the hell he was doing it. Instead of my words, a long whine came out, followed by a slight growl. What in the entire fuck happened?

"Dax?"

"There she is, I didn't think you would have figured out the mental speech so quickly, but I should have known. To damn stubborn not to have done it."

"Wait...hold.." I had trouble stringing together a sentence when memory slammed its way back into my head. Scene after scene played as I recalled in vivid detail everything that had gone down, including the pain of it all. I cried out or howled at the pain and fury that I almost died because I thought we had time. This demon wasn't only here for the wolves now, it added to the plan, and it wants my soul. I could feel it deep inside and see it in the eyes of the rogue wolf who would have claimed my eyes for the demon if...if Dax hadn't shown up in time.

"Devana!" Dax darted forward but shifted in mid-movement. He wrapped his massive arms around my neck. I knew that werewolves were larger than ordinary wolves, but him doing this without effort was wild to me. I instantly felt better as I let myself calm, feeling Dax's presence helped. "Now that you are aware of what is happening, you should be able to shift back sexy. We need to get back to the Pack. I need to figure out who we lost and find out where we can find this bastard and take his ass out," Dax grunted. He was speaking out loud this time, and just by doing that, it helped make everything normal. My breathing slowed as the memory of running off into the woods last night hit me. Dax chased me, never letting me get too far away but also letting my wolf come to terms with itself. A flash of memory had me looking into the water and seeing my reflection from the light of the moon and seeing white fur with glowing mint green eyes with a hint of light brown. They seemed to swirl and change color, just like looking at my face as a human in the mirror. I shook and felt the popping of bones and rippling of skin as I shifted back into my human form for the first time.

"I...I didn't think...I didn't think one night of sex would change my world like this." My voice sounded scratchy and rough to my ears.

"Well, I mean anything less than turning you out fully would have my Alpha status in question." The rumble of his voice sounded richer, smoother than usual. I had no clue why I was joking around because I knew it wasn't time for it, but I never saw this shit coming.

I turned my head to look up at him with a smile and saw that he wasn't smiling but looking at me so intently I pulled back slightly.

"What?" I asked. Before he could answer, I felt it. I knew exactly why he was staring at me this way and that Daxton Rayne was terrified for the first time in his long-lived life. If I could feel his emotions like this already, then he should feel mine as well. The Bond was intense, but I couldn't understand why he still looked so afraid. That's when I got it. He felt it, but he also needed me to say it. To confirm and take away his fears and doubts that he may have fucked everything up, he wanted to build with me. His fear was clouding what he should already know. What he already knew from the moment we locked eyes was that I was his Mate, and it was nothing either one of us could do about it.

"I ᴋɴᴏᴡ you did what you had to do. I'm not sorry that you marked me, Dax. What I am sorry about is what we both will have to endure once this is all over," I said. Dax pulled me closer and stood with me in his arms.

"You honestly believe I care what anyone has to say? All I needed to hear was that you weren't sorry that I changed your life completely." I stared at him because I knew he could care less about what others may think, but we will be put out front after all of this. Hell, if we made it through this situation. I don't regret what happened, but I knew confronting House Okar would be hell.

"I figured you wouldn't care. I know there is a lot more that I need to know and so much that I need to be taught, but..."

"We don't have the time. Lucky that you're a Hunter and will catch on quickly." I noticed we were moving, but it felt like we were standing still. I didn't feel the breeze or the morning chill as I usually would. Then I noticed I was naked, but this fool had clothes on.

"Wait! Why don't I have clothes on, and you do?" I frowned. I still felt drained and starving at the same time. Dax chuckled and smirked down at me. I just noticed that his jet-black goatee had a few white hairs. They weren't gray but pure white like his wolf's fur.

"As I said, you will have to learn your new nature quickly. Although we still haven't talked about the book, you have about my family, but we can discuss that later. Did it happen to mention that shifting is a type of magic on its own? You, Hunter, will have to learn to control it and use it to your advantage." He looked down as we came to the edge of the Pack property. "Once I kill the rogue, I will teach you slowly everything you need to learn about your human body and your wolf form." I swallowed at the promise in his eyes which had me wondering what would be different. His words had me almost forgetting the feud between our species and making me remember the words of the Wolf Deity.

"You have been chosen to walk in both worlds as Hunter and Shifter. Your fellow Hunters may choose to turn their backs on you, but you will bear that cost."

I didn't know if I could bear that cost if that meant my family and House all turned away from me. I didn't know if **Kannuck** had been right or if I should have died last night as a sacrifice?

DAX

There is no time at the moment for Devana to learn her new shifter gifts. Strength, speed, hearing and smell were the usual things each shifter possessed. I knew she possessed gifts as a Hunter, but they may advance further now that she has been changed. I looked down as I made my way through my property because she fell silent. Devana was asleep with a frown line on her forehead that I wanted to erase. I didn't want to wake her because I knew she needed to sleep as much as possible. This moment would be all that I could give her to rest. Usually, when a person is changed, we give them as much time as possible to get used to their wolf. I, as Alpha, would take the time to show them everything they needed to know about who and what they were now. I couldn't even give my Mate that courtesy because of this fucking rogue.

"Alpha. William is now awake. Are we allowed to leave medical?" Jayla asked. I sensed her fear laced in her words. I didn't want my Pack afraid, but it seemed as if I needed to clean house because someone helped to let them the fuck inside. William was caught, but where there is one, there is more. It was time to find the traitors who dare put my Pack in danger and take them all out.

"No. I will be there to speak with both of you. The enforcers will ensure your safety until Jarod gets to you." I cut off whatever reply she was ready to make. I didn't want to hear excuses or denials. I didn't want to reinstate my Zeta, but I had no choice. I reached out to a mind that turned my way instantly. There was something to say about having siblings that are Alpha's themselves. It makes for an unstoppable Pack army.

"Jarod."

"You're back? Is she...she is good, right?"

"My Mate is well, brother. I am not speaking to you as your brother at the moment."

"Then tell me what you need, Alpha." Jarod could joke around and be a loner when he wanted, but when it was time for War, I would let no one else plan my battles.

"I need my Zeta. I need my general. William is awake, and I want fucking answers. I'm done fucking around and giving these wolves the benefit of the doubt. Find the traitors and get me answers to take this War to that ROGUE who thinks he is an Alpha."

"Done."

I tried not to look at the damage done to my land once again as I moved up the stone steps and entered my home. I didn't look around or note who was there. Dali stood at the door leading to the room where Devana was staying, but I bypassed that to put her in my bed where she belonged. I laid her down gently, wanting to take the time to clean her up and make sure her body was completely healed, but I knew time was tight. I wanted her to rest as much as she could until I needed her to wake. She is now my Bonded

Mate and will be Luna to this Pack. So when I went to War, she had to be by my side.

"She's...she is healed?" I heard the catch in Dali's voice, but I had no time to soothe her either.

"My Mate lives, but she is exhausted," I said, turning to look at the woman. She resembled Devana, but her eyes weren't that cat-like shape, and her hair was long and pulled into a tight ponytail. She closed her eyes and swallowed hard before standing taller as she visibly calmed herself.

"There is nothing I could do to repay you for saving her life."

"I don't need anything from you. If you weren't here, I still would have done it. If she hated me, I still would have chosen to do it. I am not now or ever looking for repayment for making sure my Mate lived." I moved forward, but she stepped back, still looking me in the eye as she put one arm across her chest.

"It doesn't matter why you did it, but the fact that you did. As a Hunter from House Okar, you have my word we will forever ally with you and yours." I only heard a vow like that spoken once before, and it had been broken. However, I could sense that this...this time may differ from the last.

"Stay with her until we have no more time to rest," I nodded and moved past her, and left the room. I could feel my wolf's hesitation of leaving my Mate vulnerable, but I knew her sister would die before anything happened to her. I looked around and spotted my two enforcers that moved to stand in front of the closed doors. As Alpha, everything they sensed, saw, heard, or smelled, I would know all those things as well. The enforcers were the eyes and ears of my Pack and were loyal to me and tied to this land.

WHEN I HIT the ground floor, the first thing I wanted to do was rip Peter's throat out. I scanned over the broken and burned furniture to see another Witch in my home. The growl left my lips before I could stop it. Right now, I trusted no one, especially a Witch I didn't fucking know.

"Hold up, Dax, she has nothing to do with Peter or his family. Quinn sent Journee to help us out. How he knew to do that, I have no clue," Dimitri stated. He moved to get in my path, clearly trying to protect this female, which was unusual for him. Dimitri protected those who couldn't defend themselves, but someone Dimitri didn't know, and a Witch had my brows going up. His eyes narrowed at me, but he looked away, not trying to show that he was challenging me. That was deliberate because so many lower-ranking wolves were around and other shifters I didn't know. I knew his ass would have something to say about my conclusion. He knew me just as well as my brothers what I was saying without words. He was interested in a Witch that his Mother hadn't chosen. With everything that is going on, I needed that momentary distraction. It helped to calm my anger enough to think logically and figure out where I needed to start. I knew killing Peter at this moment wasn't the right move.

"Did you confirm that story?" I asked as I stepped around my Beta.

"We were all going to meet in your office to discuss the next steps, Alpha." I laughed because he was on one right now. He knew that I caught on to his attraction, which got even better when I saw the small boy holding the Witch's hand tightly.

"Where is Thomas?"

"Making sure our prisoners are secure while we figure out what needs to happen next," Dimitri stated. The Witch stood up and faced me, and that was when I caught a scent that I had earlier. I was too far into my wolf and Devana's changing to really put two and two together. The female shifter who sat next to the Witch was the one who I saw outside. Her lavender eyes caught mine as her scent and age pressed against me. She wasn't an Alpha or Beta. She was something else that is rare in these times. I knew this scent as if it were my own family, and I had to see if I was correct about who and what this wolf could be.

"I am the Alpha of the Rayne Pack, but you may call me Dax. I get from my Beta that our True Alpha has sent you here. Why?" I could tell the Witch was nervous, but she stood tall and held her head up. She didn't meet my eyes but focused on a point directly over my shoulder.

"From what I was told is that I would be needed. My set of skills and abilities will help you now and more likely in the future."

"And he knew all this?" It wasn't that I was questioning Quinn and what he did, but I wanted to know the reasoning. Why this Witch? Her eyes shifted slightly, and she stared into mine. I knew it wasn't in any form of a challenge but for me to see the truth in her eyes.

"He asked for a Witch to go to be on the safe side. His wife and my Circle leader said that I would be needed, and my place is here. Since the Premier, or you may call her Queen of Witches Council, divined it here I am. I would have come either way just because I owe them everything." Her eyes shifted again, but this time they darted down to the boy. His dark brown eyes weren't looking at me, but he was watching Dimitri.

"Thank you for coming, Journee. I feel that this Warlock has done more damage to my land than I believed. I don't know why I couldn't sense it, but I need to rectify it immediately. The first thing I would ask is if you could ward this house against everything. After if you could start on the property. I will have my enforcers escort you while you set those wards for safety."

"I think I have a pretty good guess as to why no one sensed what was being done, but I need to make sure I am correct before I say anything else. I have already started on this house, and that will be done soon. If I could speak with the Hunter, that would help with the wards for demon attacks."

"I don't have a problem with that. I will let Dali know that you would like to speak with her. Until then, please continue in protecting this house."

"Not a problem," she nodded. I turned to Dimitri and caught his quick glance. I knew he would take care of that while I spoke to the wolf who shared the same blood as someone who died over five years ago. To my knowledge, he and one other were the last of that bloodline, or so we thought.

DAX

CHAPTER *fourteen*

I wasn't entirely sure that I could or should trust her, but I figured he read the situation when Alex came into the room.

"Dax, this is Maeze. She brought a group of female shifters along with pups for safety. The others are down with the others, but I kept three enforcers there just to be on the safe side." Alex stated. I looked his way, and he switched to mental speech when I caught his eye.

"Is she what I believe she is? She also scents of Stiles bloodline, but that shouldn't be possible right?"

"Nothing is impossible. Shani smells the same, and we know she is his daughter."

"Maeze, how were you caught, and why didn't you escape long before?" I watched as her brows raised in surprise as she darted a quick glance at Alex, then back to me.

"I refused to leave the defenseless behind. When I figured out what was happening, I couldn't leave the pups and females that weren't fighters behind. They would have been abused, used, or worse. They could have been killed. I couldn't save them all no matter how hard I tried."

"For you as a Zetagamma, I wouldn't think you could leave anyone behind." Her eyes narrowed at the mention of what she is because such a thing didn't exist, or it was so rare you rarely came across it. "You have information on the rogue and his Pack. I want to know everything you do and if you would work with my Zeta to prepare for War."

"You just trust me to help? You don't believe I could be a trojan horse?" She folded her arms across her chest as her eyes hardened. Her energy felt so raw and powerful. It was almost as if she were an Alpha, but I knew instinctively that was not her wolf's nature.

"What I do know of your bloodline trust is not an issue for me. You serve our True Alpha even if you have not met him. That shit is good enough for me." I stared down at the female as she searched my eyes before looking down and away.

"Then everything I sensed through Aeron's visions was correct. I was right in coming here. I will help you and your Pack in any way that I can. He...Aeron must be destroyed. The demon is possessing him..." She shook her head in disgust. "Aeron is nothing but a pawn in this game of chess that he will lose. He can't take any more of us with him. His soul is lost, and I refuse to let him bring down any more innocents with him."

"All his bullshit ends here," I said. I looked at my brother, and he nodded as I turned away. I wanted to find out what Jarod got out of William. I felt his mental touch as Maeze spoke, informing me that he had already gotten something out of the wolf. There were more shifters on this land that I couldn't trust, and that was going to end now.

I MADE my way toward the house that made it through all the violence that held the wounded. I could feel the fear coming from the home in waves. I knew Jarod was in full battle mode and did whatever he thought was necessary to get the information we needed. The door flew open, and I saw a partially shifted, Jayla, struggling with an enforcer.

"Let her go, Ezra."

"Dax...",

"Ezra! Let her go and find out what Jarod will need from you," I ordered. At my voice, Jayla froze. Ezra dropped the female, and she fell onto all fours as she shifted. I didn't command her to stop; I knew Jayla would be in pain if I forcibly stopped her shift. She howled out a mournful sound as Ezra took a significant step back.

"Dax, I don't know if even you will be able to fix this." The rumbling words from my enforcer had me looking up. He met my eyes for a second and looked past me. It didn't matter because I saw the anger, betrayal and rage he was holding back.

"I am the Alpha of this Pack, Ezra. I will fix it. Now go."

"I got you, Alpha," Ezra grunted. He wanted someone's

head for whatever Jarod pulled out of William. Jayla's howls began to transform into whines and whimpers of a lost wolf. It was as if she were a pup.

"Alpha. I...I didn't know he...I..."

"You need to go to the house, find your pup, and hold her close. I don't know what he has done to the full extent, but I know you had nothing to do with it. That being said, when this is over, we will speak again. You will be the first to know what my judgment will be for your Mate."

"Yes, Alpha."

There was nothing else I could give her until I knew what happened. Whatever it was, he will be judged by Pack Laws, including exile for his family. All wolves know the consequences of breaking Pack laws, and it wasn't anything that could change it. Not even me as the Alpha of this Pack. The only one who could wipe that slate clean would be Quinn, the True Alpha. The door opened again before I could go through, and Ezra came out with Jamel behind him. The two brothers were identical, except Jamel was a foot shorter with one pale blue eye and the other brown. Ezra stood nearly my height with deep dark brown eyes that seemed to glow as if blue flames flickered behind his irises. I felt Jarod enter my thoughts as he told me about Tucker, Wayne and Dustin. It was more information-sharing, but I felt his shock before he spoke.

"Brother, I need you to confirm this. He has trap doors in his mind I cannot bypass. If this is true..."

"I will break through the traps."

I refocused on my enforcers and nodded at them, ensuring they saw I meant what I was about to say. "Take them without harm. I will deal with whoever Jarod has sent you to get.."

"Yes, Alpha," they said at the same time. They both moved in opposite directions, like the passing of the wind. I didn't need to look to know that they both were already out of sight. I stepped into the house and immediately saw William pinned to the wall with silver spikes in each palm and with Jarod's shifted hand wrapped tightly around his throat. William's bloodshot eyes seemed to notice me as I shut the door. He still looked as if he had some defiance, but I watched all that drain away once he met my eyes.

"William, William, William. I hope the thoughts running through my brother's mind are not true because that is a death sentence for you and your family," I growled. I felt my body shifting and growing taller than my six feet and seven inches in height. Jarod hadn't moved or twitched as I shifted, and I knew the power of it weighed heavily on him as well. I saw when William began to crack under pressure, and his mind broke. Every secret he kept and other things he didn't know came pouring out of his mind. I reached with one massive, clawed hand and placed it on top of his head as Jarod moved away.

"A...Alpha...I...Alpha, please. I didn't..." I flexed my hand, and he screamed as conversations, memories, and the hidden instructions in his mind flashed in my thoughts as if they were my own.

DEVANA

I knew I was dreaming or having another vision, but it looked like I had this one before. The vision moved and shifted around until the shadows became clearer. I stood in a large open wooded area where motor homes made a circle around something. This time I wasn't in human form, but wolf form. I was looking up into the night sky on all fours, but it seemed familiar and different. I took a step forward, and I could see the shifters inside of a circle. Some were in wolf form like I was, and others were still human. One man stood taller than the rest, and when I saw his face, I knew it was Aeron. I wrinkled my nose at the scents filling my nostrils and knew precisely what fragrance I was smelling.

Along with the scent of death, loss, loneliness and demon came another one that was also familiar. I felt as if I should know what it was, but this vision had me feeling all over the place. I knew it was because I was in my wolf form and wasn't used to it yet. I didn't understand how to control all of my senses, but...maybe it would help me figure out what was different. Something was familiar about this area that I didn't feel before, but it still holds a heavyweight of evil surrounding it. The closer I got to the circle and other wolves, the more I began to understand the words being spoken. I already knew who it was and what lies Aeron and this demon would speak.

"As we take down Alpha after Alpha, we show who is the True Alpha of this nation. I will give the faithful the gift of power and the ability to transform into the third form. We kill those who stand in the way of this Pack! We kill the ones who aren't pure in blood! We are the chosen, and we will own it all. Now it's time to show how my ultimate strength will have every other Alpha kneel at my feet. Once we take the Rayne Pack's Alpha down and destroy a family of Alpha's that are un-pure, they all will bow. This so-called True Alpha Quinn is nothing more than a puppet propped up to control you. He claims a Witch as a Mate, and she has birthed bastard un-pure pups. Follow me to cleanliness and to rid this world of the abominations of half-breed wolves. Follow me, and your children will have a chance to live as the dominant species of this world. Disobey and suffer just as the un-pure wolves in your Packs. Follow me as I become Alpha to all Packs across this nation. We must take out the ones who stand in our way. The ones who protect the barriers that will lead us to our great power!" The words he spoke switched into another language I didn't know before when I was here, but now I understood. It was the language every wolf shifter instinctively knew. I focused back again on the rogue as he continued in the language of wolves.

"We take this land and this house, and it will start the chain of events to take the rest of the Packs as our own! We have laid the groundwork to start this War, and we will execute it once the Aenocynon dirus Pack has killed the ones who have been sent to stop me. Who can stop the True Alpha?" Aeron roared.

"Alpha! Alpha! Alpha!" The wolves all howled, and the men and women that stayed in their human forms screamed. Aeron's crimson eyes burned with malice and hatred, but the cunning I saw was all fucking demons. He had no clue this demon was feeding off every bit of his soul and everyone tainted with his poisoned blood. How could I have missed this information or these smells and this sky that reminded me of somewhere I knew. Things looked different in this form, but I knew I was missing something glaringly obvious. This demon knew I was here and of my gifts, so it's fucking with me. I turned back toward Aeron as his speech switched back as if he never said what I just heard.

"Once that is accomplished, we will make this country and make everyone bow at our feet. I Aeron Alpha of the Breaker Pack True Alpha to all wolves will wash this land in the blood of all who stand in our way! We take the un-clean Rayne Pack, and then we kill the man who calls himself the True Alpha Quinn Savir. Who's ready?" I watched the man grinning at the howls that filled the air. His scowl was aimed at those who stayed silent. I moved closer to get a better look at Aeron as he looked over his crowd. His dark brown eyes held a crimson ring, just like Quinn's. The difference was that ring wasn't from any natural-born power but one of a demon. I remembered this was when he would look at me, but I was no longer in human form. When his gaze landed on me, he moved over me, but I wasn't that damn lucky. It wasn't more than a minute his eyes snapped back in my direction, and I knew he could see me for who I am now.

"Hunter! Impossible! Come here!" Aeron leaped down from the platform he was standing on, coming directly at me. I didn't throw up my arms this time, but I used my new agility and moved out of the way. Everyone and thing around me stood stock still as if they were on pause. I started to search for the tie to my body to pull myself out of this vision. "No! You died! You will die, and I will…" His voice faded as I felt my thread to my body. I used my teeth to grab hold of it and pulled. As I tumbled, I flipped around, and I saw the familiar lights of a large mansion styled to look like a castle. It was my home and the place he truly wants to attack. I saw the sky as my body flipped once more and I saw that the moon was full and hung like a spotlight on the hundreds of wolves readying for an attack. All of my people would be there, along with two other Hunter Houses, to welcome the graduating Hunters on the night of the full moon. That action would be considered as War. It would become War amongst the Hunters and Werewolves. "Shit!" I lost sight of the sky, my home and the demon as everything went from a bright white to green and then to a warm baby blue as I was plunged back into my body.

"Vana! Oh, sis, talk to me." I knew it was Dali, but I couldn't open my eyes. I could barely make my lips move. Everything was swirling around in my mind as I tried to pull all the pieces together. I had to warn my Mother and Father.

I had to tell Dax to tell Quinn what this demon was trying to accomplish.

"Vana, just rest for a little while longer, sis," Dali said softly. There wasn't time for rest because this attack was going to happen, and soon. I tried using the mental touch to Dax, but I slipped into the blackness that called my name.

DAX

CHAPTER *fifteen*

I felt as if I was moving backward in his thoughts as I watched him and Lindell set explosives around my home. The most were where we kept the pups and the non-fighters of the Pack. As images flipped through my mind, I saw him infect three more wolves whose job was to make sure the cell where we would keep our prisoners had a way out if no one was watching them. I almost squeezed his head clean off when I saw William and Lindell trying to infect another wolf who lived off this property but still was one of mine. This wolf wasn't weak in the mind, and when it didn't happen, Lindell came out and shot him in the chest. It was a direct hit in the heart, so I knew it could take time to heal. Fabian didn't move, and I knew then that it wasn't regular bullets they used. When his wife came running into the house with their baby in her arms, Lindell also shot her. When William reached down and took the baby from its Mother's arms, what twisted my stomach. They left the bodies in the house, taking the child with them. That was the house I was going to last night, but they were already dead even if I had made it. I pulled my claws out of William and let his body fall to the ground.

"Where is the child?" I growled. William began to whimper as Jarod started to shift. I tried to see what they did to the child and everything after that scene, but it was blank.

"I didn't know...I didn't know..." William repeated. I felt Jarod's fur brush against my hand as he stalked forward. I had no time to argue because I could feel the time ticking on the detonators for the bombs placed everywhere. Not only was my entire Pack basically inside that house, but so was my Mate. I leaned over as Jarod, with teeth bared, growled in his face, ready for the word to rip his throat out.

"You have one second to tell me what you remember about that baby," I growled so low it would have been inaudible to a human ear. I was his Alpha, and I should have been able to rip through his mind to find the answer, but I knew if I tried, the trap doors in his thoughts would alert that bastard Lindell.

"I...I can't. I don't know! It's like it's not there! I don't know..." I howled. I knew everyone could hear it and wouldn't mistake it for anything but my rage. "Dear God, I don't...wait...Lennox...he. It was odd because he asked Jayla about formula..." I grunted as I spun in place, not needing another word from his lips. He may have done a thing without knowing, but he willingly chose to help Aeron and his Pack.

"Jarod. End him and have Ezra and Jamel find the brothers Lennox and Lindell as well. One of them has the child." I focused my thoughts on my other brothers, touching each mind as I slammed through the doors of my home. It was as if every heartbeat was a second that we had left to find seventeen explosives. With my wolf senses, it should be easy. Being an Alpha would be child's play if only they weren't spelled to be hidden.

Everything was in chaos as I went to the first one William had hidden. He only had five that he hid, and the brothers hid the rest.

"When the fuck is this shit going to go off?" Alex mentally shouted as he tore everything apart.

"Minutes, we have minutes! Get everyone out! Now!" I roared. I could withstand a blast, but no one else here except maybe Remi and Maeze could handle something like that.

"We have no time! There is no way we can get everyone out!" Dimitri growled in my mind. I found three of the devices William had hidden so far. I had an enforcer take each one far away from here, but we still had too many to go and not enough fucking time. They were spelled, but it didn't feel as though they were demonic when feeling the ones William had hidden.

"Dax! What the hell is happening?" Dali shouted as I handed the fifth device off to an enforcer to get rid of it. I spun around in a panic because she and Devana should have been out of here!

"What the hell are you still doing here?" I moved and had her by the arms and back into the room. The enforcers weren't at the door, but I called to anyone who was near to get here right the fuck now.

"What the hell? Dax, what is going on? The two giants at the door burst in here and told me to leave! We can't..."

"This fucking house is going to blow up! It would be best if you got Devana and yourself away from here. Now!" I said, moving to lift Devana into my arms.

"NO! No! Don't touch her!" I stopped and pulled back. I

didn't fully understand why I listened to her words, but it had an underlying tone. My wolf was on alert and peering through to look at Dali. "She was having a vision and didn't fully awaken. If we move her right now, she could be lost trying to find her body. I don't know if she made it fully back, and I won't until she wakes. We can't move her, Dax." Dali stated. Her eyes were wide, and I could tell she was hoping I understood, and I did.

"Fuck!" I turned and headed for the door because time was running out, and no one found the ones Lindell and Lennox hid.

"Ezra!"

"They are on the run, Alpha. We are on their trail as we speak."

"You need to move faster. We have a problem, and those bastards know the location of it."

"Consider it done."

"Dax!" Dali had been saying my name a few times, so I focused on her now. Devana wouldn't want her sister here if she had the chance to live.

"You need to get the hell away from here, Dali."

"Fuck that! This is my sister, and I think you forgot something. You have a Witch here, correct?" I turned around to give her a nod and ran for the doors. I knew everyone in this vicinity heard my mental shout. I made it to the ground floor, and Journee came through the broken doors in the arms of Dimitri.

"Fuck Dax, I just thought of it before you said it." Dimitri put Journee down, looking as if his movements scared the hell out of her by carrying her here.

"Journee, we need to find spelled devices that are planted around the house by the Warlock. They could go off any minute now." She looked shellshocked, but she said nothing and closed her eyes. I could feel the ticking throughout my body and hear my inner clock getting louder and louder. Suddenly Journee reached out, grabbing Dimitri's arm, and squeezed it tightly. The marking on her hand that signified that she was a Witch began to move and grow. She whispered words I didn't understand and was so quiet I couldn't pick it up. I watched her for what felt like hours and flicked my eyes to Dimitri. His eyes rolled into the back of his head as he mumbled incoherent words, and the small, barely noticeable mark on the right side of his neck began to expand. This was taking too long, and maybe I could be getting more people out of here instead of standing around. I knew there were few minutes left, and I would have to get back upstairs to protect Devana and Dali the best I could from the blast. I started to do just that when Dimitri stopped murmuring, and his eyes flipped open to stare into mine.

"Time is too slow for those who can't feel it, too swift for some, so they fear it. As the time draws near, the glooming, the dread beyond, darkens around what doesn't belong in this home. Tick, tick of time we stop you now!"

Journee opened her eyes and held her breath as she looked around. She noticed that she had a death grip on Dimitri and pulled her hand away. I focused on my inner senses, trying to see if I still felt that impending doom. It had eased, but something still was off.

"We have them, Alpha!" Ezra's voice boomed into my thoughts.

"Bring them directly to me," I grunted.

"Journee, thank you. Are they all stopped?" I asked.

"There were sixteen of them, and they all have been

stopped," Journee said, looking around the house. I was already turning away to check on everyone else when her words penetrated.

"Sixteen? Seventeen, you mean seventeen, right?"

"No, sixteen. The only spelled devices were sixteen, and they are stopped. I can't feel anymore." She said, looking at Dimitri and me.

"She's right, Dax. I feel nothing at all..." I turned around, trying to figure out what and where would the last device be hiding. I calmed myself and thought back to the scattered memories inside William's mind, trying to make sense of his thoughts. There was something said about the last device and how it was meant to open the door. The words weren't meant for William to hear or understand what they meant, but I did. I turned around to face Journee and Dimitri.

"Journee, you said the Warlock was making a portal gate to Hell or something on this land, right?"

"Yes, but what..."

"It's not a bomb! It's a trigger to release what is needed to finish the gate," I said with fury. I was going to stomp the shit out of Peter and then his bloodline.

"Fuck! Shit, oh shit...they are going to make a sacrifice! If you aren't a demon or a Shade, the only way to get that down would be to kill an innocent. Oh, Goddess!" Journee gasped. Her large, dark eyes looked around frantically as she mumbled. She gripped her necklace as she swayed.

"What the fuck are they sacrificing?" Dimitri growled. It didn't take me long to figure it out, but Ezra came through the door with Jamel behind him. He held Lindell by the throat and threw him at my feet. I cracked my neck and eyed him when Dimitri shifted his hand into a claw, reached down, and grabbed the shifter by the shirt. Lindell screamed as Dimitri's clawed hand dug into his flesh, and his brother shook in fear as he realized they both were fucked.

"I don't give a shit which one of you tells me, but one of you better spit out where you hid the baby."

"Dax! You need the location now. I can't hold this spell back much longer...I..." Journee screamed and fell to her knees, holding her head as she began chanting once more.

"Journee!" Dimitri shouted, but she held up a shaking hand.

"Fuck it!" I growled and moved. I was right next to Lindell, who sneered in my direction. I didn't give his ass time to talk his bullshit. It took nothing for me to rear back and smack his head from his body. I knew I had blood covering me. The blood sprayed everywhere as the last beats of his heart pumped out his life's blood from his body. Dimitri dropped the body to the floor and turned his two-colored eyes onto Lennox. It didn't matter because my point was made. "Now Lennox. You are the only one left, and since he is dead, only you have what I want. His death was in an instant, but yours will last for an eternity if you fuck with me." There wasn't a need to shout my words or repeat myself. Everything in his mind spilled out and opened to me like the pages of a book. Lindell had only marked the spell called the seventeenth circle here in the house, connecting it to the child. That would give the direction to open a gate on this property with no way to close it before all our souls were taken. The baby's location was where I wouldn't have felt it off my land, but close enough to get the job done. The baby was at William's home, along with Jayla. She had been the one in charge of this shit the entire time. She had gotten to each pack member who turned traitor along with her and her husband. She was even willing to bring Lindell along with the promise of power and sex. She managed to persuade some wolves, but in the end, she was ready to kill them all to power up the opening of the Hell gate to this earth. Everything would look as if we planned to do this, causing untold death and probably starting a War between supernatural species and humans.

"It was always Jayla!" The words left my lips, but I was already gone.

DEVANA

I felt as if I was crawling on my hands and knees across glass. I could feel Dax's anger, anxiety and rage, making me push harder to find my way out of this darkness. I knew this because it happened once before and not that long ago. What was different was the pain I felt trying to move in this realm.

"Pain is in your mind. The pain you are feeling is the representation of what Dax is feeling."

"I need to get back! I need to help him through all of this." I didn't have time to sit and talk when I knew what was happening. I knew the actual reason why this demon was here and what he was trying to do.

"YOU WILL NOT GO UNTIL I SAY IT IS TIME!" The growl of the words vibrated my bones and made me pay attention. I knew where I was and who I was talking to, so I knew to keep my damn mouth shut. He isn't God, but he is a god. One who gave me the chance to fix shit that went wrong.

"What do I need to do? I understand what was asked of me now, and I fully accept that responsibility." I said.

"Nothing, I did not divine myself. This is not why you are here, Devana Okar. If you were to return at this moment, you would have been tainted by the demon." His words made no damn sense. The demon hadn't touched me or gotten near to me, so how...

"He touched my tether?" No wonder I was in pain. The demon was trying to attack my spiritual form, and he now had a grip on it.

"Correct. What this demon has failed to realize is that you are now mine. The rules do not apply to me or my chosen. It cannot have you this way. Not in your spiritual wolf form. That is mine. How do you feel now?"

I didn't speak immediately as I worked through **Kannuck's** words and what they meant.

"If I were there in the flesh, you wouldn't have interceded on my behalf?

"No. There are clear lines that must be followed, but ...this falls into a gray area. There is no need to worry about that now, child. It is time. Do you hear that?"

I did feel better, and the pain was a faded memory. I tuned in to his words, and I was confused. There was nothing to hear in this place except I heard faint crying.

"Who...where is that crying coming from, and who is it?" I asked while looking around in the darkness. The crying was getting louder, and I knew it was a child for some reason. I felt light-headed, and I had sudden pressure on the backs of my eyes. I pushed forward, needing to stop this kid from crying and also to see my Mate. Just thinking that word now felt natural and normal. I moved forward as if I was moving through a thick jungle, and every inch was large plants. I could start to smell and immediately cataloging each scent that I could but not finding the one I wanted the most. Yes, it was there, but more of an echo, and I needed the real deal. I could scent Dali and her fear. She was or had cried as well, and that wouldn't do. I pushed harder, fighting through the thick cobwebs in my mind, trying to get back to the living. I had to do it and fast because I had no clue how long I had been out. Did we get attacked again? Did Aeron attack my family already? Did Dax manage to stop him, and Dali killed the demon? I shook my head no because I knew that wasn't right. "Damn it!" I screamed, and the crying sounds stopped. Things began to get quiet as I pushed forward another step.

"Devana?"

I knew that voice. It was Dali, but the sniffling I heard had to be from a child. Meesha, maybe.

"I'm awake," I said, trying and failing to open my eyes.

"Devana, are you in pain? You're moaning," Dali asked. I opened my mouth again and said I was awake, but I heard the moaning sound for myself this time. Okay, so I wasn't quite there just yet.

"Is she awake?" A small voice asked. I knew it had to be Meesha, but I don't understand why they had her in here. I had to look like shit.

"No, but getting close. She will be waking up soon," Dali said.

"Dax..." I knew I had spoken this time. I could smell Dax slightly around me. I could feel the soft sheets around me, and I knew I had to be in his bed.

"There she is. Open those eyes for me, sis," Dali coaxed.

"Devana! She's awake!" Meesha's little voice screamed. I could feel my sister's soft hands checking my pulse and body for any wounds. I knew there weren't any, and she didn't need to worry. I didn't know how to explain all this to our parents, but it had to happen soon. Dax was my Mate, and they will have to accept and deal with the choice I made.

"Vana, we have so much to do you need to get your lazy ass up," Dali sighed. I took in a breath to say something smart out of my mouth, but everything came crashing back into my mind. I wasn't laying here because I was turned. I had another vision. The vision! Shit! My eyes flew open to see a white ceiling with lights coming from another part of the room. The vision came back to me at speeds I didn't know I could comprehend, but I guess things were different now that I am a shifter. I sat up and swung my legs to the side of the bed.

"Whoa, whoa, slow down, babe. You have been through a lot..."

"Did I miss the full moon?"

"What?"

"Dali, did I sleep through the full fucking moon?"

"No...why..."

"That bastard is going to start a War with Hunters against the wolf shifters by killing our House!"

"Shit!" Dali snapped. She had the same feeling that I did.

This would be a disaster that will never be able to be fixed. Meesha made her way towards me, looking terrified.

"Devana, will you stop the bad man?" Meesha asked. Her eyes were wide, and I could tell whatever happened in the house scared her to death.

"We all will keep you safe, Meesha. We will keep you and every other shifter in this Pack safe," I said. I scooped the little shifter in my arms and hugged her. I felt tiny arms wrap around my neck and squeezed. I felt her lips at my ear.

"I'm so glad you are our Luna, Devana," she whispered. I felt a quick kiss on my cheek before she wiggled her way out of my arms and was gone. I felt my wolf's eyes open at that moment, and I felt that she was ready for whatever needed to be done to keep our Pack safe.

DAX
CHAPTER
sixteen

I didn't wait for anyone, but I knew Thomas, Jarod and Remi were close behind me as I made it through the wooded area and leaped out of the tree line. I knew this was going to go viral because there were way too many cars on the highway. Highway 195 was busy at the best times, but I had to cross it to get to Jayla faster.

"Did Journee say how far she could be from the house?" I asked Dimitri. Car horns sounded, and screeches of tires and screams filled the morning. I dipped and dodged vehicles as I made my way to the other side.

"Only twenty miles away. Anymore, then the spell will not work. Where the fuck is she?"

"I can feel her, and she is moving. She has to be in a car."

"Where the fuck is she going?" Thomas asked. At first, I thought she would go to their home, but I could tell she wasn't near there as I focused. Jayla was on the move, and I tried to push into her thoughts, but something had me blocked. I should have had access because she was my Pack member and belonged to me, but something or someone was keeping me out. They just couldn't keep me from tracking her movements. I leaped over the sound barrier wall and landed in my human form on the ground. I knew that would be all over the news, and Quinn might have some explaining to do, but if I didn't stop this shit, things would turn apocalyptic for everyone.

"She doesn't have a destination, but she has stopped. She probably believes she is far enough away to escape the Hell hole herself." I growled. I moved through the trees as I came upon a dirt road with a single red Honda sitting there. The front doors were left open, and I saw Jayla kneeling on the ground with her hands held high as if to stab down at something beneath her. I felt a wave of sudden doom and fear. I knew it was coming from Thomas, and that feeling would have a lesser wolf cowering in fear, not an Alpha, but it did affect Jayla. Her entire body spasmed, making her lose hold of the knife in her hands. I reached out as I passed her and grabbed her by the back of the neck. Remi caught the blade and threw it to the side as she scooped up the child. I threw Jayla headfirst into the ground.

"No! She has to die! He has commanded it! You don't know what or who you're dealing with here! I have..."

"Shut the fuck up." I knew my voice was deadly, and the ring of command had her breath seizing in her chest. It seemed that when I was close enough, the spell meant nothing because I could read every thought in her head. If I had focused on her earlier, I would have seen what she was doing.

"I don't want to hear anything you have to say." I took a step as Jayla began to scoot backward on her hands and feet as she watched me in fear. I felt Jarod in wolf form by my side.

"He will come for me! Aeron will..."

"You have violated every Pack law. Your judgment is death. Zeta." With a normal eye, you wouldn't have seen Jarod move. I saw each of his movements as if it were in 4k. His massive paw slammed into Jayla's chest as he began to pull her body apart. I turned away and moved to Remi so I could check the child. Once I reached her, she held out the tiny baby girl, and I took her into my arms. I looked her over physically and then scanned her for any internal damage.

"What did you get from her thoughts?" Dimitri asked. His eyes never left Jarod until he howled.

"I think it's time we have that meeting and also bring Quinn up to speed," I said. I could not unsee the future this demon and others like him wanted. Even if we stop this one, it will not be the end.

~Alpha's Claim~

We arrived back on the property, and the first person I saw was my Mate. She stood tall in all black, next to her sister, who seemed to pace. I blinked, and she was already off the steps and coming at me. I could feel the joy, relief and the Mating bond humming, but I also felt her fear. Something had happened in the time we had gone after Jayla.

"Dax!" She was wrapped around me, but I didn't stop. I just picked her up and kept moving. Almost everything on my property needed rebuilding, and those who died in defense of it needed burials. "What the hell happened?" She asked. I made it to the steps of the house as she moved to slide down my front.

"We will all go over what happened, but I need to handle some shit." Every Pack member was out and around the house. There was no time for the pit. Everyone who was involved in this would pay the consequences. I saw Journee come around the corner of the house, followed by Jamel and Ezra. Devana turned to face Journee as they approached us. I felt Thomas at my side, and I could feel the intense anger he had to release. I knew my brother, and it took a lot to get him to this point.

"Thomas, bring Peter and the wolves you caught to be judged with the rest." He said nothing, just moved and disappeared. Devana turned to me as she ran a hand through her hair. "I know we need to deal with Pack business, but it is way more going on than we believed."

"Yeah, we know all about the gate to Hell. We have that covered and..."

"I helped Journee in getting rid of that and setting down additional wards, but that isn't what I am talking about," she said.

"Devana! No one is answering the damn phone! We need to leave now if we are going to make it before dark. They are probably preparing for the ceremonies already. No one will have a cell phone on or even think to check text messages. Shit, shit, shit!" Dali swore while she redialed her parents, I assumed.

I noticed Max look up from helping some of the female shifters. I wanted everyone out here, so we knew once and for all who the traitors were. It did not matter if they were wounded or not. I saw Lennox, Tucker, Wayne and Dustin kneeling in the dirt with their heads down, and hands were bound together with silver chains.

"Shit! Shit! We have to go." I turned back to my Mate as I felt the spike of fear and irritation.

"Talk to me. The fuck is going on? We need a plan to go at this rogue and figure out where the hell they will be next."

"That's just it, Dax. I know where they are going. It was about you and me, but my visions weren't always correct."

"What? They attacked here and would have killed everyone if..."

"No, no, I mean everything. Yes, I got what I was supposed to get right, but I didn't understand what was happening. The demon manipulated my visions, so I would have never figured out unless...unless I was a wolf shifter. I had the same vision from the day before when I passed out, except it was slightly different. Aeron spoke words I wouldn't have known as Hunter or understood even if I was taught it."

"The language of wolves, **Kannur.**"

"Yes! He wants a war Dax between us. He wants you, Dax, and the souls of every wolf here. Your family prophecy says that you could stop this from happening, but if you were fighting your own War, why would you help a Hunter? A Hunter who came to help and died doing it while wolves attacked her home."

"That would start a War between all wolves and fracture what Quinn and the others have been building." It all began to click in place as the screaming ripped through the air. We both spun around and watched as Thomas pushed Peter in front of him while the Warlock looked like he had a heart attack. His face was a tomato red, and his eyes darted around wildly.

"None of you will live! They will finish what I started! This land you call yours will not know peace!" He raged. I saw the moment Thomas was just about done with everything. After seeing that female shifter about to execute a child, a newborn baby had fucked with him. Before I could move Devana out of the way, Remi was up in Thomas's face as she side kicked Peter down the rest of the steps. I moved to Peter and pulled the small man to his feet, and dragged him over to the others.

"You're nothing! You will never be the wolf the scrolls say you will. You're weak!" Peter spat. Devana moved between us as if she were made of fluid and wrapped her fingers around the Warlock neck.

"As a Hunter, Peter Johnston, I am in my full authority of eradicating your entire bloodline, and I will start with you. You have committed the highest of crimes here, Peter. You placed the entire world in danger, granting me to sentence you to nothing but an endless death. Do you know how we accomplish that Warlock?" Her voice was as smooth as silk but as deadly as the blade she held to Peter's jugular. I heard a vehicle approaching and the tires as they screeched to a stop.

"No, you have no authority over me, HUNTER!" Peter said as the spittal flew from his lips. Devana smiled as the shouts of protest came from our right. Alex had the rest of Peter's family. He has a sister, her husband, and two nephews. They were all in on what was happening. All of them were old enough to know this shit was wrong, but they chose to go along with the plan to open a gate to Hell on my property.

"We do not answer to your Pack rules!" Patrice, Peter's sister, screamed. I couldn't believe I thought she was the better of the two. I didn't know how their family had strayed away from good.

"Your parents and their Circle would be disgusted at what you have become," I stated. Devana dropped Peter back to the ground as the rest of his family joined the traitors.

"As a Witch of the Grey Circle here on behalf of our Premier, I can speak for what I think is best. No laws by anyone will be broken because I give my permission for the Hunter to serve justice." The eyes of Peter's family widen at the mention of the Grey Circle.

"This isn't..." Peter started, but Devana cut him off with a punch to the face.

"As the Hunter who is here, I leave your fate at the hands of those who you tried to murder. You now belong to the Pack." Devana said, taking a step back. She looked around at the wolves, who stared at her in disbelief.

"Now that all that is out of the way, let's get on with it." I shifted as my power began to build. I knew the violet of my eyes grew brighter and more intense as I howled. All of my anger was directed at those who would give their Pack up for promises of power. My power was directed at those who committed the crime. It didn't matter because everyone who was near could feel my wrath. It would remind all who would think of choosing this path what the consequences will be. I shifted into the form I took with William, stood over every one of them, and moved down the line. I quickly turned through their minds, seeing the same in each, just as I saw in William's thoughts. None of them were innocent, and none would live. It was always harder for me to speak in this form, and I knew it shook everyone around me when I used this form to issue out the sentencing. "You all have been found guilty."

DEVANA

It was a straight-up blood bath and something I would never forget. I saw the horror through Dax's eyes that he saw in their minds. None of these people were worth trying to save, and I didn't feel bad about what happened. Peter and Patrice dragged their family into this mess, but they went along with it even knowing the shit was fucked up. The only two that were left stood watching as the others were judged. Thomas and Remi stood on each side of Aeron's Pack wolves. I could see on their faces that they were scared shitless. As Dax returned to his human form, he was still covered in blood. I looked over to my sister, and she stared at the carnage that was just released on the traitors of this Pack. Her eyes darted to my mine, and she shook her head minutely, telling me she couldn't get a hold of anyone. We both knew the chances were slim at best, but we had to try. I looked back toward Dax, feeling that he was about to speak.

"I dislike tearing into the minds of my Pack who are my family, but this left me little choice. Use this time to prepare for the War that is ahead of this Pack tonight. We may have stopped one plot that the rogue has thrown at us, but that doesn't mean shit if he is still out there to do it again."

No one said a word in protest at his invasion of their privacy because he was right. From my knowledge, as Alpha, he could do it whenever he pleased. The remaining Pack member was scared, but I could see a plan for times like this where you would typically see people looking around for guidance. That wasn't the case here. These wolves, bears, cougars, and whatever else was in this Pack knew what to do.

"We can't get through to anyone, Dax. We need to get there as soon as possible." I stated. I started to walk in the same direction as him. It didn't matter that I was tall for a female at this point because standing next to someone who was damn near seven feet tall dwarfed just about everyone. His arm snaked out and wrapped around my waist, and I didn't think he even realized it. I started to realize that most shifters were very tactile in stressful situations and that almost everyone was touching someone, even if it was just a hand on the shoulder or just standing close to each other.

"I think I might have an idea of how to get us there quickly, but we can't rush into it without having a plan. Aeron and this demon have planned this thing out from the beginning, so we need to outsmart them."

"Yes. I agree with you on that, but I can assure you that Aeron doesn't know the true reason for this demon's end game. Demons will always lie, cheat, and trick whoever and whatever they can. They will always have another agenda no matter how things turn out."

"Yeah, I seem to remember Cassandra saying something like that," Dax said as we entered the house. We took the stairs up and entered his office, which thankfully escaped the carnage downstairs.

"Cassandra? So you knew her, I take it."

"I did and thought I knew her better than anyone else, but maybe not. I once held very high respect for Hunters but completely lost it when she deserted us. She was supposed to be my friend. It was fucked up, but maybe things are correcting themselves." I wanted to know more about his time with the Hunter, but now wasn't the time to go into his history. I was sure that the books and journals didn't know everything, and I wanted to know every detail about his life.

"Just as I will know every detail about yours when we have time," Dax said, looking down at me. I looked up, but he was already looking over everyone who gathered in his office. We were all looking rundown, dirty, and bloody. Dimitri stepped forward with Journee by his side. My sister and I helped the Witch remove the spell work for the Hell hole and gave some of our blood to lay proper protection around this property against demons.

"Alpha, I think we should get what we need from these two and then get cleaned up." His eyes found mine, and he nodded once before finishing. "I mean Alphas." I opened my mouth to correct him because I was not an Alpha when I felt my wolf move inside me. She was now paying attention, and I could feel the power coming from her that I was just noticing.

"We are Luna. We are Alpha."

My mouth fell shut at the growling of words in my head. I felt Dax squeeze my hip as if he heard it as well.

"You have a way, Dimitri?" Dax asked as he let me go.

"We may have a way which we will need to get started on as soon as this meeting is completed. I am long out of practice, but it will get done." Dax eyed Dimitri for a moment before nodding.

"I got you, Tri. I know you will get it done and as soon as possible." I almost laughed at Dimitri's expression, but I bit it back. The same couldn't be said for Malic and Max, though.

"Fuck all of you," Dimitri said, turning in place. He walked over to the two wolves that had been watching and hoping we would forget about them, but that shit wasn't happening. The door opened again, and the wolf with the lavender eyes stepped through. The two wolves started to growl and tried to shift at the sight of the female.

"Maeze! You betray your, Alpha?" One of the wolves hissed in a low growl. I couldn't figure out what rank of the wolf she was, but she didn't flinch. She looked at the two wolves and then around at all of us.

"I can tell you that these two don't know shit. They were in it for the powers and the access it gave them...to younger females." Maeze said. I could see the barely controlled rage she hid well, but she didn't want to be in the same space as the wolves.

"Are they a use for any information?" Dax snarled. I saw Thomas's eyes shift to obsidian, which made even me shiver slightly.

"I can tell you they have ingested the Alpha's blood," Maeze said. She looked at Journee and Dimitri, who looked at each other. That was when a flood of voices and information hit my brain.

"**We can use their blood for a more accurate location,**" **Dimitri said.**

"**Let me handle these two wolves, Dax. I need the release.**" **Thomas growled.**

"**I will go with Thomas,**" **Remi stated.**

"**Let them get to work on that while we bring our true Alpha up to speed about everything,**" **Max said.**

"**I have spoken with Maeze, and from her information about this Aeron, we can come up with both defensive and offensive plans.**"

"**I will work with Dali and figure where the weak points will be and who else will be there we have to protect,**" **Max stated.**

"**Agreed.**" Both Dax and I said at the same time. It felt natural, but it was entirely a new feeling for me. There was no hesitation in coming to this decision with my Mate, and it felt as though we were one.

MAEZE
CHAPTER seventeen

The speed and decisiveness of this Pack stunned even me. I wasn't sure how so many Alphas could work this closely together, but it seemed like they had all of it down to a science. The Beta Dimitri didn't seem so Beta-like with his skill, power and abilities that aren't normal in most wolves. My opinion was taken with no question. Let me know why the True Alpha trusted this family to deal with an enemy of this nature. I didn't know what was happening, but I got some information about Quinn familiar to me. His scent and how all the Rayne brothers carried themselves in his name told me they respected him and his judgments.

"Maeze, tell us everything you know about this rogue, please." I hadn't noticed when Dax made a call or heard him talking on the phone. I still felt out of sorts coming back into the world like this, but everything snapped back into place when I heard his voice. I felt the command in his voice and heard the tone of patience, but with power. All of that was through the phone. He sounded so much like all the True Alphas that came before him. I instantly knew that he was the reason I came back. Quinn's coming into his power and the world going to battle ticked off the boxes that marked me returning to help him through the coming fights.

"When I was first taken, it happened at night, and it happened on a full moon. That is why I didn't understand why we were attacking the Rayne Pack last night. I just knew it would happen when he used my blood as a conduit for the demon. I believed he was using the full moon's magic, but I could have been wrong, and it was just another ploy. I knew he did not have any knowledge of my powers, so I didn't fight it. Part of my role in a Pack is to care for the members of the Pack, and I could not leave the ones who truly did not belong with Aeron. The male wolves who didn't join him or serve him were killed. The ones who just wanted to hurt others or believed in his lies went along with anything. When I was with them, I noticed that the Alpha's who joined the Pack started to disappear. It didn't happen all at once, but it was often enough others started to talk."

"What do you think was happening to them?" Dax asked, leaning forward. I wasn't sure, but I had to tell each of them what I thought. My eyes moved to Devana and Dali as they shared a look at each other. Devana turned back, holding up a hand with a look of disgust on her face.

"There is only one reason they would go missing at this point. Maeze, did he make everyone drink his blood?" Devana asked. All eyes focused on me, maybe thinking I had ingested that foul shit, but that did not happen.

"The only ones he had to drink his blood were the Alphas and the Betas. They would keep everyone else in line. It also lets the others see what powers they could look forward to if they only follow him as the True Alpha. I can say that he does have an army even with Alpha's disappearing. It was north of two hundred, but I think it has been cut in half after last night." I growled. I squeezed my fisted hand in my lap, trying to erase the horrors of what he did to the Alphas that fought back. I wanted to unsee the atrocities Aeron committed to the wolves that were changed, to the pups and females that couldn't defend themselves.

"The Alpha's that disappear are being used for power. A sacrifice to the demon to keep the strength he was given." Devana said, shaking her head. I could see the frustration written on everyone's faces, but what could they have done. No one knew this was happening.

"From what I know about demons, the more they kill, the more power they gain. So I take it the demon is also devouring the souls of these wolves." Quinn growled.

"Exactly, and we should have seen this coming...we should've..." Devana broke off when Dax put his hand up.

"None of us saw this happening. There has been so much crazy shit happening the demon knew the perfect time to start this up." He said, leaning back in his chair.

"Maeze, you did everything that you could without a Pack to have your back. If I had known you were out there, I would have come to find you. I didn't have a father to tell me about things like this. With your knowledge and guidance, I hope to bring our species together and form a stronger nation. Dax, to accomplish this, we have to end this rogue and destroy this demon."

"We got this, Alpha. You came to me, and I told you that we would handle it."

"I do not doubt that one bit," Quinn stated. I kind of tuned out and thinking about the words Quinn spoke. It had me needing to know what happened while I was gone. What the hell went on that his father couldn't prepare him for the responsibility of being what he was destined to become. Either way, I knew where I belonged, and the feeling of peace and home were at my fingertips. Before I went off to join this new True Alpha, I also knew that I would help Dax and his Pack put down this rogue and free the other prisoners if we weren't too late.

"Quinn! Is everything good?" I heard the alarm in Dax's voice bring me back to the conversation.

"Shit! I don't know. Finish this Dax. I would be there to help if we didn't have shit to hold down over here. I trust you to get this done. I know for sure all of you will bring that rogue down." The line disconnected, and we looked around at each other.

"He's right. He gave us this responsibility, so we need to take care of it. At least they will try to warn the Hunters if possible, but after that abrupt ending to the call, it seems like they got some other shit going on. It doesn't matter because we got this." Dax wrapped his knuckles on the table and stood. I felt the tension, anger and excitement in the air as we all stood to prepare for a fight we all will die from or come out with the head of this possessed wolf who thinks he is a True Alpha.

AERON

I was already on my fifth Alpha before the rage in my blood cooled enough for me to think straight. The demon was silent, but I knew that shit wouldn't last too much longer.

"She isn't dead! Peter and the rest of them haven't made it back with her body or Dax's body!"

"Your weakness is what sets ussss back!" I snarled as I ripped through another wolf that was closest to me. I threw the empty shell of the wolf into the fire with the rest.

"I am not weak, **Abadozui**, nor have I ever been weak! I am the True Alpha!" I roared. I knew my wolves were eyeing me in fear, and that was good for them. They should feel fear and remember who their leader is! They need to remember who their God is!

"You will do well to remember who gave you this power, Aeron. You were nothing when I found you, and you can be again if you don't fix the mess your people created. You chose that Warlock's Circle. All I asked was for the eyesss. Sooo closse to everything you want, but..."

"They are still alive, aren't they! You will have the seer, and I will have the white wolf's eyes! You will have your

War!" I roared. I knew no one heard the demon or understood what I was talking about, but that didn't matter. They followed me and did what I said because they all know their True Alpha, and now everyone will know my name. I turned to face the remaining of my wolves. I still had about one hundred wolves at my command, but I could see that they were all beginning to lose their nerve. I still had those who were loyal, but I needed every last wolf on the battlefield. I looked to my left and caught Maurice's eyes, and he made his way over quickly. His larger body had no issue with getting through a crowd.

"Yes, Alpha." His smooth midnight skin shined, but the slice across his face from the claws of our enemy wasn't healing.

"It's time. It is time for everyone to take part and gain new gifts," I said. I made sure I pitched my voice so everyone could hear it. Most of the wolves here were here because they sought power, and I promised to give it to them.

"Yes, my Alpha!." He grunted. He turned away and howled into the sky. "Line up! Let our True Alpha give you the gift of power you should have gotten when you were born! Only a real True Alpha can share power, and I have been a recipient. Now, who will follow our True Alpha into battle?" The loud roaring howls and screams set fire to my blood. I could see the blaze of eagerness in Maurice's black eyes when he looked back at me. He had a taste of it before, so I knew he wanted more. We were going up against Hunters, and that would be no easy thing. These wolves would die, but it will kick start a War to end all others. How could Quinn allow that to happen and enable a Hunter to die while helping the very shifters he asked her to assist. That was no True Alpha. I turned away and stood close to the fire as the blood of the wolves I just consumed fueled my power. I began to shift into the other form that gave me greater height. I was larger in this form, standing on two legs almost nine feet tall. My head shifted into my wolf form as I howled. I could feel all eyes on me as they chanted my name. I turned, and Maurice already had two large bowls waiting, and the first wolves lined up to take what I was offering. It was too bad they would realize their mistake until it was too late. It didn't matter as long as I got the results that I needed. There were many more wolves ready and waiting to follow my lead.

"Drink!" I growled. The low rumble of my voice had many of the wolves whining and pacing, but none ran as the blood began to flow. They all could sense the power just as I could when **Abadozui** the Black Dog came to me that night. It was a power I had never felt before and one I was willing to kill to have. The first that had to go was my Alpha and his Luna, which were my Mother and Father. I felt no regret at that decision. Their blood and power will live on through me. It was just exchange for a soul they no longer needed. I was chosen, and all pure wolf shifter Packs will belong to me.

DAX
CHAPTER
eighteen

After the meeting, I took Devana into my room and closed the door. We didn't have much time, and I knew her mind was spinning about her family.

"How long did Dimitri say it would take?" She asked, pacing the floor. I watched as she twirled two blades around in her hands. It seemed like a nervous action she wasn't aware of doing.

"They aren't sure. They aren't getting a clear location because it had been a few days since they ingested the blood." I said. I started to strip out of my clothes, leaving them in a bloody pile on the floor, when Devana ended up walking toward me when I finally managed to pull the sticky sweats from my body.

"My parents and everyone there are skilled at what they do. I mean, they are very much prepared for attacks such as this, but..." The blades in her hands disappeared quickly into the sleeve so she could run her hands through her thick curls. Her cat-like eyes flashed as tears appeared at the corners.

"Come to me, Mate," I said, holding out a hand. I knew I

still had dried blood places, but I couldn't see her cry, not this Hunter who took down a fully grown wolf without killing him. She came without hesitation. I knew she wouldn't have just yesterday. This world we lived in moved quickly, and if we didn't grab on to the good in it when it showed itself, God only knows when it would come back around again. "They are Hunters, Devana. They are all Hunter's, and I am sure that all Hunters ward their land against demons and whatever else is out there." I said as I lead her into the ensuite. I kept one arm around her as I reached into the massive shower and turned on the water, letting it run as hot as possible.

"That's just it, Dax. Tonight is a New Moon. Yes, we do ward and spell our lands better than most, but to capture the magic of that night, you can't be behind wards. That night is special to us as it is to you shifters. They will not be ready for a battle or have the weapons needed to fight. You have to enter into this ceremony without weapons if you want to make a weapon. That is what the spell requires."

"They may not have weapons in hand, but I know a Hunter is a weapon themselves. I didn't know that Hunter celebrated the New Moon as we do," I said, helping strip her naked. Her full curves and silky skin begged for me to take her in this shower, but now wasn't the time. We had so little time together that I had to make sure she knew that this was real, that when I said she was my Mate, I meant that shit. Everything else went out the window, like the amount of time we have known each other. None of that mattered when two souls became one.

"Yes, we do, but not the way a wolf would, I guess. We take the magic it produces and turn them into spells for protection. I never really understood why it turned harmful to wolves, but it is mixed with wolfsbane and silver. It gives it a powerful punch when needed. I know that it is true that we are trained to be weapons, and it will help, but it will still be a disadvantage to shifters who are ten times bigger, fast, and hopped up on demon blood." She explained. I stood underwater while her soapy hands glided over my body, but her eyes never left mine.

"I agree with you, Devana. That is why we will balance those scales. As far as why it's harmful, it probably has something to do with the fact that the New Moon brings out our weakness in full force. That will also help the Hunters as well. We celebrate wolf shifters because it reminds us that we are not invulnerable to harm. That we still need to be grateful for the life that was given to us." I leaned forward and planted my hand on the opposite wall as she stroked my length, never taking her eyes from mine. I could feel my wolf coming to the surface, and I saw my Luna peeking out as well.

"I think there will be many things I will need to learn when this is over," she panted. Her tongue darted out, and I didn't waste time letting it get away. I pulled her to me and took what I wanted. I accepted and gave what we both needed. I had to feel that she was still alive, and she needed to feel grounded. Our bond was getting stronger and steadily growing, but I can imagine the Alphas we would become together once she is settled in her full power. I pulled back, trying not to take this any further.

"Oh, I am going to teach this ass a lot of shit you never knew existed. Maybe you will tell me more about how you came into possession of that journal," I growled. She swallowed hard as her fingers played along my skin, making me rethink not fucking her up against this wall.

"I will tell you everything you want to know about it. Just know that I know I have loved you the first time I saw your drawing in that book. I didn't know what it was at first, but when I saw you come out of the door, the first time...I knew...I just..." We both turned our heads to the door before the knock came. I knew it was Max, and that meant our time was up.

"I want you to tell me all about how you fell for me before you even met me once this is over," I said.

"Really? I was just saying all that cause I was caught up in the moment." She laughed. I grabbed the plush black towel from the rack and wrapped it around her body before grabbing the other and covering my own.

"Naw, I want to hear all about you touching yourself when thinking about me. I know you did because I caught you once, so I know damn well it has happened more times," I grunt. I saw her wide eyes and the shake off her head as she tried not to laugh. That was precisely what I wanted before reality sat in again. I wanted her to have something ordinary, even if it were just a moment.

DEVANA

Dax moved over to the door as I picked up my clothes. My dragon suit was destroyed, and I prayed that Dali had another one with her when she came. Dax closed the door and turned back, holding a bag that looked exactly like my own.

"Max says Dali put another dragon suit in here for you," he said. Dax handed the prized bag over, and I said a mental thank you to my sister. I was pretty sure she was trying and failing to see if she could contact anyone.

"I guess all her snooping can come in handy at times," I said while rummaging through the bag and pulling out a one-piece dragon skin suit. She loved this style, while I preferred a two-piece set. Still, it was better than wearing regular clothing going into a fight.

"Dali isn't a seer like you, but she does have some type of ability like yours, right?" Dax asked as he made his way over to the armoire in the corner. I let my towel drop so I could pull on the form-fitting suit. Once I finished, I looked up while pulling my hair out of the collar to see Dax eyeing me. His piercing violet eyes raked over my body, and I smiled.

"Dali is...she is not a seer, but she can see certain things. She is what is called a Remote Viewer. Dali can perceive information or imagery of remote geographical targets. She can sometimes see events right before they are about to happen." I dug around in the bag for more weapons and began arming myself. Dax remained quiet as he dressed in all black.

"Did you know that Cassandra could use astral travel?" He said, studying me. I found my two pistols on the bedside table, and I put them into their holsters. I frowned because I didn't know that and even doing something like that as a Hunter was dangerous as hell.

"I didn't know that. I don't know a Hunter who would do it willingly, anyway. It takes intense discipline and skill to do it. Then even if you can perform it without another Hunter, being present is crazy," I said, shaking my head.

"Why crazy? I never really understood what it could do as an advantage, but I never asked about it. I have known no one else who could do that." Dax held out his hand for mine, and I moved instinctively to him as he pulled us both out of the door. I thought about his question and the conversation, wondering why we even had it when I realized what he was doing. Dax was still trying to keep my mind from straying down the rabbit hole of being too late.

"It would be more of a scouting type of thing. It isn't usually done alone or at all unless we have no seers or RV Hunters around. Our souls give each Hunter the gifts, speeds and senses, and our bodies have been formed for our souls. Having our soul leave our body asks for a demon or unclean soul to take our physical form leaving our soul unprotected. A powerful demon could then capture our soul," I explained. We made our way down the stairs and out-the-doors leading to the front of the property.

"That is what demons do, though, right? That is all they want is souls." Dax said as he took in his beaten and broken land. I could feel his anger and hurt at seeing it, but pride at the shifters, who were already beginning to put things back together.

"It is their ultimate goal at gathering souls, but when you have a soul of a Hunter, it is worth a thousand human or supernatural souls." Dax stopped at that information and turned to me when Dimitri called out to everyone.

"It is almost time!" We both turned our attention to Dimitri, and I felt the rush of anticipation and fear. I looked up at the sky, realizing that it was getting late, but I could see everything as if it were mid-day. I shook my head because I had to remember what I was now, and the mission I was on wasn't just to save my family but to bring two families together. We had to help them in this fight so that Dax and I could bridge the gap between wolf shifters and Hunter.

DAX

There was no more time that I could give my Mate to keep her emotions in check. Devana's newly changed status was the one thing I was worried about because we had no time for her to get to know her wolf as one should. I was banking on the fact that she is a skilled Hunter and that her discipline in that life will help her when it came to her wolf. Just by this small conversation, I realized how little I did know about Hunters, even though I claimed one as mine long ago. Devana had given me far more trust and knowledge than that one I thought could have been my Mate. Cassandra hid so many things about herself that she would close up and leave even when pushed. My mind kept going back to the Astro projection and the many times I saw Cassandra do it. Every time she did it, she would come back just a little more different from before. Listening to Devana had me thinking that I may have missed something important all those times. Each time that Cassandra left her body, where did she go, and what did she do? Maybe the more important question was who or what was riding back with her as she entered her body?

I looked down at Devana, who stared at her sister. I followed her gaze and saw Dali with her head down and hands clenched into fists. Max stood close to her with a hand on her shoulder and speaking so softly I couldn't make out the words. Dali shrugged her shoulder, dislodging Max's hand as she walked away. I started to say something to Devana about what the hell was up with those two, but we both turned as Journee's chanting turned into shouts as her body jerked. The tones and pitches in her voice weren't a natural range. It also held an accent that I know wasn't present when I first met the Witch. Dimitri sat in the middle of the large circle formed on the ground as Journee held onto his shoulders. His shock of white hair in the front began to glow brightly as the mark on his skin that was barely noticeable just yesterday grew and seemed to form into the head of a snake.

"Malic, this land is left to you until we return." Malic looked at me sharply, and I knew his ass was about to protest until he followed my gaze to a still-healing Leodora.

"Also, Thomas needs this," I stated mentally. We all

could feel Thomas's rage as if it were our own, and he needed this outlet.

"I got you. We can handle things here," Malic nodded. I saw Ezra and Jamel nod as well, with two other enforcers who would stay behind. Many were hurt, but many more died last night. We have many shifters going with us, but not as many as Aeron has, but we differ because we are a genuine Pack.

"We do this for those who we have lost. We fight to protect the meaning of the word Pack. Aeron is a demon-possessed wolf who thinks he is an Alpha and calls himself a True Alpha. We know this is wrong, and what he stands for is not the "Pack" way of doing things. He and his followers have broken Pack Laws. It is time for them to pay the consequences of their decisions." The commanding tone hit every ear and reinforced their courage at what we faced tonight. I turned to look at Dimitri, who was now standing and chanting along with Journee in this strange language I didn't know. I knew my Beta's bloodline held Witch blood, but I didn't realize that he may be more potent in witchcraft than we both thought. I smelled the sharp tainted scent of demon blood in the air as the droplets of blood in the circle raised into the air and spun counterclockwise. We all watched as the blood droplets formed a dark mirror that shone in the center of the ring. It was like we all stared into a mirror that had been fogged over, making it hard to see our reflections inside of it. Dimitri stepped forward, holding up an arm, and began to shift, but I could tell that it wasn't voluntary. He let out a howl so loud and long it split the dark mirror in half, making an opening for us to step through. Journee stopped chanting and swayed slightly without Dimitri there to hold her up.

"Go! Go now before it closes. Dimitri can only hold it but for so long." She said, falling to her knees in the dirt. Remi was beside her, but she waved us on. "Hurry!" She cried. I heard two blades slide in Devana's palms as we both took a step forward in ending this shit once and for all.

DEVANA

CHAPTER nineteen

It wasn't where I expected it to be wherever we came out. We were close, but we weren't on the property. We had homes spread across the world, but this one is used for the ceremony of the New Moon and to initiate the new Hunters into the family. Two families would come together to gather the energy from the New Moon to be used in our weapons. This time it was House Okar and House Diya. At the least, it should be ten from each house attending the ceremony.

"Devana, we are nowhere near the house," Dali said suddenly next to me. I wasn't surprised or surprised by her appearance. My wolf seemed to notice her angling toward me, and my Hunter instincts didn't feel a threat. I could feel the two halves of myself trying to click in sync and merge all my instincts for a more effective predator.

"Yeah, I see that. I know our house is to the west of this location, but why would we end up in the middle of the woods?" I said. I felt Dax move, and it was eerie because he moved silently as big as he was. No one else had moved or said a word as they all took in the scents of the land. We were still in Maryland but now in the city of Brunswick. We were close to the state's border that could go into Virginia.

"Journee said that it wouldn't give us an exact location, but it will bring us close to the intending target," Dimitri said. I looked over at him, and he was in human form but completely naked. I raised an eyebrow because more experienced wolves knew damn well how to materialize their clothes on, but he just smiled. Dax didn't even look at us or acknowledge Dali, and I am staring Dimitri down because damn. His body had nothing on Dax, but that didn't mean it wasn't perfection to its finest. The wind shifted at that moment, and the scents of over thirty tainted wolves flooded my nose, making all of us except Dali turn to the east as one.

"They are coming," Dax growled. "If we can smell them, then they can scent us as well," Dax said as he scented the surrounding air. His violet eyes seemed to make things brighter than what I saw as his eyes lay on what was around us.

"Yes, but he isn't with them. Something isn't right," I stated. I stepped forward toward where I would go to our property and felt something slightly off. "Dali," I said sharply. She moved and was standing close to me with one of her Glocks in her right hand.

"What?" She said, but I could tell that she was staring off in the direction I was watching and seeing something entirely different.

"What do you see?" I asked. I could feel the loosening in my limbs as I prepared for the run. Things were off, and the night was entirely too quiet.

"It's happening! The battle is already happening, and the Hunters are not on the winning side!" Dali shouted. She took off toward our people, and Max was beside her in an instant. I hadn't noticed that he was standing close behind her, almost as if he was her shadow. Like Max was a part of her and wouldn't be seen unless she wanted it to happen. I turned back toward Dax, just as he sent Alex and half of our Pack to deal with those coming up from behind. He sent Jarod and the others along with Max and Dali to help the Hunters. I was ready to go. I knew my people were going to need help and would be confused about what was happening.

"We need to go!"

"We will Mate, we got this, but we need to think first. Where is the demon, and what is it that we are missing?" He asked. Thomas and Remi stood back to back, looking up into the trees at the sky. The moon was full, but it wasn't at its full power just yet. Why would Aeron or the demon that is riding him wait until his Pack would be slightly weakened? That just made little sense to me whatsoever.

"Dax! Do you see that?" Thomas growled. My eyes moved over toward him and Remi at his words. I followed both of their gazes up, and I scanned the trees. I was about to ask what they meant and tell them we didn't have time for this when I saw it. There were winged forms in the trees looking down at us and as I focused on them. They were not natural at all as they stared at us with their seven eyes. Three were black, and the other four were crimson. Hundreds of birds lined the trees. Just as I was about to go for my pistol, they all opened their beaks to screech. All you saw were rows and rows of needle-like teeth.

"Oh shit! Vucub-Caquix!"

"What the fuck is that?" Remi yelled. Her teal eyes grew

wide just as her hands covered themselves in a bright teal glow with a razor's edge.

"Demon birds! They are demon birds!" Dax growled. He didn't shift or turn his hands into claw-like, I thought. That was good because the only thing that was going to take these things down was Holy water.

"We need to get to the river! Now!" I screamed. We all took off as hundreds of birds dove from the trees after us. One look into their eyes and your soul will get caught as they tear your body piece by piece and devour you. "Do not look into their eyes!" I warned and prayed I remembered the words to bless the waters.

WE CRASHED THROUGH THE TREES, and the birds were hot on our asses, but we were fast. I was never so grateful to have the speed as I was tonight. As we burst into the clearing, I knew why things felt off and exactly why these birds were here. Aeron and the demon didn't want a repeat of last time when I broke their spell. They knew if I didn't kill these demon birds, all of us could be at risk. I saw the Hunters, wolves and our group fighting in an all-out battle. I figured they didn't have the time to set up the spell barrier like they wanted but had enough time to block some of our senses from the battle.

"Dax!"

"We need to get there now! I see him!" Dax growled as the first of the birds came swooping down to an attack. I looked back, seeing Aeron in human form cutting down Hunters left and right as his crimson eyes glowed. I whipped my head back around, knowing what had to be done but hating that we had to be split apart.

"Go! Let us handle this, and you go after Aeron. We will join you as soon as I take care of this!" I said, pointing. I fell to my knees by the edge of the river. I rolled onto my back and started to fire. I hit each bird that arrowed down at me as Dax swatted them away and tore heads from the giant creatures. It would matter how many wept down because they would just keep raising again.

"No! You're fucking crazy if you think I will leave you..."

"You have to! If you don't stop him, he will get what he wants. I just need Remi and Thomas to keep them off of me until I can send their bird flu asses back to Hell!" I rolled to the left, dodging birds that crashed into the ground next to me. They were using their size and becks as weapons, trying to keep us pinned down.

"Devana!"

"Dax! Go! Please trust me!" I shot three birds in a row and threw a blade from my other hand at a bird flying down to attack Thomas in his blind spot. My eye flicked over to Dax for just an instant, but that was all that was needed. He knew without words that this was exactly what the demon wanted. He knew we were coming, and the best defense was to split us apart.

"If you die, I swear I will drag your ass back here. Finish this and come to me!" He growled. I shot eight more of the bird demons, so Dax had enough time to move. He didn't even have to bend his knees much as he launched himself into the air to leap over the lake. I felt when he crossed over because I couldn't feel our bond anymore.

"Remi! Thomas! Cover me!" I screamed.

DAX

I landed inside of the barrier, and I instantly felt that Devana wasn't near me. I could see her, but this barrier made it look like she had been ripped from my soul. I moved as wolves and Hunter fought each other and caught sight of Jarod taking down a wolf that was an Alpha once before. I could gauge the power of the wolf, and it wasn't as strong as Jarod, but the taint and power of the blood it carried gave the wolf an edge.

"What do you wolves want! My daughter went to your aid, and this is how you repay us!" A tall golden skin man gritted when I caught his eyes. He stared into mine as he cut down a wolf by using what looked like a shovel. His green eyes seemed to glow with hate and pain as he saw me.

"This isn't what you think, Cassius! Look around, or can't you tell that this isn't us!" I roared. I didn't have time for this, but the Hunter gave me no choice. He came at me, ducking low and sweeping out with his leg as he brought the handle of the shovel up. I moved and knocked away the shovel, snapping it into pieces. That would have thrown a lesser being off their feet, but Cassius wasn't just an average human. He was old just as old as me and has been a Hunter the entire time.

"I cannot feel my daughter! I felt her pain and then nothing! I thought she just cut herself off so we would not worry. Dali would have called and told us if anything happened. Then we were attacked by these wolves! Dali returns, but no Devana! You!" I knew nothing I said would get through to him. All he could see were werewolves attacking and killing his people. I couldn't understand why he couldn't sense the presence of a demon.

"It's a demon! Devana is alive! We are here to help you! Just look around and feel for a second." I said. The fighting raged on, and I couldn't see Aeron anyway. I tried to sense him as well. There was nothing, and I didn't know why until Cassius spun on his heel, whispered three words, and blew white dust into space.

"DEMON!" Cassius roared. The white dust covers the invisible form of Aeron, who stepped out of a now visible Hell gate. Cassius snapped out in two fast kicks, dropped low, and punched Aeron hard in the solar plexus. It did absolutely nothing. That hit would have thrown an entirely changed wolf across the field, but Aeron just smirked.

"I haven't tasted Hunter's soul in millennia," Aeron

hissed as he reached out grabbed Cassius by the throat. I moved, but not fast enough as he ripped Cassius's head from his body and devoured it in one swallow.

"NO!" A long, pain-filled cry tore through the fighting, howling, and screaming as Cassius's body fell to the ground. I saw a tall woman that was dressed in white that was now covered in dirt and blood. Her face was a mask of rage and hurt as she began fighting her way over to us. Wolves dove in between the grieving woman and Cassius's body, separating the Hunter from her Mate. That all happened in a second, and I wasted no more time. This piece of shit had to die, and this demon needed to be sent back to fucking Hell. I moved and used my arm to take a laughing Aeron down as I punched him while we landed hard in the dirt. I heard the grunts and knew my hits were being felt. I felt him shift and throw me off him, making me fly backward. It didn't matter because I twisted in the air to land on my feet in a crouch so I could charge at him again. Aeron was already up, and his hands were transformed into red-tipped claws.

"All I need from you is those eyes, Daxton Rayne. Once I have those and **Abadozui** has Hunter's eyes, I will be at the top of every food chain." Aeron growled as we circled each other. We made our way toward each other, taking down any member from the opposite side until we were finally across from each other once more. I stared at my opponent, knowing that he wasn't an ordinary wolf and that this fight had to end and quickly. "I see that you lost yourself at seeing my superiority amongst our kind. I came to claim your worthless Pack and to take out these Hunters. Hell does not need our enemies to be allowed to come together," Aeron said.

"I'm not here for all the chit-chat you wanna do. You ran

from my Pack and me. It will not be any different for you this time, either. The only difference will be you won't get the chance to live," I said as I charged at him. I shifted my hands into claws as I allowed my body to take the third form.

"My Pack! Who do you follow? Stop him!" Aeron screamed. He began to shift, and it didn't take much time for him to do it. I had to stop him right here and now!

"I will make the first move!" Aeron growled. His words were grabbed and grated in my ears. I slashed at the wolves who threw themselves in front of me, trying to slow me down. Aeron was now shifted into a third form I had never seen from any wolf. I let my claw rip through the stomach of a shifter as I leaped to attack Aeron on his head with my claws, but Aeron moved slightly to dodge the attack quickly. I kept a consecutive series of combos aiming directly to cause critical damage to Aeron, but he kept sliding off the attacks with little effort. "An Alpha this weak! You are not worthy of leading anyone! Just like your worthless True Alpha!" Aeron growled.

"What!" I roared. I jumped left, using my feet to spring off the side of a tractor, and aimed myself at Aeron. Aeron caught my hands and pulled me close, and I head-butted him in the face. He let go with a snap kick out, then spun around low, kicking me in the knee. I went down on the other, and he reached out, pulled my head to the side, and bit into my neck. I roared, and I felt the violet of my eye blaze as the next thing I knew, he took us into the sky. Aeron speed was unbelievable, and I knew it was because of the Alpha sacrifices. I twisted, using my hand to rack my claws across his face and my other hand to dig into his shoulder so I could spin myself onto his back. He bucked and threw me back toward the ground. I used the momentum of the fall to arrow myself at a mass of wolves who started to surround Dali and Max. I crashed into them and grabbed them one by one, ripping them to shreds, but I had no time to keep helping them as Aeron crashed by to the ground. The smokey dark wings folded back, and his crimson eyes burned with malice. Everyone froze for a second upon seeing Aeron barely hurt. I knew they noticed my wounds and the bones that started to snap back into place. That didn't matter, though, because I was not about to let this thing win. However, the speed and power of Aeron were stronger than I thought. I had to find a way to fight a demon and a wolf.

"Ohh..., I think I underestimated you a little. You can take some hits and keep coming, but how long can you hold up to someone like me?" Aeron said with a sneer.

"You aren't shit without that demon lending you power! You had to get it from a lesser being because you just weren't strong enough on your own. So weak you have to go around stealing wolves to form a Pack. What you have isn't a Pack, and you are not an Alpha!" I shouted.

"You don't know shit! I thought you understood from the beginning I am no Alpha, but the True Alpha and all will kneel to me," Aeron snarled. I growled and ran towards him. I let my full energy go and embraced my wolf. "That power you have is not enough!" He shouted. I got into his face, and Aeron moved his wings upwards to work simultaneously as an attack and defense. I directed all my speed to move fast and turned around as Aeron flew up. He didn't see me move to get behind him, so I thought when he shifted and landed behind me. I felt my wolf pull me to the right, and I dodged a blow and used his outstretched arm to leap up and over him to get behind him. I bit Aeron's neck ferociously as he tried to move his wings back and forth to make me let go of him. My fangs curved into hooks in this form, and the more he trashed, the deeper my fangs sank into his flesh. Aeron growled a strange and mighty roar simultaneously as if two voices screamed out while his crimson eyes went brighter than I had seen before.

All the fighting on the field stopped, as they couldn't ignore what was happening around them.

That's right! Bring the demon to the forefront. With that thought, Aeron got more and more difficult to control. He ripped his neck from my teeth and shot up into the sky as tainted blood rained down on the ground. I could see that he was healing, and I didn't want to give him that chance. I started to leap up to grab at his ankle when Aeron opened his mouth, and a deep red fire shot out and came toward the ground directly at me. I moved, and the flames seemed to start spreading across the field, lighting everything it touched on fire. The howls of pleasure came from Aeron's wolves while I looked for my own Pack. I saw the wolves and faces of my Pack members and saw that they couldn't believe the abilities this demon had given Aeron. Mixed feelings of fear, confusion and wonder got a hold of them, and my wolf did not like that shit.

"This is not a normal flame! Get the hell out of here!" I shouted. I caught the eyes of Jarod, and he howled for our Pack to gather closer to him. I knew he had a shield, but I didn't know how long that would last. I saw the woman dragging Cassius's body toward her as Aeron's Pack began to circle around the Hunter. I moved, then backhanded the wolves that were circling out of the way. I used my other hand to toss her over to where Dali and Max were standing.

"No! No!" The woman screamed, but Dali wrapped her

in her arms, pulling her behind the shield Jarod was creating.

"Now, I will make you pay for me to become the superior being! I will be the only True Alpha and the only Alpha to every wolf on this planet!" Aeron snarled. He spread his wings wide and lifted his arms.

"I think I said this once before, you are no Alpha and never have been!" I roared. Aeron used those bat-like smokey gray wings to lift high into the air. His eyes turned to pitch black, then bled back to crimson once more while looking over the destruction he brought to this land.

"RUN!" I shouted to my Pack because I realized what Aeron was about to do. I knew more flames were coming, and this time, he would aim it for my people no matter who was in the way of it!

DEVANA

CHAPTER twenty

I knew that we had to end this and end it now. I knew we were needed on the other side, and right fucking now. Remi and Thomas kept the birds away, but I had to stop every so often. I shot one to draw what I needed on the ground. So many of these demon birds should have been impossible to get here, but I did not know how long the demon had worked to bring them over. The screeching and flipping of wings had me wanting to cover my ears. I heard Thomas howl and knew he had shifted. His massive paws swiped over my head as I drew the symbols that needed to turn the entire Potomac River into Holy water. At least for enough time to put these birds down.

"Few more seconds!" I screamed before I started to chant the words that I needed to make this happen. I would never question my father again about the need to learn such prayers.

"Hurry! The wolves are coming!" Remi grunted as a bird dug its talons into her arm. I noticed slightly that her face rippled and shifted. Her mouth widened as she used gigantic teeth for ripping the bird into pieces. She didn't even pause as she pulled a double-barrel shotgun off her back and fired.

"Take the pistol in my thigh holster. Tell our Pack to back off before you shoot! Just wait long enough for all the wolves to get closer." I said. I slammed both hands to the ground when I heard an agonizing scream. The scream had the barrier crumbling piece by piece, and I felt it like a punch to the gut. I felt my heart crack down the center. I spoke the word that I was taught by the man who had just lost his life. My father had died because I didn't see this coming. The rage, pain and heartbreak almost consumed me. The symbols lit up where my hand was pressed into the earth. The blue light burned before exploding into a golden glow that rolled over the water, making the dark water shine golden. I turned back, seeing the birds had lifted away from the light, but as the golden light began to dim, they arrowed back down toward us. The wolves came through the trees with dimly lit red eyes as they snarled. I felt the tears rolling down my cheeks and the anger at the one who killed my father rise in my chest.

"Remi! Now!" I roared. My voice deepened, and I felt my skin rippling while my teeth began to grow. I heard the shots, but nothing else mattered as I shifted into my wolf. I lifted my head and let out a long howl as I turned to make my way over the river and towards my Mate. This had to end tonight, and I would destroy this demon if I had anything to say about it.

"Use the river! Stop the birds."

I sent the command mentally to Remi and Thomas. As I made it onto the other side, I turned back to see Remi knee-deep in the water, as her teal eye glowed and swirled like a storm. She moved her arms in what almost looked like a dance, making the water from the river shoot up. I turned away, leaving it in their hands. Remi seemed to be way more than I believed. She held tremendous power over water, and I don't think that even scratched its surface. I leaped into the air and landed beside my mother and Dali. I saw the rage and anger on her face when she saw me, thinking I was a part of this attack. She reached out and grabbed a gun from Dali and pointed it at my massive head.

"Mother! No! That's Devana! It's Devana!" Dali said, holding her arms out between us. My mother's hand shook uncontrollably, and her tears streamed down her cheeks.

"Wha..what have you done? Wh...why..," she stammered. Just her thinking I had anything to do with this shit had me barring my teeth.

"No! She has nothing to do with what's happening! It is because of a demon! This is all because of a demon! These wolves are not with the True Alpha or the Rayne Pack, Mother." Dali tried to explain. I didn't have time for it, though, because I had to get to my Mate. This fight wasn't meant for him to fight alone. This had to be won together!

"RUN!" Dax roared. I looked to Max, Jarod and Dali. I nodded and jumped over my mother and the other wolves. I felt Jarod's shield buckle and come down. I didn't look back to see if they followed Dax's orders because I knew they would. Hell, I prayed they listened, but the scent of the demon was so strong that I didn't think anything of Aeron had to be left. Most of our Pack heard him and moved away. I saw a young wolf still standing in the middle of our Pack fighting its way out of this field. He looked stunned and unable to move, and I realized that this must be his first battle. He hadn't even shifted or noticed the flames coming toward him. I saw Aeron breathe flames out of his mouth, and I knew instantly what they were. This demon could breathe Hellfire, and if that touched any part of the body, it would consume it on sight. If this demon controlled this fire, things could get even worse from here. The flames came down at the field, aiming to burn everyone. Thanks to Dax's warning, most of the ones who stayed were Aeron's Pack. The only one who couldn't seem to move was this young wolf who was stuck in place as the ashy red flames were approaching. I saw the moment Aeron's wolves realize what their so-called Alpha was doing. I saw the betrayal and ingratitude roll over their features as they saw the flames ready to turn them to ashes by the powers of their own leader.

I moved across the grass to the wolf that stared in horror at what was happening. I dodged around stunned wolves who watched their Alpha in disbelief. Some shifters ran and tried to get away, but I knew we had a split second before the breath of Hellfire touched the ground. I leaped up in the air and knocked the young wolf out of the path of the flames. The young Pack member hit the ground as the first of the fire consumed everything in its path. I saw the ashy red of the fire cover the ground. I dodged out of the way of the flames as screams of torment rose all around me. Each victim it reached crumbled, and I caught the eyes of the young wolf that saw that the inferno was still coming to wipe him out of this world. **"No!"** I screamed in my mind. My howled pierced the night, cutting through the screams and whining of pain.

DAX

I felt Devana before I saw her, but I knew the barrier was down. I turned and caught sight of Devana as she knocked Kendrick out of the way of the flames. I shifted into my wolf form as I bounded my way over to the kid. A sense of helplessness covered the young wolf's face as another wave of blazing fire went in his direction. I heard the mental screams of my Mate when she caught sight of what I already saw happening. I was already on the move and snatched up the pup in my jaws without hurting him. I moved us out of the path of the flames that would have engulfed and caused unbearable torture before he burned to ash like the rest of the wolves who got caught up in the Hellfire. I dropped the boy to the ground and shifted back into my human form to scan the pup for any damages that I couldn't see. Kendrick opened his eyes as I looked him over.

"Al...Alpha? What the hell is happening? What was that shit?"

"Are you okay, kid?" I asked. I looked around to see if I spotted Devana. I could feel her, so I reached out mentally.

"Dax! You have him. God, I thought I got him out of the way!"

"He's all good, but we have to stop this. How do we stop this demon? It seems more to the surface now the moon is at its peak. It's suppressing the wolf inside of it and is taking over." I said, looking back at the field of fire.

"He didn't spare his own Pack. What type of Alpha does something like that? He cries for purity but kills his own Pack! He isn't worth being called a wolf, let alone an Alpha!" Kendrick spat.

"Exactly! As long as you know the difference between right and wrong in this world, you will do fine, pup." I saw Devana leap across the fire that hadn't died out and quickly reached our side. She was pure white like my wolf except for the light brown fur on her paws. Her burning green with a hint of brown eyes landed on me and then the kid. The giant wolf sniffed at a wide-eyed Kendrick to make sure he was okay, like I said.

"Lu...Luna. Thank you." Before I could say anything, Devana shifted into her human form but couldn't keep her clothes. The pup looked everywhere but at either of us as I took my tee shirt off and gave it to her. It was covered in blood and dirt but better than nothing.

"First thing I need you to teach me is how do I keep my clothes! Dragonskin is hard as fuck to come by."

She turned to Kendrick, who stared at the lumps of ashes that were covering the entire area. "Kendrick, I need you to get a message to my sister. You know who she is, right?"

"Yes. The Hunter with the big ass guns."

Devana smiled as she looked away from him and up to the sky. I saw her eyes go hard and knew this little moment had to end. Some of my Pack members didn't make it away with Max and the others, but they were still alive. I sent the message to follow Kendrick and get to safety on the other side of the river.

"Exactly! I need you to tell her to make sure everyone is in the river. The river will protect everyone long enough for us to finish this."

"The river?"

"Yes! Now go!" Devana shoved the wolf in the direction he needed to go as I turned to stare up at the sky. Aeron descended slowly from the sky and onto the ash-covered ground. The crimson of his eyes gleamed as he saw the burned and burning bodies of his Pack. Some turned to piles of dust, and some were still standing like crops. Others were still alive and were still screaming as they burned and fell to the ground. The demon looked at the dead without remorse or regret. He walked through the corpses as he began to suck in the souls of the dead.

"We have to stop this bastard!" Devana growled. There was a moment of silence as the demon-filled himself with souls of wolves and Hunters who had fallen.

"Still not enough! War is what we need to take this world, and tonight will mark the start of it. Hunters and wolves are notoriously known to hate each other. Who was to blame neither will believe it was their people who did it, thus leading to Warrrr!"

The voice sounded as if it were over one demon. It sounded like many. Aeron's remaining Pack was baffled at the atrocity and cruelty. I saw the understanding dawning in their eyes as they genuinely saw what they had been following. "All worthless in body, but the soul is another matter altogether. The power of a Hunter's soul and the strength from the Packs soul was all I needed to take you out for good. Peter and his family were worthless, but this just gave me a better opportunity to devour the Dire Wolf myself." The demon growled in our direction, and I stepped out and in front of Devana. I looked at his Pack, who were still alive as they pushed to their feet and gritted their teeth. They all turned to face their hatred at Aeron as the one in human form began to shift into their wolves. Aeron stood still. The wolf from Aeron's Pack jumped to attack him, to which Aeron swung his wing, creating a strong wind current stopping his attacker before biting him mid-air, tearing out his throat. I saw him pull back to launch another breath of blazing flames at the rest of his Pack. He caught some in the path of the flame, but some still managed to evade the fire.

"Devana, what can we do?"

"Demon blades won't work. If they did, he would have been killed already." Devana pointed to the ground, and I saw a blade that laid there covered in blood. My wolves were trying to leave the scene, but some stopped beside Devana and me.

"Alpha, we can help end this." Brandon, one of my enforcers, stated. He was flanked by another two of my enforcers who eyed the demon.

"Nothing you have will stop me in this form, not a demon blade or the stench of that Holy water. At least not for much longer," it hissed, looking directly at us.

"Brandon, get the hell out of here and get the rest of the Pack safe. You need to make it back to Malic and contact Quinn!" Brandon stared at me for a moment but bowed his head and lowered his raging eyes.

"Got it, Alpha!" I could tell he was battling the decision to leave, but the command made it all but impossible.

"Dax, he is going to attack! We have to hold them off so they can get out of here!" Devana said as she shifted and ran after the demon. I didn't waste another moment as I shifted and followed. I caught up to her when that bastard spoke again.

"The Hunter turned wolf. You want to save your new Pack?" The voice of Aeron and the demon growled. We launched ourselves at his wings, but he flew higher toward the retreating Pack with incredible speed.

"He is coming!" Brandon shouted. He screamed for the others to move faster, and I knew I had to give them time. I leaped again and shifted into the third form going straight for his ass. Devana ran on the ground dodging his wolves, but they moved out of her way. I saw Aeron getting closer and in range of attacking. I didn't think he would drop and spin around to breathe his fire toward Devana and me. As he breathed the Hellfire, he used his leathery smokey gray wings to create a wind current directing it right at us! I let my height pull me down to the ground, and I grabbed Devana and rolled us over. We hit the ground near the river. We were further away from everyone else. I felt Devana twist, and she rolled us both into the water. We sank below the water as the flames came over us, but they didn't reach us. They seemed to try but bounced off the surface of the water. We came up both gasping for air and both in our human forms. Aeron wasn't anywhere in our sight.

"Shit! He should not have control over this fire on this earth. Only Hell Hounds have that ability, or so I thought," Devana said as we pulled ourselves out of the water. I turned to make sure the others made it when I saw him attacking them with his claws one by one. He was on the ground now using his massive, clawed hands to take members of my Pack and his own down in one movement.

"Devana!" I shouted before taking off. I knew she was on

my heels, and as soon as I made it within a few feet of him, he spun. I lashed out with my clawed hand, pulling him toward me as I used my other and rammed it into its chest. I felt his heart, and I pulled as I roared in his face. I could see the slitted eyes that burned crimson narrow as he tried pulling my arm out of my socket. Then his wings snapped out, and he began to flip them taking me into the air with him.

"Now, time for another snack." Aeron was still present in the body, but he was fully invested now. He believed in what he was saying and the lies told to him by this demon. He flapped his wings taking us higher into the sky.

"Naw, not tonight," I said with one last yank as I removed his heart. I watched as his eyes went wide and his grip loosened, and I fell from the sky. As I fell, I twisted in the air and saw the ground approaching rapidly. I hit hard but landed on my feet. I jumped out of the crater I created and caught Devana as she rushed me.

"It's not over! I feel it! The demon isn't through."

Her mental exhaustion was showing. She wasn't used to fighting in this form. Her tolerance was very low for all this, but she wasn't backing down. I didn't bother to answer mentally because it would take her more energy to hear it.

"I know, but it bought us time. Is everyone okay? Did they make it?" I asked, looking around.

"They are fine. Just a few scratches but nothing that would infect them."

"Good. Scratches we can handle. Now, where the fuck is he, or maybe he is dead? I know the demon didn't let him die," I growled. Then I heard the brush of wings, and we both spun around.

"Just scratches. I will wait here and enjoy the action!"

Aeron said with a deranged smile. Devana turned away just as I did to see our Pack swaying strangely. The members of Aeron Pack that he cut down were getting to their feet as well, but something wasn't right with them.

"We need to get to them!" We moved and headed to the Pack, and then I saw Devana starting to drag behind. I looked back, seeing her wolf form beginning to shrink as she shifted back into human form. She didn't stop running, and I was out of a shirt for her. It didn't seem to matter as she stopped long enough to rip clothes from a down Hunter to wrap around her body. I never stopped moving.

"Hey! Brandon! Simon! Are you okay?" I asked, getting closer. I saw Jarod jumping over the river to help another Pack member who had fallen to their knees. I noticed neither wolf responded when I suddenly felt my torso scratched severely. For a moment, I was surprised and couldn't believe it. I lowered my head and saw blood dripping from Brandon's clawed hand. It was covered in my blood.

"Dax! Don't let them touch you! Don't touch them!" Devana shouted. I heard Dali saying the same thing, but Brandon stared at me with a blank expression.

"Wha...what the fuck? Brandon!" I said in a shaken voice. My body felt off, and I knew something was trying to invade it.

"Dax!" Devana screamed as she kicked Brandon so hard, he flew into another wolf. "Dax? What...let me see!" She growled, but I didn't want her to touch it.

"No! No! it's too late. Get everyone out of here!"

"No, hell no! I am not leaving." She cried as she pushed my hands to the side. I looked up and past her to see

Brandon and the other wolf climbing to their feet, and I saw their eyes all turn crimson as they howled.

"Now you see the power of what souls can do! One more species that will come to the end of its existence," Aeron and the demon laughed. "I now control your Pack and you Alpha," he spat like it was a curse. "Didn't you wonder why I didn't kill them? Hunter, don't you understand what is happening here? Others have failed where I will succeed. Wipeout wolf shifters and Hunters alike," the distorted voices screamed. "Wolves kill Daxton Rayne and his Mate!" He ordered.

"NO!" I roared as I fought the tainted blood that was trying to take hold.

"Dax, we have to move!"

"Devana, get out of here NOW!"

"You didn't leave me, and I will not leave you!" Devana shouted as every shifter began to charge us.

DEVANA

CHAPTER twenty-one

I spoke in a barely used language, but what I learned in the journal that Cassandra had written. My hands began to glow a mint green as I chanted. I knew time was short, But I had to try. Dax did not leave me to die but did everything he could to save me. I knew that something like this wasn't meant to be done, but I wouldn't want to share my soul with anyone else.

"Devana! Move! They're coming!" I didn't even reply as I stuck both hands inside of his wounds and pushed with everything I had inside of me. I gritted my teeth at the burning pain his mixed blood caused, but I knew it had to be done. I felt the wolves closer and heard Dali screaming as she took shots that missed. I knew Dali didn't miss. I knew she was trying to warn them away. She was not about to harm innocent people even if they were being used. "Devana!" Dax growled as his eyes burned an intense violet that slowly bled into the mint green of my soul. I pulled out my hand in time to turn in place, catching the clawed hand coming at me. I bent it backward as I stood up and kicked out. I sent the wolf flying, but it wasn't dead. I moved in the middle of the crowd that came at us, trying to lead them away from a screaming Dax. A mixture of violet light spilled from his mouth and eyes, burning anyone who got close. It even kept Aeron at bay, but he soon turned those crimson eyes to me. The sneer on his lips and slitted eyes made my skin crawl.

"I'm coming, Devana!" I heard the brothers shout. I flicked my eyes to Aeron as he sent a wave of fire in their direction, keeping them firmly on the other side of the river. I ducked and came up with my left palm, grabbed Brandon's chin, and threw him headfirst into three other wolves.

"Stay back!" I growled, and I knew my voice took on a commanding tone. I went low and rolled to the right, sweeping out and catching another wolf in the back of the knees. I backed away as the wolves all stopped to look at me, and Aeron made his way to the front.

"The things I could do with the eyes of a seer. I could effectively hide from any Hunter with a gift such as that. Times up, Hunter, you lose." I knew that the screaming of my Mate had stopped, but I don't think any else knew. I smiled.

"The lies demons tell themselves is real. I don't think so." I grinned as Dax howled.

DAX

I could feel the blood burning out of my system as I sat up. There is so much pain still, but that shit did not matter. Devana was fighting alone, and I refused to let that fucking demon touch her again. I could feel her Hunter's soul twine around my own as I moved. I shifted into my wolf and howled as the last of the demon blood faded out of my system. I moved when they all turned toward me as one. They all came at me as I dodged left then right of their attacks without harming them. There was still a chance we could save them, so I would not kill them until then. Still, their numbers were a problem because they weren't going down. I would not kill my Pack and add more souls to the count. Dodging them was getting harder and harder, and I did get clawed a few times. It didn't matter to me now as the gift from Devana kept the blood from taking hold. It still was causing me damage because of the blood loss I continued to endure.

"Please keep running while I attend to what is more important because they will keep this shit up for as long as it takes," Aeron growled. I had to find a way to take them down without life-threatening injuries. I dodged the attacks coming from my Pack and the rogues. Those I wanted to kill but needed to answer their crimes and tell the supernatural world all about it. Brandon was in front of me now, and I knew he could take more damage than the rest. I bit down on the back of his neck and threw him at the others. This move quickly created an open space.

"Dax, down!" Devana screamed as a shining bright light lit up the space between us. Aeron jumped back but launched a blast of fire in her direction. Devana had already moved out of the way. I saw Dali in a shooting stance on the other side and noticed she waited to use the Moonlit bullets until our Pack was out of the way. This move didn't kill them, but it blinded them and still hurt to a degree.

"Still refuse to harm these clowns? Are you so protective with your Pack that you would refuse to harm them even though they are attacking you?" Aeron said, confused and angry. He was never an Alpha, and he thought of himself as a True Alpha. He was a fucking joke.

"Aeron!" Devana shouted. He turned away from me as she formed a sign with her hand and pushed a white light in his direction. That blasted his ass away from her and gave me a chance to get closer to Devana. I leaped over the down Pack and landed next to a heaving Devana. "What the fuck?" She panted, and I looked back to see the wolves all suddenly stood up and still. I looked from left to right. I began to growl because Pack members or not, I would not let them hurt my Mate. If I had to take everyone down, I would do it as their Alpha because I knew not one of mine would lay a finger on what was mine. None of them stepped forward, and strangely enough, they stepped back. They made more space between them and us which made absolutely no sense. Aeron stepped through the crowd covered in blood, with piercing crimson eyes staring daggers at Devana. "Did that hurt, bitch?" She said, spitting out blood. I moved to keep her hidden from their gazes, but Aeron just smiled.

"That little stunt will cost you. You did damage which I will need souls to repair. You protected them so far but how about now," Aeron growled. Brandon and Simon marched forward with red glazed-over eyes and turned to each other. "No! You can't fight your own battles, you piece of shit!" Devana roared in anger at the sight. My eyes widened at the scene of brutality they were dishing out to each other. It almost made me lose it. Only Devana's hand gripping my fur tightly held me together. I had to stop this before more gets killed, and he feeds on their souls. The instinct to protect engulfed me as the words of my father filtered through my mind. **"As a leader, you must protect all who need protection, even if it is from themselves. As an Alpha, you must protect your Pack at all costs."**

I howled as I never did before because I was their Alpha, and no one commands them except our God, the True Alpha, and me. I was the one put in charge of their lives and the one they trust above all. I felt Devana's energy inside of me, and her hand dropped from my fur. The power I put forth filled her enough that she was able to shift once more. My howl and the light that powered from my eyes bathed over Aeron and the fighting shifters. A bright light emerged from within me, blinding everyone as it covered them in my protection.

"No, we killed all of you! Your line was severed!" Aeron shouted. I knew Aeron was no longer there or in control and that the demon was speaking. He shifted into his massive wolf, and still, he had the wings. He covered himself from the light with his wings, but it was pointless. He was right, though, about my line. I knew we came from the **Aenocyon dirus,** but the ability was lost hundreds of years ago, and now we know why. The last was killed without passing down the knowledge of how it was done. After a moment, the light started dispersing little by little. I felt completely different. I stood on both legs, just like in my third form. My clawed hands become more prominent and my ears much longer. My fur shined bright white with mint green symbols that I could feel moving on my forehead. They went down my body, emitting a comfortable and warm aura around me. I knew the feeling, and it was my Mate. She was all around me and inside of me. I looked to where she stood, but she wasn't there.

"Our soul is one. To take this form, I think…"

"We had to save each other to become…"

"One." We both stated, and my head snapped up

"This is impossible! This…" The demon screamed. The voices sounded as if they were trying to flee. I raised my hand, calmly looking at it and how he changed. I moved, and the demon backed away, letting the wolves conceal him. "Kill…"

I didn't give Aeron a chance to finish his sentence before I was up in his face. Aeron breathed Hellfire directly at my face. I lifted my hand and pushed through the fire, grabbing his mouth and crushing it shut. The rows of sharp teeth pierced through his jaws, but the demon kept his wings moving, still trying to free itself. I didn't realize I began chanting until I felt the words coming from Devana. I let the words flow as I used my other claw to slash at the right-wing, tearing it apart before releasing him to fall back to the ground. I never lost contact as the chant went on, but I continued to pierce him with my claws. I pinned him with such brutal force that the surrounding ground cracked as I pushed deeper. I saw the crimson start to bleed away, and Aeron's dark gray eyes were staring back at me. I knew the fight wasn't over for Aeron, but the demon wasn't gone. I pulled my hand out of his chest and placed it on his head. We spoke the last of the chant as one.

"We will make you suffer for every life you stole, and every soul destroyed. There is no place for you here, **Abadozui.** Now you will burn." We said as screams filled the night, and then all went quiet. Aeron took his final breath as his body slumped to the ground.

DEVANA

I felt myself being lifted, and I knew Dax was carrying me in his arms. I could barely open my eyes to see who was still alive and who we have lost. I was drained, but I knew everything wasn't said and done. There wasn't just one demon riding along, but many, and their plans hadn't changed. Everything was meant to happen the way it should, but I knew that it was only the beginning for this family.

"Devana! Give her to me!" I knew the voice even as I slipped in and out of consciousness. My mother was a force, but she may have just met her match with Dax. I could feel that he wasn't about to let me go no matter who was asking, but I also knew he would go out of his way to smoothing some things over. I knew she was grieving for our father, and she just wanted her remaining family close.

"Mother, please just let Dax get her somewhere safe. Then you can look her over for yourself. Plus, I don't think even you could take his big ass down," Dali said. My sister always had my back even though she got on my last nerve, but I wouldn't have it any other way. I had to pull it together because I needed to let them know what I saw and what would come. The shit that happened in the last few days didn't seem to be finished with any of us.

"Tyshria, I know we all have a lot to talk about, but let me get Devana cleaned up and rested," Dax said with much respect, but I think everyone heard the finality of the statement. I wanted to help. I wanted to see everyone to make sure we saved who we could, but my energy was gone, and I tried my hardest to cling to each conversation.

"I think maybe you are correct, Rayne. Rayne Pack, you are welcomed into our home."

I knew she was worried when she invited non-Hunters into our home. That hadn't been done in over one hundred years. I knew I was going in and out, so I tried to push against Dax's chest, but he held tight, and his warmth and scent had me giving in.

"Rest, Mate. We will have time to explain everything to your mother. Just rest." His deep, soothing voice had my eyes sliding shut.

I rolled over, opened my eyes, and noticed that I was not in Dax's home. I knew the room instantly as I took in the scents and furniture in the room. The soft gold and cream bedding and the smell of the home had everything come crashing back to me. I knew it was time to get up and explain what happened and what was to come later. I wasn't sure how my mother would react to the fact that I am a shifter now, but I wouldn't change what happened for anything, even family. I honestly wasn't sure how the death of our Father was going to affect her or what I could do to atone for it. If only I could have seen this from the beginning, everyone would have been prepared and not caught slipping. I let out a sigh, knowing it was time to face the music and face the other Hunters. My choice could effectively change the way all Hunters would look at me. As I swung my legs to the side of the bed, I knew there wasn't anything I could do about that shit. After last night, there was a reason I became what I am, and I would be the bridge to bring both sides together. Hunters and shifters are being attacked, and they are willing to use our long-time hatred of each other to take us down. I knew that the first thing I had to do was see if my mother and the House of Okar would back me on this, or would they turn away?

I felt Dax before the door opened, and I pushed to my feet as he slipped inside of my room. I just noticed that I was washed and wearing only a white tee shirt that was way too big for me. I knew it was his, and it automatically made me feel safe and...at home. I had no clue how he could get clean clothes here so fast, but I was not complaining.

"It's about time you woke up. I feel like you slept so I had to deal with all the 'why the hell did you change my daughter' questions," Dax grunted as he moved closer to me. I couldn't help the smile that formed across my face because I could see my mom cussing him out no matter what or who he was. That woman rarely held her tongue, and that shit got passed right down to Dali.

"Maybe I did. I mean, I didn't want to get in the middle of grown folk's business," I laughed. He was close, and his scent had me catching my breath, but his violet eyes pinned me to the spot. I watched as he removed his black tee-shirt and tossed it to the chair that sat in the corner. My eyes followed the tattoos that marked his body and had me licking my lips.

"You are not so young, Devana," he chuckled. I mean, he was right, but I was not as old as him and my mother.

"Young enough," I sighed as he grabbed my hips and pulled me closer. As I looked into his eyes, I couldn't believe that I once didn't believe in destiny or fate. I once thought that would mean that some sort of higher being predetermines everything you do without free will. Now I understand that we always have a choice of how we want to live our lives. It's just that it's always a happier road if we are willing to do what is needed. The thought of not having a choice made me insane and made me hate the gifts I was born with, that is...until Dax.

I believe in destiny and fate because that would mean my Mate was chosen to be my perfect half. It would mean all the others never worked because it just wasn't time for it to happen. Maybe neither one of us was ready, but now....

"You're overthinking. No one is trying to hurt our Pack, family or trying to kill us. I think it's time for those lessons," Dax growled into my ear. I knew my eyes rolled as the heat of his breath tickled my neck and his hands gripped tighter.

"I need to speak with my mother. I should...I should get this over..."

"No need. We can do all that later. Your sister and mother are preparing for the Hunter meeting about this situation. So right now, all you need to do is rest and heal. I am here to make sure all that will happen."

"Wait...okay, I get why they are calling the meeting, but the Pack we need..."

"Our Pack is and will be fine. My brothers are there, and they understand what needs to be done here. So again, are you ready for these lessons because I know I need to claim you? Again. I need to make sure that you are okay and..." I put my finger to his lips as I reached between us to grab at his length. I knew the feeling he was having because my wolf was whining about feeling his bite once more. Honestly, I'm not going to complain about that, especially when he likes to remind me who's the Alpha in the relation-ship every now and then.

After all, I seem to forget my place as his other half, his Mate, his Luna. I can be just as bold and Alpha with what I want as well. Everything inside of me wanted to test his dominance by pushing his buttons and clashing with him head-on. I knew he liked it, but him being an Alpha, he couldn't help but react. I could feel the Alpha inside me, but I couldn't front like I didn't crave his dominance. It was a drug, and I'm addicted. I knew that everything wasn't solved, and there was so much I still needed to learn, and that we had to learn about each other. We had time to go through it all, but he was right about now. I needed this, and so did he. I wasn't about to waste this moment we had because I knew all too soon this small peace would be over, and all hell would break loose once again.

"Okay, Devana. I can see the wolf peeking and testing me. I got you sexy," he growled, staring into my eyes. I knew what that did to an Alpha, but now I could feel how the wolf responded to a challenge. I knew it was different for others because he grew even harder in my hand. Dax looked at me with lustful violet eyes that burned with the knowledge he knew I was his. I was his Mate. Before I could stroke him again, Dax stepped back. He looked me over from head to toe as I began to pant. I had no clue what his ass was doing to me, but his scent became stronger as he slowly smiled. I couldn't help but admire his body as he looked at me, rubbing my thighs together. I knew he could smell my heat, which made me almost moan at the knowledge. His body was so built it should be a fucking sin just to look this damn sexy.

I'm a skilled Hunter, and I reigned in my lust for his ass. My medium-length hair was still slightly wet and beginning to curl as usual. His hand reached out and grabbed the back of my neck as he lifted the hem of the tee-shirt I was wearing. I did really leave little to the imagination. At this point, I was happy that I wasn't decked out in Hunter gear because that shit would have been in my way. His nose flared as his lips pressed into a thin line.

"Already wet for me, Devana?"

"You and I both know you want to tear this into shreds. Why are you stalling? I thought I needed your so-called lessons," I point out, only to have him grinning at me. His eyes flared brighter, and the violet shade seemed to burn a line of heat over my skin. He smiled when my wetness began to run down my leg. He had no fucking remorse.

"You're mine," he possessively growls. "At least now I know you like that pull on your hair. Every time I tug…" Dax drew in a long breath and licked his thick lips. "You get even wetter."

"I know," I moaned. "Which was why I didn't. I can't tell you everything. You should be able to figure that out on your own, A-L-P-H-A." I bit off.

"Get naked and on your knees, Mate," He growled. I controlled the urge to follow his orders as he let me go and stood back. I would not fall to my knees, not yet anyway. I guess he knew exactly what I thought because Dax's lips curved upward in amusement. "My Mate likes the fight. I wouldn't have my Luna any other way."

"Just a little," I confess before stepping forward to wrap my arms around him. I could feel him pressed against me and his length digging into my stomach. I tilted my head to the side when I looked up to catch his eyes. "You mad I didn't just fall at your feet, Mate?"

"Nope," he grunted, "I think I need to remind a certain Hunter who's the real hunter in this equation. The one who owns every single inch of you. The one who has a body that is built just for me to make it come."

I swallow at his words, my nipples pebbling under his

shirt as he closed the slight distance between us. He pressed his nose against my neck. His teeth grazed on my skin before trailing them lazily up and down. Then he made his way to my collarbone as his tongue snaked out to taste my skin. I know he could practically smell my arousal as he hums gently.

"You taste so sweet," he said as his hand moved to rip his shirt from my body. His other hand went to grab a handful of my hair, yanking it hard enough that a moan slipped out. The slight pain I felt was all pleasure. I didn't mind the pain as much as I thought I would. It just made me want more of it. His mouth traveled along my sternum, his breath hot and molten. Each trail set a fire in my chest that burns into my heart as I whimper in response. "My Mate, it seems like you don't need to run off that mouth. I bet you're dripping if I swipe between those legs, right?"

I feel his clawed hands now on my bare skin, which just made shit worse. His breath hitched as he looked over my body, just waiting for what he wanted to do to me. I'm practically dripping on him; my nipples hardened to peaks. Gently, I balled my hand into fists around his belt, trying to rip them off like he did the shirt I was wearing. "Dax, more. Now!"

"I don't think you have the right to say that. You're mine, sexy, and I am teaching the lessons. I am your Alpha," he growls in my ear. "All of you, it's mine. Mine to touch and to taste. To fuck."

"You...you don't own me," I whisper breathlessly. I knew that was bullshit because he did own me, just like I owned him. Our souls were one and the same, and nothing could tear them apart.

"Your marking, body and soul say otherwise," he

chuckled darkly. His mouth just barely brushing against my nipple as he leaned down, "I guess I have to remind you after all. Especially since I can tell you and your wolf likes to challenge me."

"That's...," I said with a breath of laughter. "You can't know what my wolf is thinking."

"Do I look like I'm fucking around, Devana?" he growled lightly. "You are my *Mate*. I know what your wolf wants just like you know what mine wants." He was right because I could feel every emotion his wolf had as if it were my own.

I could feel my wetness between my legs at this point as it trickled down my thighs. I'm nothing more than a quivering mess, but I wasn't about to let him see that shit. It'll be so easy to submit to him by lowering my head, but my stubbornness wasn't going to surrender without a fight. So, I'm rather proud when his finger slowly trails up my quivering thighs, and instead of bucking into him, I swallow and straightened my back. "I guess you got that one. I can feel you as well. I can feel that you want to fuck the shit out of me, and your wolf needs to bite me. Needs to claim me..."

"Devana," he growls quietly.

I sucked in a breath as he threw me over his shoulder, then onto my bed. He crawled onto the bed and grabbed my legs to pull me down towards him. He pushed my knees apart, spreading them open for his gaze. I know he could not only see, but he smelled my arousal while I stared up at him. Then I watched as he removed the rest of his clothes in one swift, fluid motion.

Jesus.

Even to this day, I don't think I'll ever tire of seeing his body. His muscular, broad chest and tattoos of different animals adorned his body. It made me breathless by how powerful he looks, especially when his large body cages me in like an animal.

He doesn't waste time latching onto one of my nipples and sucked hard, making me gasp and moan at the same time. His muscles ripple as one hand goes to knead my breast before going to explore my ribs, the flat of my stomach, and then to my hips while he practically eats me alive.

He hunts me, and I loved it.

I loved the way his large hands were holding me around my waist. The way my body fits his in a way no one else can because I am his perfect half, his Mate. His possessiveness is only reminding me that not only am I mated to an Alpha, but someone who knows what he wants and will stop at nothing to get it. He knew it the moment he spotted me, even when I denied him. He knew it even when I lied to him and myself about my feelings.

He transferred his attention to my other breast, closing his mouth over my neglected nipple as I moaned, my hand going to clutch in his jet-black hair.

"You denied me at the start, and that just made me hard because I knew I would make you mine, Devana. That fierce side of you called to my wolf, and no one else has ever been able to do that," he says almost threateningly when he released my nipple with a loud pop. "I knew you would try to defy your Alpha as well."

"You... you will get over it," I whimper out, knowing how much trouble I would be in if I kept pushing his dominance. Yet, I didn't want to give in too easily to him because I craved his dominant side even when it was irritating.

"I suppose I will after you beg me to fuck you, won't I?" he taunts while trailing his tongue at the center of my body before settling right between the V of my thighs. He inhales deeply, his eyes seeming to glow as he grinned. "Though, something tells me that you'll like that shit, anyway."

"Dax," I buck my hips in hopes he'll get my point. But he tightened his hold on my waist and practically nailed me onto the bed as I continue. "Dax, I want you now."

"Maybe if you beg a little better and convincingly, then I'll give it to you. As I said before, you have lessons to learn, Mate."

I'm practically ready to give into him when I feel his tongue latching onto my swollen clit before I feel his thumb making small circular motions around the bundle of nerves in between licks. Pleasure zips through my body like electricity. I feel it in my toes, my fingertips, and then my entire body. I didn't bother to hide my moans as I begin to shamelessly fuck myself on his fingers as two entered me. My hips bucked on their own off the mattress. Dax leaned away to watch me as I moved like a woman possessed. His eyes never left mine as he licked his lips while I work myself to climax.

"Dax," I cry out. "I...oh, I'm close."

He lazily grinned at me because he knew what he was doing to me. "You want to come on my fingers, Mate?"

"Yes!" I arch off the mattress, back bowing as I'm practically feeding myself to him.

And then the fucking bastard withdraws his fingers from my heat with a chuckle. "Well, you're going to have to beg for it. I don't just give these good lessons away for free."

"Are you serious?" I scowled, narrowing my eyes until they were slits. I'm deliriously high on my ruined orgasm. Rather than answering, Dax leaned down in a fast motion and worked with his tongue, teasing on my opening but never delving right inside alongside. It was torture and pleasure as he worked in a frenzy with his long, sensual licks.

I'm more than frustrated as I'm writhing, squirming, and arching under him. The words are at the tip of my tongue to cave in. I'm on the fence about just begging him for it. Instead, I try to escape his hold, but his hands only tighten as he feasts on me like a starved animal while his claws dig into my skin, almost as if it's a warning. The rumble only shoots pure vibration to my core, causing me to become utterly breathless. I sucked in a breath, but I couldn't help the moan that slipped through my lips.

"Fuck, Dax!"

I'm ready to smack him over the head or flip his ass over when I feel the lashes of his tongue on my clit moving at speeds I didn't think possible. He swirled his tongue once more as his finger spears inside me. I'm melting away, my knees falling to the side weakly. Then, abruptly, he shoves another finger inside of me without warning as I jerk and cry out.

"Who is your Mate?" he asks. He growled the word, and they were heavy with desire. "Tell me, sexy."

"You!" I reply, almost sobbing. "You, Dax."

"What else?" he snarls.

"You are Alpha," I rush out. I stared at his with lustful violet eyes, "I need you," I growled. I didn't even recognize my own voice at this point. My hands had turned into claws as I gripped the blankets.

"Soon," he practically growls out as his nose flared. He curved his talented and skilled fingers upward, hitting a part of me that makes me see stars and want to howl. "Who do you belong to, Devana? Just give in, and I'll give you what you want, Devana. However, and whenever you want, Mate. It's yours. Well, so long as you understand this," he snarls while plunging his fingers hard into my tight channel. "You may be an Alpha, but I am your Alpha."

I bit down hard on my lip to stop the words he wanted to hear. I said I needed him, but he wanted more, and I will only bend but so damn far.

"You got something to say? Let me hear you."

"I..." I swallow and try again. "You are right. I am an Alpha, but I need my Alpha, inside me, inside my heart, and my soul." The words just fell from my lips, but I didn't care anymore. They were true.

"I told you that you would learn something." He smirked, and I wanted to smack his ass, but then he moved away.

"Hey..." I started to say, but my mouth closed.

Damn, but it's like every inch of him was carved out of marble. He is swollen, dripping in slick pre-cum with a curve that hits a part deep inside of me that makes me forget my own name. Dax is perfect in every way, with the right amount of girth to make me feel stuffed to the brim and stretched when he's inside of me. He gripped himself hard, giving it a few strokes before he climbed back over me to start teasing at my entrance. I sucked in a breath as his tip slide along the slickness of my folds, coating and mixing our juices.

His eyes find mine again.

"This is just the beginning of us. You know that, right?

"Yes."

"I love you, Devana," His words were guttural as his hand slide up my chest and around my throat.

"You are my Mate, my everything I never knew I needed," I gasped out, almost beginning to shake. "I love you, Mate, and—*ah!*"

With a throaty grunt and a sharp snap of his hips, he shoved the entire length inside me in a single motion. It knocks the breath out of me, as I have no other choice but to bite down on my lower lip to keep myself from crying out at how full and stretched I felt. Yet, something about all this feels different. It's as if he's reminding me who has my heart. It was a mixture of pain, pleasure, love, and it was unfamiliar territory for both of us.

I'm blown away by how he takes me. It's so animalistic and downright dirty as he tangled his hand into my hair and pulled, so I crane my eyes open to stare into his. The low moan of that action was ripped from the deepest parts of me. It's so raw, the different types of emotion swarming in his eyes.

"I love you, Devana."

He wasted no time in thrusting at the ruthless pacing I love so much. My back hollowed out as he speared even deeper into me. I could feel my walls clamping hard onto his length as he continued to slam himself in and out of me because I was made to take it. It's something about the thought of being made for him to use makes a moan rumble out of my mouth, causing him to chuckle.

Dax rolled a nipple between his fingers. "You're made to handle every part of me perfectly. So snug and tight because you're made to be my Mate. I know how to make you cum, how to make you submit to me. No one will ever know how you cry out my name like this, how your full breast bounce when I take you this way. No one but you can handle the wolf inside of me."

He groaned when I tightened around him as he

continued to plow into me with every inch of him, so much that I openly moaned as he slammed into my cervix. I swear I could feel him in me everywhere at this point. Dax's eyes began to glow as a faint green entered his gaze, and his canines began to lengthen. He was right because I loved that shit. I wanted him to take me in any way possible.

"Please, Dax," I whimpered out. "I want…want…I want to come."

"You're close, aren't you?" He grits out. Wordlessly, I can only nod in response.

He grunted, and I can feel his hand on my back and his claws digging into my flesh, but not enough to break the skin. It may have harmed me a little if I wasn't a shifter, but my skin and bones are tougher than before. "I know, and I will let you soon."

"Now," I demanded. "I want you to come with me now." I heard the ring of command and the growl of my voice. His ass just smiled as he leaned away from me and put my legs over his shoulders. "Oh…shit…oh God!" I moan as he hit my spot. I knew I was done, and I couldn't hold it back.

"Come with me, Mate," Dax growled as he leaned down and sank his teeth directly where he marked me. With that, he pushed in deeper as he jerked and became more erratic with pacing. In just a few thrusts, he tossed his head back, giving me exactly what I wanted. I could feel hot thick ribbons of cum erupting and flooding me, just like I asked. He snapped his hips back and pushed in deeper. I know I'm going to feel this for days, and I couldn't care less.

It's enough to trigger another orgasm to follow shortly as he presses my clit hard with his thumb. Just like that, I became undone again. I threw my head back in euphoria, bucking my hips up to him for all I'm worth and taking everything that he could give. Neither one of us said anything for a while as he rested his forehead against mine, catching our breaths.

Finally, he pulls out of me, and we stared at one another, trying to come back to reality before he smiled, searing a kiss over my mouth that stole my breath away. My heart skipped a beat at how he looks at me with burning violet eyes. He pulled the blanket over us as I contently sigh, nuzzling deeply into his chest.

"Does that mean I am fully claimed by you, Alpha?" I teasingly murmur. Dax looked at me with a raised brow.

"Sexy, you were claimed the moment you stepped foot on my land. You and I were only going to end one way."

"Which way is that? Fighting off a crazy-ass demon and rogue wolf, or did you mean still having to deal with the politics this Mating will cause?" I sucked my teeth just thinking about it. "But I can't say it wasn't worth it. I didn't imagine anyone could accept me with these gifts I have and believe the feelings that I felt until you."

"As I said, the only way it was going to be is you being my Mate, so if you need to hear it, then I have no problem letting it be known. Devana Okar, you have been Claimed by this Alpha, and I dare anyone to challenge me about it. We will make our own path in this life because I know, and so do you, that this is not the end. It's just the beginning." There wasn't too much to say because he was right on all accounts. We weren't done with just this mission, and he was right. Dax, the Alpha of the Rayne Pack, claimed me just like he said he would in the beginning.

THE END

GLOSSARY

Hunter- A Hunter is a human that has been given unique gifts and a mission to keep the peace of all species on earth. A Hunter's primary mission is to hunt demons and send them back to Hell. Five Family Houses lead and train Hunters: Cross, Ryder, Okar, Diya and Wellsley.

True Alpha- A True Alpha is a wolf from the bloodline of the firstborn wolf shifter. They have abilities far past any wolf shifter. The True Alpha is over all wolves and is the leader of all Packs across the world. The True Alpha must protect and guide the wolf shifters according to the laws set by their Deity at the beginning. The True Alpha has Alpha beneath him/her to help accomplish the task and help him/her lead the wolf shifter nation so they may prosper.

Alpha/Luna- The Alpha of the Pack is the leader. He/She is the main one in control and sets the laws of his Pack. They are not required to hunt with the Pack, but most typically do. They demand respect and are in the position to exile, banish, or even kill those who do not show it. Though it is rare, this position can be challenged, and if the challenger wins the fight, the challenger, being the new Alpha, can do what he/she pleases with the previous leaders. This does not usually happen because it would result in a considerable change within the Pack.

Beta- The Beta is the second in command and enforces the law when the current Alpha is not present. If both Alpha dies, the beta(s) take the Alpha position and lead the Pack unless the Alpha has said otherwise. This position cannot be challenged without the alpha approval.

Sentinel- There are four sentinels, two mated pairs, in the Pack. The alphas and betas specially choose each pair. The Alphas and betas train the sentinels to take their places if anything should happen to them. Since becoming one can start as early as one year, the sentinels don't usually have authority over the Pack unless the Alpha or beta have publicly given it to them. They are respected, though. Messing with a sentinel is messing with the Alphas and betas themselves. This rank cannot be challenged whatsoever.

Assassin- Assassin is the most fitting name for this rank because it is self-explanatory. They are also spies for the Pack. There can be a total of only three assassins in each Pack.

Lead Warrior/Enforcer- The lead warrior takes his/her orders directly from the Alpha and sometimes the beta. They are the main leader, general or captain of the warriors in the

Pack. They are appointed by the Alpha and are the best of the best of warriors.

Pups/Cubs- I'm pretty sure that this is self-explanatory. They are the children of the Packs.

Gamma- Those holding this position are usually, if not always, the oldest and wisest of the Pack. They pass on their stories and phrases to the others within the Pack their pearls of wisdom. They delight in telling stories to pups though sometimes what they tell is just legend. Still, each story usually has some moral to it. At one time, they may have been the Alpha, and usually, that is true. However, the current Alphas may put others here should it seem right to them. Those who hold this position are much respected and loved by the rest of the Pack.

Delta- They are the messengers of the Pack, the go-between among the allies, and sometimes even the axis. They risk their own lives by doing so, but it is their duty to make sure that those who need to know are told. Those seeking this position must be agile, patient, and even tempered while speaking with other packs.

Zeta- They are the war general of the Pack that takes direct orders from the Alpha in case of a war. The Alpha may be the one to declare war, but the Zeta leads the army and come up with the war plans. They also train recruits for a position as an Enforcer and train younger wolves for this position to take their place in the future. Typically, there is only a single Zeta, but there can be as many as three if the populace is high or the Alpha declares it.

Gammazeta- A Gammazeta is a cross between a Zeta and Gamma. They must be born of the two wolves who carry those titles and the True Alpha bloodline. These wolves are very rare, and if you have one in your Pack, you have a wolf full of knowledge of Pack lore and the strength of an Alpha.

Kannuck- Kannuck is the Deity and creator of wolf shifters. He is also the moon god and chooses if you will be an Alpha/Luna and grants each Alpha/Luna some of his powers.

Rogue- Rogues are werewolves that have either been kicked out of their Pack or left on their own free will. Rogues are usually the wolves who have gone against Pack laws and the True Alpha.

Lone Wolf- A lone wolf acts independently or generally lives or spends time alone instead of a Pack. Usually, wolves that have left their Pack are described as lone wolves who is an individual who acts independently and prefers to do things on their own. They primarily prefer solitude or works alone. They are still part of the Pack and will come back when called by their Alpha.

Cadejo/Black dog- A Cadejo/Black Dog will cause disease, destruction, confusion, chaos and death. It may appear as a dog but do not mistake it for what it truly is a possessed shifter. Once it has possessed a shifter, it can now walk like a human. It will no longer need to hide in the shadows of night to whisper poison from afar. It will now have a voice and a willing soul that will feed it the power of life.

AUTHOR'S NOTE

Thank you for reading. I hope you have enjoyed the series so far! Please review I love them or feel free to contact me on Facebook, Twitter, Instagram, good reads, book bub, or through my website. Thank you again for reading, and keep looking for more Deadly Secrets, Dream Walker and The Rayne Pack Series!

Follow or contact me at the links below to see what is coming up next!

www.ebowserbooks.com

www.facebook.com/authorE.Bowser

https://www.bookbub.com/authors/e-bowser

https://www.goodreads.com/ebowser

Twitter: @ebowser0110

IG: @e.bowserbooks

TikTok: @ebowserauthor

ABOUT THE AUTHOR

E. Bowser is an author of paranormal romance, mystery and suspense. E. Bowser loves to come home and write whatever stories come to mind. E. Bowser always wanted to write a story that people would like to read and give their feedback to make her next better. She loves to read herself and takes great pleasure in doing so. In middle school, E. Bowser started writing short stories about life, anything horror or paranormal. E. Bowser loves to write whatever her imagination can come up with over a cup of tea.

BOOKS BY THIS AUTHOR

Deadly Secrets Brothers That Bite Books 1-5 The Deadly Secrets is an exciting series focused on Taria, Michael Quinn and LaToya are friends and lovers fighting against evil forces.

Deadly Secrets Awakening Book 1

Deadly Secrets Revealed Book 2

Deadly Secrets Consequences Book 3

Deadly Secrets Consequences Book 4

Deadly Secrets Royalty Book 5

Deadly Secrets Novellas

This collection of stories will give you a glimpse into the lives of Taria, Michael, LaToya and Quinn, along with many others. Sit back and fall back into the paranormal world of Deadly Secrets.

Desires of the Harvest Moon

Twice Marked Witches and Wolves

Rise of the Phoenix

A Vampire and His Alpha Mate

A Hunter Touched My Soul

Brothers That Bite Chronicles Volume 1

The Crown Series Books 1-3 On-going series

This series would be best read if you start with Deadly Secrets Series Brothers That Bite books 1-5 and other novellas.

Taria, LaToya, Michael and Quinn are back together again in Deadly Secrets Hunters Regin: The Crown Series. Taria Cross was turned into a Vampire by Michael Vaughn, and she became his Queen. Not only does she have to figure out this new part of her life, but she is a Hunter as well, and that is a whole other list of duties.

Deadly Secrets Hunters Reign Book 1

Their Sirenian Queen

Deadly Secrets A Vampires Temptation Book 2

Deadly Secrets When Queen's Are Crowned Book 3

The Rayne Pack Series On- Going

Follow the Rayne Brothers as they find their Mates and fight the forces of evil. See how Dax, Max, Malic, Alex, Jarod and Thomas fight for those they love while being attacked on all sides.

An Alpha's Claim Book 1

Dream Walker: Visions of the Dead On-Going Series.

What if you had the ability to see things before they happened? Saw a zombie outbreak unfold before your very eyes? Could you embrace visions of the dead coming back to life? For Kaylee, who has been chosen to receive this gift, these visions are the beginning of a nightmare.

Dream Walker: Visions of the Dead Book 1

Dream Walker: Visions of the Dead Book 2